After the Spirits Come
A Continuation of Dickens's A Christmas Carol
Beth Ford

Copyright © 2025 by Beth Ford

All rights reserved.

No portion of this book may be reproduced in any form without written permission from the publisher or author, except as permitted by U.S. copyright law.

Chapter 1

On a cold New Year's night, from a confluence of shadows in the lee of a building, two men watched Ebenezer Scrooge's front door. Both men were about forty, but anyone seeing them in the light would think them at least ten years older from their deep-etched wrinkles and the steeliness in their eyes.

"Do you think he'll even read it?" The man who spoke was tall, with a pockmarked face.

His shorter companion scoffed at the first man's doubt. "Of course he'll read it. The man has never received a letter in his life." He hunched his shoulders against the cold and jerked his head toward their destination. "Let's go. We're going to need to plan for a lot more than one lousy note and a shovelful of horseshit. It won't be easy, taking everything from a man the way he did to us."

Meanwhile, in a middling house in a middling London neighborhood, two young people stood in front of their fireplace in a parlor crowded with celebrants.

"Remarkable, isn't it?" Fred Williamson asked his wife, Clara.

"No more crowded than last year." She kept her gaze on the guests filling the space. A coy smile tugged at the corners of her mouth, showing she knew that was not what Fred referred to. Fred had only one thing on his mind during the week between Christmas and New Year's. Now, with two hours left before they rang in 1844, she knew the trajectory of his thoughts would not change.

"You know what I mean." Fred lifted his glass, shining with a fresh helping of punch, in the direction of a gray head across the room that Fred glimpsed only when the man's two companions moved in time with their laughter.

"You win the bet on that one. Your uncle managed to maintain his new demeanor for this whole week." She swiveled her face toward her husband, beaming. Her sausage curls bounced merrily against her cheeks. "How long do you want to wager next?"

"I think I have more faith in him than you do. Maybe Easter?"

"That's bold of you. All right. I think he'll be back to his old self long before then."

They shook hands to seal the wager, then watched Fred's uncle, Ebenezer Scrooge, as he chatted in a small group squeezed behind the sofa.

"Still . . ." Clara began, "do you think he's all right?"

Fred shrugged. "He refuses to talk to a doctor, of course, but I spoke with Dr. Smelton last week—you know, Helen's cousin?—and he said an apoplexy might cause odd symptoms—personality changes, hallucinations . . . and if he's had one, he's more likely to have another that won't be so kind."

Clara's sister, wrapped in lavender silk and cream lace, tugged on Clara's arm and led her away, eager for Clara to join a game starting in one corner. Fred laughed and gave a quick nod at the two women. He watched his uncle awhile longer. It was unlike Fred to be pensive, and he didn't like the feeling. He drained his glass of punch and determined to leave what had happened in 1843 behind. In the new year, he would enjoy whatever time he had with his uncle and thank God for it. With a grin, he dove back into the crowd, joining a group of his fellows in a song.

At five minutes before midnight, Fred dashed back to the clock on the mantel at the front of the room. He rapped his punch glass. When that didn't get everyone's attention, he stuck two fingers in his mouth and released an ear-piercing whistle. Instantly, everyone turned toward him, though a few grumbled to their companions about the shrill noise.

"It's almost time!" he shouted. "I just wanted to say, I'm happy I knew all of you in '43, and I hope our acquaintance will continue in '44." He raised his glass. Others followed, and one man cheered, "Hear, hear!" Everyone took a drink. But Fred had called for everyone's attention too early, and the remaining few minutes suddenly felt like a very long time to fill. His guests started to return to their conversations. Fred watched the clock hands. "Thirty seconds!" he yelled at the appropriate time, then, "Ten seconds!" Everyone joined him in the countdown.

Midnight struck. The great dongs of the nearest church bells drowned out the tinny chimes from the parlor clock. There were embraces all around, and some kisses, mostly with the appropriate partner. A few young men started a round of "Auld Lang Syne" that did not catch on.

Scrooge found his nephew in the mass of bodies and clapped Fred's back three times. Fred had received more hugs from his uncle in the last week than he had in all the years of his life put together.

Fred smiled as they pulled apart and wished each other a happy New Year. "This will be a wonderful year, Uncle. I can feel it!"

"Yes, my boy!" Scrooge agreed. He turned and shook hands forcefully with the other men near him and even dared to give one of their wives a friendly peck on the cheek.

Fred also greeted his fellows but kept an eye on his uncle. He had commented on the great things 1844 would bring partly to convince himself. One thought still nagged at the back of Fred's mind.

This all might be too good to be true.

An hour later the guests cleared out. Fred and Clara waited at the door. Like monarchs in a reception line, they shook hands with everyone as they left. During a gap between farewells, Fred noticed that his uncle hung at the back of the line along with a man Fred had seen chatting with Scrooge earlier. Fred had to search for the man's name a moment before it came. Dr. Norman, a friend of one of Fred's coworkers who had wrangled an invitation. But Fred and Clara were not stingy with their company and welcomed everyone who joined them. For a fleeting instant, Fred dared hope his uncle had made a friend—and in the next, he wondered if Scrooge even knew what it meant to have a friend. Scrooge's closest association prior to this week had been Jacob Marley, and through that relationship, both men had sucked the humanity out of each other.

Eventually the line ended. Scrooge took his last leave from his nephew and his wife, pumping their hands with both of his. "This year is going to be the best of my life," he said. "I just know it."

"We'll endeavor to make it so," Fred said. Beside him, Clara stifled a yawn but nodded in agreement.

Scrooge glanced behind him at Dr. Norman, now the last guest.

"I just want to have a quick word with your nephew before I leave," the doctor explained.

"Then a happy New Year to you." Scrooge paused in the doorframe to put on his hat. "Praise the spirits!" he shouted, without looking back to direct the comment to anyone in particular. Then he waltzed off into the dark, his "Happy New Year" to passersby heard faintly as he disappeared.

"I hope I'm not being too bold," Dr. Norman said once the room was silent, "but I found my conversation with your uncle this evening fascinating."

Fred's smile wavered. Perhaps the two men had not gotten on as well as he had hoped.

"I don't mean that as any sort of a veiled insult. I'm actually doing some research on people who believe they've met ghosts, angels, and the like. I wondered if I might include your uncle in the paper I'm finishing. All anonymous, of course."

"Did you ask him?"

"Oh, he loved it. But I find it's usually a good idea to check with the family as well."

"Right. I suppose it's fine as long as it's all anonymous and on the up-and-up." His heart sank to hear his uncle treated as nothing more than an interesting case study. It would take time for others to see his uncle the way he did, Fred reminded himself. Scrooge's decades of avariciousness were well known in London. Only time and concerted effort would erase that reputation.

"Excellent." Dr. Norman donned his hat and stepped toward the door. "I'm hoping it will be my entrée to the Royal Society. I'll send you a copy." He beamed and went out.

Farther down the road, Scrooge walked home. The crowds thinned as he neared the odd, hidden square fronting his home. The lack of friendly greetings for the new year along this final part of his journey left him feeling lonely in the dark.

He tried to shake the feeling as he pulled his house key out of his overcoat pocket. On this winter's night, the cold metal bit sharply, even through his glove. He stepped onto the front stoop. His foot landed in a wet pile, releasing a sucking sound as he pulled his shoe free. From the stench, it could only be manure. Strange that it would end up on his step, where no one but himself ever came. But no matter.

Except when he put the key into the lock, his hand bumped a sheet of paper rolled between the knob and the jamb. He unrolled it, but unable to make heads or tails of it in the dark, he pushed on inside.

At the hall table, he fumbled for a candle. Once he had one in hand, he hesitated. It seemed a shame to waste a match and a bit of candle to read this scrap that could be read just as well in the morning. But no, he had to know what it said, or he would get no sleep that night.

"It can't be from the spirits," he muttered. "They've never left a physical token such as this."

And indeed, it was not.

The messy scrawl consisted of only two lines.

You can act nice all you want, but we won't forget. You can't be forgiven that easily.

The warning floored him. After a few seconds, he reminded himself to breathe, and a huge, shaking breath entered his lungs. In the week since Christmas, he had made no formal declarations of his change in outlook and his newfound intention to help rather than take advantage of the poor. But acquaintances had remarked on the boisterous change in his demeanor, and he had not hesitated to explain to those who asked. His recent charitable donations, though ostensibly anonymous, had also attracted rumor and notice. As a known man of business in the city, his actions affected others—a fact he had just begun to acknowledge. Even so, provoking such rage in someone shocked him. He couldn't let it slow his resolve. He would have to make reparations, that's all. He would have to work even harder to overcome those who opposed him changing his life.

He crumpled the note up and dropped it into the candle flame. He watched it curl and burn until it was no more than black dust on the candleholder, like the ashes of his old life.

Chapter 2

In the bright hope of a New Year's morning, Scrooge easily forgot the threatening note. As soon as he was out of bed and lit the fire in his bedroom, he tossed the missive from his mind. Instead, he focused on what he would bring to the new year. Having much to do was overwhelming. Knowing he would be comforted by neat rows of words, he dressed and went downstairs to his small office. He pulled a sheet of paper from a desk drawer and began writing a list of resolutions.

The list was creeping onto a second page when the morning's silence was broken by the sound of boot steps in the courtyard. Even with this warning, the knock at Scrooge's front door startled him because it occurred so infrequently. He hesitated as he passed the table in the foyer, the ashes of last night's letter still resting in the base of the candleholder. Would the caller be someone like the writer of the note—or indeed, the very same person? He squared his shoulders. Whomever it was, he would face them. Such confrontations were the penance he owed the world after so many misdeeds.

He swung the door open and was pleased to see Dr. Norman standing on the front steps. Scrooge, relieved that the prospect of confrontation had dissipated, welcomed him gregariously, with one hug on the step and a second in the foyer.

After Scrooge pressed a small glass of port into the doctor's hand—hair of the dog and all that—they settled into the sitting room. Like the rest of the rooms, this one was sparsely furnished and rarely cleaned. Scrooge felt the lack keenly as Dr. Norman swiped a hand across the dusty seat of one of the rough chairs before the unlit fireplace. The room was so rarely used that Scrooge never found it worth heating.

"Let me go get some coals," Scrooge said before sitting.

"No, no. I won't be long."

Scrooge sat. Dr. Norman didn't unbutton his coat. Instead, he pulled a handkerchief out of one pocket and repeatedly dabbed his nose, dripping in the cold air, while he talked. "I hoped to ask you a few more questions. About your time with the spirits."

"I'm always happy to discuss it, but I think I told you everything."

"I'd like to go over a few things to make sure I'm recalling everything correctly now that we're all sober." He smiled and, without moving his gaze from Scrooge's face, pulled out a small notebook and spread it open on his right thigh.

Scrooge answered questions amiably for several minutes. Then, while Dr. Norman scribbled his notes, Scrooge leaped out of his chair like a man inspired and raised one finger in the air. "Am I right to assume that you are a man who has made his own New Year's resolutions, Dr. Norman?"

The doctor looked up from his notebook, startled. "Yes, I suppose so."

Scrooge walked to the doorway that connected the parlor to the small office where he had written his list before Dr. Norman arrived. He turned back and said, "Resolutions to do good, perhaps?" Before his guest could answer, Scrooge disappeared into the room. He returned a moment later with the list he had prepared that morning. He sat across from Dr. Norman again and ran a finger slowly down the list as if searching for an item of inventory. When he found what he wanted, he tapped the page twice.

"Perhaps you could help me complete one of mine," Scrooge said. "I have an employee, a clerk, a poor man with—well, I can't think exactly how many children right now, but far too many children. One of them is very ill. Medical care is difficult to get for a child in such a situation, you see. Would you consider helping him as a favor to me? For your interest in the spirits?"

"I don't see why not—"

"Good!" Scrooge jumped out of his chair again. The paper floated, forgotten, to the floor. "We'll go right away."

Dr. Norman fumbled with his notebook, handkerchief, and hat as he scrambled to keep pace with Scrooge's preparations to leave.

At the front door, Scrooge paused. "We'll walk, unless you object. I have resolved not to scrimp on carriages for a friend." He muttered to himself as he searched his pockets, but not finding the list, he waved it off and reached for the door handle. "No matter."

Outside, Dr. Norman said, "I have no objection," but by the time he had completed the sentence, he had to dash ahead to catch up with Scrooge's long, determined strides. They talked no more for the rest of the way, except for their occasional calls of "Happy New Year" to the strangers they passed.

Their knock at the Cratchits' door set off a scuffle inside. There were a few whispers, one turn of the knob that was not carried through, and one peek through the window by two pairs of small eyes before Bob Cratchit appeared in the doorway. He was a thin man, of average height, with watery blue eyes whose color seemed prepared to disappear completely at the slightest provocation. The cuff of the sleeve that held the door open was ratty around the edges, the last mending having come partially undone.

"Bob, I'm sorry to disturb you on New Year's Day, but I just couldn't pass up the opportunity to bring Dr. Norman when he came to visit me this morning. He's here to take a look at Tiny Tim."

"Oh!" was all Bob said, but he stepped aside nonetheless.

The room they entered was little better than a hovel. Despite Scrooge's several visits over the last week, it still broke his heart to see it every time. The leftover holiday greenery and the remains of the previous night's feast, recently served for breakfast and still spread on the table, put a brave face on the room.

The children and Mrs. Cratchit stood arrayed around the edge of the room. In such a small space, anything said at the door had surely been heard by all. Still, the looks the family gave their two guests were hardly welcoming.

Dr. Norman scanned the row of Cratchits, his gaze lighting on the small boy with bright eyes and the crutch at one end. He knelt in front of Tiny Tim. "May I have a look at you, boy?"

After a quick glance seeking his father's approval, Tim stepped forward.

Dr. Norman handled him gently, looking at his eyes and in his mouth, manipulating his shortened limbs, and listening carefully to his lungs. This short examination conducted, he stood, patted Tim on the head, and motioned Bob and Scrooge to one side of the room. "I don't think he has anything that can't be cured," he said in a low voice.

"Wonderful!" Scrooge shouted. Across the room, Mrs. Cratchit jumped and held a hand to her heart.

"What do we need to do?" Bob asked.

"Daily doses of cod liver oil should help."

"How much?" Scrooge asked, pulling a small purse out of his pocket and rooting around in it, not heeding the grating jangle of metal on metal. Having never spent a penny on medicine for himself, preferring instead to suffer through any cold that took him on, Scrooge had no guess as to the cost of such an item, delivered daily.

Bob and Dr. Norman exchanged unsure glances.

"Here, Bob, take this for now." Scrooge settled a few coins in his employee's palm.

Dr. Norman cleared his throat. "A more varied diet could also help. Along with better air—fresher and with more sun."

"There now, Bob," Scrooge said, beaming, "we can work on all that, can't we? Easy enough." He pumped the doctor's hand in an overenthusiastic handshake. "Thank you so much." He turned to Bob and settled a hand on his shoulder. "Now we'll leave you and your family to enjoy the rest of this fine day."

"Thank you, Doctor." Bob reached awkwardly around Scrooge to shake the other man's hand. At the door, Bob asked, "We'll open the office tomorrow, Mr. Scrooge?"

"Yes, yes, now that the major holidays are over, I suppose we must. I'll see you in the morning."

Once they had said their goodbyes and were in the street, Dr. Norman asked, "Has all your charitable work begun since you were visited by the spirits?"

"Yes. They showed me the errors of my ways, and now I must make up for it. Now will you head home?"

Dr. Norman nodded, but he scanned Scrooge's face, as if puzzling something out in his mind.

"I think I'll continue my walk," Scrooge said.

The two men shook hands and parted ways.

Inside the small house they had just left, Bob Cratchit and his wife continued their vigil at the window, watching as the two men stopped and chatted briefly, then walked in opposite directions.

Mrs. Cratchit held her arms across her chest. She was a handsome woman rubbed raw by hard years. "Do you trust him?"

"Trust him? Why wouldn't I?"

With the two men disappeared from view, the couple turned toward the interior of the room, switching their watchfulness to their children.

"All these promises all of a sudden? Don't you think it's odd?"

"I certainly agree it's odd. But Scrooge has never been dishonest. He's always been perfectly clear about what he is."

"I suppose that's right." She smoothed the hair of the littlest girl, Sarah, clutching at her mother's skirts.

"Besides, here's proof." Bob opened his hand to reveal the coins Scrooge had placed there.

His wife looked at them, but her expression remained unmoved. "Let's just hope it lasts, then."

"Oh, ye of little faith." He kissed the top of his wife's head.

Outside, Scrooge continued his walk through the Cratchits' neighborhood. He was still rather unfamiliar with the area, but the street was quieter and emptier than usual, which made it easier to explore. A pain twitched behind his eye. He wondered if he should be among those wise citizens staying in to nurse their hangovers. But no, he had to start on his list. His days of complacency and hiding from his duty were past. Today, the work needed to begin.

As he neared a bend in the street, the chatter and laughter of children broke the silence. Scrooge brightened as he navigated the narrow curve between two buildings jutting rudely into the street.

His mood deflated as he confronted the building from which the happy noises emanated. The building was long and low and encroached on the street as if the architect had demanded every inch of the lot be put to use. Its two small windows facing the street were black with grime. His gaze tracked down the length of the facade until it reached a faded sign timidly marking the front entrance: Hopewood Orphanage for Boys and Girls.

Scrooge took a few steps toward the front door. Maybe this was exactly where he needed to be today. Now that he was so near, he could hear undertones of unhappiness beneath the sounds that had drawn him in: the harsh shout of a matron, the wail of a child.

He rapped at the door with a heavy brass knocker. No one came to greet him. Not ready to give up, he tried the doorknob. It turned easily, and the door swung open with a creak. He stepped into the foyer. Just inside stood a pedestal with a locked metal box perched on top. It was labeled *Donations* by the same ancient, spindly hand that had made the sign outside in a long ago, more respectable time for the institution. Scrooge pulled out his purse and dropped its contents through the slot. The hollow clang as each coin landed showed it had been a long time since any other funds had dropped into its confines.

The sound of such a rare event announced his presence. A woman appeared from a dark hallway leading off the foyer. She and Scrooge regarded each other for a long moment, both startled by the sudden presence of another. She was tall, in her middle thirties. Her blonde hair was pulled back, but the loose wisps went unfought, giving her a haphazard appearance. Her stained duty apron covered a rather fine pink dress. Scrooge blushed, suddenly aware of his graying hair and clothes that felt brash in their spotlessness.

Finally, the woman stepped forward. "Alice Spencer," she said. "And whom do I have the pleasure of addressing?"

"Ebenezer Scrooge." He stuck out his hand. Miss Spencer wiped hers on her apron first, but the presence of a sticky substance still made itself known as they shook hands. A flash of something—embarrassment or annoyance, it was hard to tell—lit her eyes, but the emotion made its way no farther down her features.

"Of Scrooge and Marley?"

"The same."

Scrooge succeeded in placing her look. Skepticism. He waved his hand toward the donation box. "I've made a few New Year's resolutions, you see. I was wondering if there was some way I could be made useful."

"We could always use benefactors or assistants." She paused. "Why don't I take you to see the matron."

"I would be much obliged."

They walked down hallways and through large communal rooms. Miss Spencer talked on about the history of the place and the treats they had managed to secure for the children for Christmas and New Year's. Scrooge half listened; he couldn't draw his attention away from the children they passed. Some stood singly while others clustered in groups, but the eyes that met Scrooge's all told the same tale: of want, of despair, of a growing sense that the world is profoundly unfair. Suddenly the Cratchit children whom he had thought so destitute seemed like little princes and princesses. Scrooge recalled the two children huddled beneath the robe of the Ghost of Christmas Present—Ignorance and Want. He shuddered now to see them made real. His own ignorance, he thought queasily, had caused this want.

Soon they came upon the matron standing at the entrance to one of the dormitories. She was stout, with a grim, lined face. She moved constantly as she spoke to the children swarmed around her, the jangle of the cluster of keys hanging at her waist emphasizing every word.

"This is Mrs. Thompson," Miss Spencer said as they approached.

Mrs. Thompson broke off her diatribe to the children abruptly. "Who are you?"

"This is Mr. Scrooge."

The matron looked Scrooge up and down. The look made Scrooge feel like he was a misbehaving child, and he found himself unable to make any reply.

"He's come here to see about providing some volunteer work or some donations."

Mrs. Thompson's face didn't soften. "Get your requisite good deed done early in the year, hmm?" She flicked a hand at Miss Spencer. "You can place him where he is most needed." She turned her back on them and grabbed one boy who had stolen a treat from another while the adults talked.

Miss Spencer waved Scrooge back the way they had come. Once they left Mrs. Thompson behind, Miss Spencer said, "It's difficult to run this place alone, as I'm sure you can imagine."

"She does this by herself?"

"Yes. There aren't many people in this part of London who have any spare money or time to give. We do the best we can. I'm happy to talk with you about what projects you could best support. I work with a number of charitable organizations in the city."

"Yes, yes, of course."

They reached the front door. Scrooge tipped his hat to Miss Spencer as he left. Back out on the narrow street, he stood stunned for a moment. It had been so easy to ignore the needs around him when he kept them safely out of sight. Now that he had seen it . . . he had much, much to do.

Chapter 3

Early the next morning, on a smarter side of town than the one Bob Cratchit called home, at the corner of a square that announced its presence proudly to all passersby, another Cratchit went about her own form of business. Martha, the oldest of the Cratchit children, ducked out the back doorway of her employer's house and dashed across the small courtyard. She emptied the dustbin she carried into the refuse pile. A breeze worked itself into a frenzy. She struggled to control the shawl wrapped around her head and shoulders with one hand while maneuvering the dustbin in the other. The shawl was not an approved part of the maid's uniform, but no one in the house who was not a servant had yet stirred, so there was little chance of being reprimanded. Her employers, the Werther family, had held not just a New Year's Eve party but a New Year's Day party as well, and Martha knew they would be abed with hangovers for a few hours yet.

This task complete, Martha hurried back inside, where there was some semblance of warmth. In the kitchen, the cook and one of the other two maids, Kitty, tried to guess when they would need to serve lunch. Martha dropped the dustbin at the foot of the back stairs, then trudged back up to get the coal scuttle from Mr. Werther's study. He would want it filled and ready to go whenever he decided to make an appearance. He liked to pretend he worked hard all day in exchange for his money, but Martha knew he mostly smoked cigars and waited for his employees to make money for him. He was in manufacturing, though what exactly he made, Martha never gathered. Such concerns did not trouble her as long as her pay came regularly.

Normally, the servants were made to move quickly through the upstairs room, taking the back stairs to be seen as little as possible. But this morning, since the family wasn't awake, she took her time on the way back downstairs, walking the wide hallway, imagining the portraits that lined the walls were her own illustrious ancestors. In reality, she had never seen a likeness of any of her family members she had never personally met. *That may not be such a bad thing,* she thought as she took in the visages of the portly and sallow Werther ancestors captured for eternity.

She took the front stairs on the way back down. At the bottom, she peeked out the window by the front door, a view she rarely saw. Even though the Werthers' house occupied a corner lot, it wasn't as big as some of its neighbors. Still, to live here always in the front rooms seemed to Martha an impossible luxury. Though the fact that the family lived there exclusively and had no country residence showed their social status was not as illustrious as it could be. New money could never quite compete with old.

Coming back through the kitchen, she dismissed her silly daydreams about wealth she would never have and turned her mind to the New Year's party she had missed at the Cratchit home. Their entire house could fit inside the Werthers' kitchen, but the joy in it would fill the whole Werther home. Not able to get away for the night, Martha and the other two maids, along with the housekeeper, cook, groomsman, and butler, had clinked small glasses of sherry together to ring in 1844 before disappearing back to their rooms to rest.

Martha returned to the courtyard to fill the coal scuttle. Already, the small space behind the house was livening up, with tradesmen making their morning deliveries. As she knelt by the coal pile stacked under the eaves, one side of her shawl blew away. She dropped the coal scuttle with a clang and tried to grab the shawl.

She felt the fabric go taut and fall across her shoulder.

"Allow me," a man's voice said.

She stood and turned. The young man facing her was tall and lanky, like a piece of molasses candy stretched to its limit. Martha had to crane her neck to see his face, which was not an unhandsome one, with clear blue eyes and strong cheekbones.

He motioned to a pair of barrels nearby. "I have these deliveries to make. Do you know where I should take them?"

"Mr. Grayson usually takes deliveries," she said, referring to the butler. She pointed at a door across from them. "Go in there and you should find him."

"Thanks." Instead of heading in that direction, he tipped his hat at her. "I'm Ian Thatcher, by the way."

"Martha Cratchit." She took a few steps toward the back door, but he stayed close by her side.

"What do you do here?"

She looked down at her dress, which, despite the forbidden shawl, made her station clear. She pointed again to where he should take the barrels. "I really must go," she said before picking up the coal scuttle and disappearing into the kitchen. Ian watched after her for several seconds before he continued on his way.

Back in the kitchen, Kitty had stopped helping the cook and was instead watching out the back window. She grabbed Martha's arm in excitement as she walked past.

"I see you met Mr. Thatcher. He's a handsome one, ain't he?"

"Yes, I suppose . . . Wait, how do you know him?"

"He works for the brewer. He's been delivering beer here for weeks. Haven't you seen him before?"

"No." She laughed. "He made it seem like he had no idea where to go."

"He's a flirt, that one. Not that I mind." Kitty tucked a few loose strands of hair back under her cap.

"I don't like a flirt," Martha said.

"You'll like Ian, I think."

"And what good would that do me, hmm?" she asked over her shoulder as she climbed the back stairs once again. By the time the family stirred and the day's real work began in earnest, all thoughts of Ian Thatcher had vanished from her mind.

As Martha was studiously not thinking about Ian Thatcher, Scrooge was unlocking the door to the offices of Scrooge and Marley. As he turned the key in the lock, he realized that the previous week's break was the longest he had been away from his work since he started in business as a young man. And yet, as he stepped inside, everything was just as he had left it, and he hadn't suddenly descended into abject poverty. He chuckled at his decades of stubborn stupidity. He had to laugh at his past, or the memory would be too burdensome to bear.

He went around the few small rooms, tidying up and making sure Bob's coal bin was full before sitting at his own desk. A short while later, Bob swung open the front door. Scrooge scrambled to get up from his desk, nearly knocking over his chair in the process. He crossed over to the Tank, the small clerk's office near the front door, where Bob was still removing his coat.

"Bob!" Scrooge held out a fist wrapped around a small pile of coins. "Here are your wages for the last week while we were out, as we discussed."

Bob looked relieved at this announcement and accepted the coins dropped with a dull clink into his gloved hand. "Good morning, sir, and thank you."

"Yes, yes, good morning, too."

"And thank you for the kind assistance with Tim yesterday."

"I am so grateful to be able to help. How is he? Any better?"

"I don't think we can expect much change in one day, sir."

"Right, yes, of course." Scrooge opened his mouth to speak but could not find any words that would improve the silence. Instead, he nodded and returned to his office.

Scrooge buried himself in his account ledgers for a few hours, a welcome respite from the whirlwind blowing through his mind. His thoughts were always a slew of considerations and uncertainties these days. In this context, he especially appreciated the way the numbers lined up in their neat rows and, at the end, came to an answer no one could question.

No visitors came to the office to disturb their work. On such a bitterly cold morning, most people found it easy to put off the restart of business by another day.

Reaching the end of a set of figures, Scrooge looked across at Bob, copying letters at his small, high desk. The only difference in the scene from any other day was that with the addition of the coal fire, Bob's long scarf was slung over the coat rack instead of wrapped tightly around his neck for warmth.

The same.

Things should not be the same.

Latching on to this thought, Scrooge tapped his pen against the ledger book and stared off into some unseen future for several minutes. When he emerged from his reverie, he called out, "Bob, can you come here, please?" He congratulated himself on the use of this extra politeness at the end of the request.

Bob lingered in the doorway until Scrooge motioned to the chair in front of Scrooge's desk. Bob had never sat in that chair before; it was normally reserved for clients making a last desperate plea for mercy regarding their accounts. Bob perched on the edge of the seat like a bird, ready to flit away at the first sign of trouble.

"Bob, we will have to make some changes to the business."

"Changes? You don't mean close the business, do you, sir?"

"Close the business? Of course not. We must *improve* the business."

Bob didn't look quite as impressed by this statement as Scrooge had hoped.

"We must make it a place that people come to for assistance, not as a place of last resort."

"And how will we do that, sir?"

"We'll figure it out together. And once we do"—he paused, briefly reconsidering the power he was about to give up, but pushed forward—"I shall make you a partner!" Bob slid back in his chair as if the words had shoved him. His wide eyes showed the same surprise as if his words had.

"You've been a loyal employee for many years, sticking by me when many others would have left long ago. It's time for me to have a partner again, someone to keep me in check. It's fitting it should be you." He glanced out the window, where the corner of the establishment's sign was just visible. "Besides, it will finally make me change the sign over the door."

This, at last, cracked open a smile across Bob's face. "That is a bit overdue." He cleared his throat. "I don't know what to say. I'm honored."

"Bah! You know you deserve it. Write down some ideas. We can discuss them tomorrow."

"Yes, sir."

Scrooge swore Bob's steps were lighter and quicker on his way back to the Tank.

Scrooge and Cratchit. His name would have to be first, of course, as the senior partner, but still, it had a nice ring to it. He had made a poor choice in partner before, with Marley just as avaricious as him, but this time would be better. He could trust Bob to keep him on the right path.

Bob settled back into the chair in Scrooge's office, more relaxed this time, to continue their discussion. It was the next afternoon, and the day's most pressing tasks were complete. He had brought with him paper, pen, and ink, which he now spread across the desk. Scrooge frowned as a stray sheet grazed his sleeve but resolved not to resent this overtaking of his space. Everything in order, Bob dipped his pen in the ink and looked at Scrooge expectantly.

Scrooge scratched his neck before beginning. "I've been looking through our outstanding loans, and most of them have terrible terms. I don't know how any man on a fixed income could be expected to pay them."

Bob bit his lip but said nothing.

"We must refinance. We must talk to all the small loan holders to let them know."

Bob dutifully noted this down. "And will we still be taking on new business, sir?"

"Yes, of course. We must keep conducting business. But we can refocus."

Scrooge stopped. He hadn't heard the bell over the front door ring, but in the doorway to his office stood Alice Spencer.

Bob glanced between the two several times. Then he stood and took far too long to gather his materials. "I'll leave you to your meeting," he said as he backed out of the room, expertly balancing everything in his arms. He nodded to Miss Spencer as he passed.

"I can wait for you two to finish," she said after Bob had left.

"No, no." Scrooge waved to the chair Bob had vacated.

As she sat, Scrooge caught a whiff of roses. The scent matched her deep-red dress. This time, no hair or thread was out of place.

"I'm glad you were able to come by."

"When a notorious miser decides he's feeling charitable, there's no time to waste." She grinned at him, and while he couldn't quite smile at such an accurately aimed barb, his shoulders relaxed.

"I see my reputation precedes me."

"Why the sudden change of heart? A sense of one's own impending mortality?"

"I hope I don't seem that old." But he knew he appeared at least ten years older than he was. The dryness of his life had desiccated him, and it had been many years since he had taken any particular care with his appearance. He hesitated in answering her question. His natural inclination was to speak freely of the spirits, but something in the sweetness of her face made him reconsider. He couldn't stand to have her think him any more of a pathetic creature than she already clearly did. "I've been seeing my life in a new light, let's say. I would like to make amends."

"I assume amends have a rather large price tag?"

He laughed. "Yes, I suppose they do."

"Excellent. Because I have a wealth of projects in my portfolio." She reached inside a large bag she carried with her and pulled out several broadsheets. She went over each one with Scrooge—the orphanage where they had met; a nearby workhouse, an institution that Scrooge had so recently derided; a free hospital for the poor. Scrooge gathered that she was a spinster of independent means who had dedicated herself to lifting up others. He envied her innate knowledge of her human duty. He had much catching up to do.

By the time she left, he had pledged several amounts to her favorite organizations and promised to come tour them as well. Her handshake as she stood to leave was as confident and forthright as a man's. He showed her to the door, and when he turned to reenter his office, Bob was standing in the doorway to the Tank, one raised eyebrow silently mocking him.

"Bah! Humbug!" Scrooge slammed the door to his office shut behind him and did not emerge again until Bob had left for the day.

"What a way to begin the new year." The shorter man clapped his business partner on the back. "This shipment should put us so far in the green we never have to look back." His companion grunted in response and scratched at the pockmarks on his cheek.

They watched the dockworkers unload the ship's cargo and stack the crates on the first of three carts that would carry the load to the partners' warehouse. Spices from India, officially, but they'd fish out the real Chinese motherlode when they were safe in the dark, dank space of the riverside warehouse.

The cargo inspector walked over to them. Despite the freezing cold, he wore just his shirtsleeves and waistcoat, as if wanting to declare his high status by the fact that mundane things like the weather had no power over him.

He nodded at each of the two men in turn. "Michaels," he addressed the speaker. "Crane. All good, gentlemen?"

"Yes, sir," Michaels said, swiping a hand across the wide brim of his hat. "We'll send someone over this evening with your part, don't you worry."

The inspector nodded and started to walk off, then paused and turned back. "Happy New Year, by the way."

"Same to you." Michaels then turned back to his silent companion. "This is going to be our year—I can feel it. That miserable bastard is finally going to get a taste of his own medicine."

A young woman approached them, shivering. She wore only a woolen cape around her shoulders and no coat, but this was not the most striking thing about her appearance. Even in the dim streetlight, they could see that her left eye was swollen and half-closed, with a blackness encroaching on the skin around it.

This finally prompted Crane to speak. "What the hell happened to you?"

"Bloke tried not to pay me. Don't worry, I gave him what for."

Crane shook his head. "Well, are you coming up tonight?"

"Sure. You got anything for me?"

"I'll bring you something."

"All right. See you in a bit." She trudged slowly up the street, away from the water.

"You've been giving her product to smoke?" Michaels asked.

"She asked for it." Annoyed by his friend's lack of generosity, he added, "She just got punched in the face, for Christ's sake."

"I saw that. But still."

"Well, at least I'm trying to move on. Once all this is over, we can set up more respectable, like. Have a shipping concern with an actual office, away from the river."

"You're losing your nerve."

"Like hell I am. I can just see past my own nose." He stomped off in the direction the woman had walked. Michaels watched until the last cart had left the dock, then walked after the other two.

Chapter 4

Martha helped the Werthers' cook, Mrs. Bradley, wash the dishes from the servants' dinner when a knock came at the back door. Kitty rushed to answer it. Mr. Grayson walked into the kitchen from the pantry, carrying a decanter of brandy so that he could enjoy a glass in his office, as was his wont before bed. Voices drifted in from the hall.

"What is that boy doing here at this time of night?" Mr. Grayson asked no one in particular.

Martha tilted her head to focus on the voices, but the man's voice didn't immediately ring a bell. "Who is it?"

Mr. Grayson peered at her over the rim of his glasses. "Don't tell me you haven't met our Mr. Thatcher."

"Oh, I have, actually. Just once."

"He's always here now, distracting the maids."

Kitty leaned around the kitchen doorframe and motioned for Martha to join them in the hall.

The butler leaned toward Martha. "I hope you have more sense than those other girls," he said before walking in the direction of his office.

Martha hesitated only a second before joining her friend.

"Ah, Miss Martha," Ian said as she appeared. "Just who I wanted to see."

"Martha, you haven't finished," Mrs. Bradley called.

"I'll go," Kitty offered. She giggled before disappearing into the kitchen.

Now that they were alone, Ian took a few steps closer. He held his cap tightly in both hands before him. "Now, when is your half day, pretty Miss Martha?"

Martha retreated toward the kitchen door, and Ian made no further advances. "Sunday, like all of us, why?"

"Let me take you somewhere for the afternoon. There's plenty of exhibitions going on."

"Sorry, but I always go home."

"You have to have fun sometimes."

"Who says going home isn't fun?"

"Let me guess. You have lots of younger siblings you have to take care of. A busy mother to help. Am I right?"

Martha smiled. "A common enough story, I suppose."

"That doesn't sound like very much fun."

She shook her head. "I'm sorry, I can't." She returned to the kitchen and relieved Kitty of the duties she had taken over for Martha. Kitty returned to her own conversation with Ian. *Beaus are a distraction*, Martha thought as she scrubbed the last of the dishes. She had no desire to end up like her mother anytime soon—with a house full of children, always struggling to get by. She would make her own way for now, somehow.

Scrooge sat on a red patterned couch in his nephew's living room the next morning, tapping out a mindless beat with his feet as he waited for an audience with the lady of the house.

Finally, after a flurry of whispers in the hall, Clara entered. Her hair had not yet been done up for the day and still hung in a thick braid down her back. "You wanted to see me, Uncle?"

"Yes, my dear." He half stood and waved her to the chair across from him. Once she was settled, he continued. "It has recently been brought to my attention that my accommodations may have . . . suffered from the lack of a woman's touch."

Clara glanced toward the cracked-open hall door from which a snorting laugh emerged.

Scrooge followed her gaze to the shadow lurking in the corridor. "Would you like to join us, Fred?"

The door swung open, and Fred walked in. "You only just noticed this lack, Uncle?" he asked as he sat beside his wife.

"I only now recognize it as a negative attribute." He looked between his niece and nephew, both only partially successful at smothering their grins. "You are both laughing at me."

"Honestly, Uncle, you must learn to laugh at yourself," Fred said. "Life is not quite as dour an event as you make it out to be."

Scrooge shifted in his seat. "Be that as it may, I've come seeking assistance. Isn't that a good thing?"

"Yes, and good things are often accompanied by laughter." The gentleness with which his nephew said it brought a flash of memory of Fan comforting a young Ebenezer as he readied to leave for the boy's school. For once, the thought of his sister, gone for so many years, brought a warm spread of smile rather than the sharp bite of tears.

The next smiles that the two young people exchanged were less of laughter and more of a pleasant sweetness as they sensed this tenderness in Scrooge's demeanor. Eager to encourage it, they did not bring attention to it in case that embarrassed it away.

But Scrooge, recognizing that he never spoke of Fan, forced himself to bring her to life for this boy whose youthful memories of her had surely grown fuzzy with time. "You have all the best qualities of your mother, you know, boy."

"I am hardly a boy any longer, Uncle." He grinned mischievously. "And which of her negative qualities do I not have?"

Scrooge laughed. "I meant merely that you have much of her in you, rather than your father." Scrooge had never taken to Fan's husband, who himself had been dead a number of years. Though it was fair to say that Scrooge wouldn't have approved of the king of England as a wife for Fan. "Fan was a perfect angel."

Clara glanced at her husband. "Women are humans with faults, Uncle, not angels. We each have our own flaws, just like any man."

Scrooge waved her off. "Yes, yes. But I need you to be an angel to me now, my dear. I need to set up my household, and I haven't the faintest idea of where to start."

"I'm happy to help with purchasing furniture and decorating the space. But . . . there are other things I think will require additional help."

Both men met this statement with quizzical looks.

Finally, Clara burst out with what she really meant to say. "I mean, when was the last time anything in that place was *cleaned*?"

Scrooge laughed and admitted that such quotidian notions never crossed his mind—until recently, that is. He mentioned Dr. Norman's obvious notice of the dust when he had visited.

From this, it was arranged that Clara would also find him a housekeeper. Scrooge left a little nervous but also proud at the idea of having a real household for the first time in his life. After he was gone, Fred and Clara hugged each other in contentment. Uncle Scrooge, it seemed, was rejoining the world of the living.

With this part of his life being arranged for him, back at the office on Monday, Scrooge turned his attention fully to revamping his business. After tending to the immediate tasks that inevitably arrived with the start of the week, he determined to continue his previous conversation with Bob. For once, he entered the Tank rather than calling Bob to him. "You probably thought I'd given up on redoing those loan terms, eh?"

Bob's head shot up, a wayward lock of hair sticking straight up and leading the way. After a heartbeat's pause, he said, "No, sir."

"Oh, come off it. I'm not quite so fragile as that. I know exactly what everyone thinks of me. Let's get this done."

For the next few hours, the two men hunched over the stack of books in Scrooge's office, reviewing each loan, figuring out what would help each past-due borrower make his payments again. By the end, Bob had a stack of notices to copy, letting each man know the new terms.

While Bob started on this monumental task, Scrooge scribbled in his office, wasting three perfectly good sheets of paper before he was happy with his design. Bob was wrapping his scarf around his neck in preparation of leaving for the day when Scrooge reentered the Tank.

"Don't leave just yet." Scrooge brandished the sheet of paper as if he were executing a complicated fencing maneuver.

Bob eventually succeeded in capturing the sheet from Scrooge's waving hand. "Scrooge and Cratchit," he read. "Purveyors of small loans at friendly terms. Advisement on business and accounting matters at little to no cost to individual entrepreneurs."

"An advertisement for the papers."

"I see that." He returned the page. "You realize once this is printed, there's no going back."

"Is that all you have to say, man? Don't you like seeing your name at the top?"

"Yes, sir."

With a frustrated sigh, Scrooge looked around the small room. "We'll have to get this set up for you so that it's a proper office. I'll ask Clara to help with that, too."

With no further explanation, he turned and shut himself back in his office. Bob shrugged, blew out his candle, and left. Inside his office, Scrooge hesitated before putting pen to paper but gained steam as he wrote. He made a fresh copy of the advertisement, folded one up with a note to the newspaper for publication, and wrapped another with a note for Miss Spencer. He tried not to sound too eager, but he wanted her approval on the business direction. If someone like her believed in him, then surely, he was heading down the right path.

Scrooge froze in his front entryway. It was a few evenings later, and he had just returned home from the office. Instead of the silence he was used to, clattering came from the scarce-used kitchen. Could it be the sound of chains, he wondered? Had Marley come back to pass more judgment on him?

Scrooge took two steps inside and promptly tripped over the edge of a new rug laid down the length of the hallway. He landed on his hands and knees. "Damn it," he hissed. Since he had engaged Clara to decorate, new bits were always appearing to be bumped into and tripped over. His shins were more bruised than they had been since he was a boy.

The clattering stopped, and footsteps hurried toward him. Instead of an apparition, a middle-aged woman appeared. "Oh, are you all right, sir?"

She stooped to help him, but he waved her away. She stepped around him to shut the front door, then waited expectantly as he righted himself. Once he had done so, she stuck out her hand. "Mary Minston, sir. Mrs. Williamson hired me to come help with the housekeeping." She was dowdy, with an exceedingly pale face and a round, snout-like nose, giving her the look of a burrowing animal that rarely saw daylight.

Scrooge recovered himself enough to mutter a series of barely comprehensible pleasantries, then hurried into his bedroom to hide. He had never considered the reality that the person Clara hired would be here when he got home from work. A woman in his house! That he would have to talk to! He suddenly felt that he had been a bit too ambitious in changing his circumstances.

He was still brooding over this when a knock came at the bedroom door. "Sir, I'll leave now unless you need something else? I've left your supper in the kitchen."

"No, no, you may go . . . Thank you!" he called a moment too late, after the footsteps had already retreated.

Safely alone again, Scrooge made his way to the kitchen, where he found a plate of beef and potatoes waiting for him. The staff at the public house he normally dined at would probably notice his sudden absence, though he doubted they would miss him. He took a bite of meat. It was still warm, salty, and with a hint of some spice he couldn't place. "Well," he said to himself as he cut into the rest of the food, "maybe I could get used to this."

"You'll get used to it eventually," Michaels said, taking the few remaining coins out of a young man's hand. "Few people who stay here once decide to leave." He left the man cowering on the dirty bed, an opium pipe nestled beside him. His clothes were still fine, his pocket watch still looped across his waistcoat. A new recruit, clearly.

Michaels jangled the coins in his palm, then handed them to the proprietor. "Busy place you've got here."

"However much you can bring me, I can sell," the proprietor said, scratching at a scab on his neck.

"We'll take care of that. Just keep our cut coming," Michaels said. He sauntered toward the exit, Crane following close behind. At the door, the two men turned back and surveyed the large room they had just walked through.

"We could end up with our own little empire within the Empire," Crane said. A small smile hinted that he found his own comment rather clever.

"We're already most of the way there. But we can't get distracted from the real reason we started all of this."

"We've earned back everything we lost to Marley plus some. Isn't that enough? Do we really want to risk it all on this plot you've concocted?"

"Marley is dead, you idiot. Have you been sampling the product like your whore has?" Michaels took a step toward the door, then paused and leaned in, his forefinger tapping Crane's chest. "And yes, yes, we do. Revenge will make all this worth it."

Chapter 5

Scrooge left early for work the next morning in a bid to avoid Mrs. Minston's arrival. Despite lying awake for nearly an hour in bed last night, he still hadn't quite figured out the sort of things one should say to one's housekeeper. Maybe Clara could help him with that as well—though he was sure any advice she offered would once again come layered with laughter. It was a reaction he would have to learn to live with.

As he approached the office, an angry buzz of conversation rose above the relatively muted sounds of an early-morning London street. When he stepped through the last patch of fog obscuring his view of the building, he saw a group of men gathered in front of his business's door. The agitated men were working themselves into a swarm.

He stopped a few feet away, leaving sufficient space between him and them to dash away if necessary. He had dealt with many angry and desperate men over his years in business, but they usually came singly, not as a mob. He cleared his throat. "Good morning, gentleman."

The men turned, silenced for an instant by the interruption. Then a young man stepped forward, a sheet of folded paper in his hand. "Is this real?" he demanded, stabbing the paper at Scrooge's face a few times. He was so close Scrooge could tell he was barely more than a boy, with pimples still scattered across his cheeks.

"Mine, too!" another man called from the back, his paper held above the head of his nearest compatriot.

"Is what real?" Scrooge snatched the page from the boy's hand. With a glance, he saw it was a letter Bob had sent about the new loan terms. He relaxed and handed the letter back. "Yes, I assure you, it's real."

"How do we know it's not a trick?" a voice called, unidentifiable, from the middle of the crowd.

Scrooge shoved through the men to get to the front door. Silence descended as they waited for him to unlock the door—he had installed three locks in that previous era of his life that already felt so long ago. When he had made his way down them all, he opened the door, turned, and extended an arm to welcome the men in.

When they were gathered inside, jostling each other in the entryway, he explained his new goals for the business. The men shuffled their feet and looked around at each other, gauging everyone else's reactions. One man spat on the floor as he listened, but none dared to complain verbally about their miraculous turn of fate.

The door swung open, and Bob squeezed in. Scrooge waved him through the crowd. Quickly assessing the situation, Scrooge determined that Bob would be the more neutral party. His name wasn't loaded with the same meaning as Scrooge's, and the faded elbows of his coat made him look much more like the men gathered in the foyer. He brought Bob beside him and laid a hand on his shoulder. "My partner, Mr. Cratchit here, can show you your entries in the books and give you new signatures if you wish it."

"Partner? It still says Scrooge and Marley outside."

Scrooge didn't even bother to look for the man who had made the comment. "Well, I haven't had a chance to change it yet, have I?" he said to the crowd at large. The statement was absurd—he could have changed it at any time in the last seven years had he been willing to spend the few pounds it would have cost to remake it. No one challenged him, however. They were too focused on their own concerns.

The group turned as one entity to follow Bob as he walked into the Tank. Bob looked bewildered as he faced them, but he said calmly, "Form a line at the door." The men did as he instructed as best they could in the small space.

Seeing them mollified, Scrooge went into his office and shut the door. "Ungrateful idiots," he said as he enveloped himself in the peace and quiet of his desk and the familiarity of long columns of numbers.

Finally, there was silence as the last man was ushered out the door. Scrooge relished the moment until a tentative knock came at his office door.

"Come in, Bob."

Bob's long, thin face peeped around the door. He waited for Scrooge to wave him in before walking into the room. "Who would have thought so many people would complain about better terms?"

"They don't trust me." Scrooge pointed a pen at the street. "We need to replace the sign. Show people things have changed."

"The sign, sir? But it's always said Scrooge and Marley, even after all these years since Mr. Marley passed."

The pen jabbed in Bob's direction. "That's exactly the attitude we're trying to correct. Now, remind me. Your oldest son, what's his name?"

"Peter, sir."

"For God's sake, Bob, drop the 'sir.' If you're a partner, act like it."

Bob gulped down his response.

"Peter's old enough to be employed, isn't he?"

"He's been working as an errand boy for a newspaper."

"Hmph. Well, I suppose he can leave, can't he? I assume he knows his letters?"

"Very well, yes."

"With you as a partner, we'll need a new clerk."

"That would be an honor for him, sir."

"Not at your wage, of course, because he doesn't have your experience."

"Understood."

Scrooge looked at his employee-turned-partner for a long moment. Abruptly, he returned his attention to the account book on his desk. "It's a question, you see, of what will happen to the business when I'm gone. I don't have anyone to pass it on to, but you do." He peeked at Bob out of the corner of his eye. Bob's eyes widened as this vision danced before him. "You may go."

Bob gave a jerky little bow and backed out of the room.

Once he was alone again, Scrooge smiled to himself. In fact, he beamed. With these new magnanimous visions of the future, he might be able to redeem himself after all.

The following Monday morning, Bob arrived to work with Peter in tow. Even though Peter was close to becoming a man, he still hadn't embarked on a growth spurt, coming only to his father's chest. His greeting to Scrooge was mumbled and obscured by his overly starched collar that stuck up around his jawline.

Scrooge didn't mind and didn't ask the boy to repeat what he had said. Instead, he ushered him into the Tank and guided him by the shoulders to a small desk Scrooge had found at a secondhand store the night before. (Surely, he couldn't rely on Clara for everything.) Peter stared at the desk as if he weren't sure what it was for.

"I'll leave you to get settled in."

Peter gave a minute nod that was only perceptible because of the sound of his cheeks scratching against the starched fabric of his color.

Scrooge walked with Bob the few steps to the door of the Tank.

"Thank you, Mr. Scrooge," Bob said. "He's a shy boy, but once he warms up to you, he can talk your ear off."

"I'll be looking forward to that, then, I suppose."

"By the way, Dr. Norman came back to see us last night, and Tim seems to be getting stronger. All the children are looking better, really, with the improved diet. The extra shillings have really helped."

"I'm glad to hear it. I only regret I delayed helping so long." He slipped an arm around Bob's shoulders in a half hug. In the next instant, as Bob stiffened, Scrooge realized he had overstepped, and the awkwardness of the gesture overcame him. He hurried back to his own desk, ostensibly to allow Peter time to become accustomed to his new situation but really to chastise himself yet again for his social missteps.

Scrooge regathered the courage to leave his office that afternoon and hovered in the doorway to the Tank. He cleared his throat even though both Cratchits were already looking curiously at him.

"I have some business to conduct at the 'Change. Perhaps Peter could take these for me?" He held out a slim stack of papers.

"Yes, of course, sir," Peter said, jumping up so quickly his chair clattered to the floor.

"You're not going yourself as usual?" Bob asked. Before the events at Christmas, Scrooge had been in the habit of visiting the 'Change almost daily, his typical position on a particular corner well known to all.

"No, no, I'm much too busy." Scrooge broke his gaze from Bob's questioning look and watched Peter dart into the street. The truth was, the thought of facing his old business associates—the men the spirits had shown him held so little regard for him when his back was turned—chilled him. But still, he had to make money, or how would he be able to help anyone? Peter as a courier was the perfect solution.

The tinkle of the bell above the front door broke Scrooge from his thoughts. He turned to see who had arrived. Miss Spencer stood before him, her hair covered by a blue bonnet that perfectly matched her dress. She seemed more lovely every time he saw her.

"Ah!" he said. "What have you got there?" He pointed at the large papers rolled up into a tube under her arm.

"Some plans." She rapped them with her opposite hand, and the deep thud resonating from the thick pages filled the foyer. "May I come in?"

"Yes, yes, of course." He held out an arm, and she entered his office first. He closed the door behind them. "Plans for what, may I ask?"

"That's why I brought them here. They're plans for your—our—new campaign." She dropped the tube onto the desk with a grin.

Scrooge took his seat and untied the string. The pages unfurled across his desk with a satisfying flutter.

Miss Spencer moved the stack in front of her, then pulled the first sheet off the pile. "I've put together a couple of advertisements for papers targeted to those who need your help rather than just promoting your business services."

Complimentary services for small business owners, the first ad read. *Small loans at incredibly low rates,* stated the other. Stamped at the bottom of each was the name Scrooge & Cratchit and the business's address. Scrooge handed the sheet back to her. "Very smart. I just hope people don't think it's some sort of a scam. With my name being on it and all."

Miss Spencer set the sheet neatly back on top of her stack, lining up all four corners as she spoke. "Some might. But many others will come, and you will just have to convince them of your sincerity." She dove right into the next item on her mental agenda. "I have a couple of speaking arrangements lined up. I think you should come, to present this as a new way to help the poor."

"I don't think they want to hear from me."

"They need to hear from you. To know this is legitimate."

Scrooge saw from her firmness that this was actually more of a demand than a request. He acquiesced. "Right, then. I hope you'll give me some pointers, though."

She had clearly already prepared for this request. "Here's a page of notes you can review." She rolled up her other papers and stood.

Scrooge did not want her to leave quite so soon and scrambled for an excuse to delay her. "Perhaps we can discuss it further over dinner—a dinner party. I'm hosting a dinner party." He rubbed his chest and gave a little cough.

"Are you inviting me?"

"Yes, that was meant to be an invitation."

She laughed. Somehow, the notes of her laughter perfectly matched the brightness of her dress. "When is this dinner party?"

"Saturday night." He realized he was still rubbing his chest and brought his arm down abruptly.

"All right. I'll be there."

Once she had left, Scrooge laid his forehead on the cool surface of his desk. His whole body vibrated from the pounding in his head. Dear God, what had he done?

Clara just laughed when Scrooge explained his predicament that evening. "Fred and I will be there, and I'll find you a few more guests. We'll get to test Mrs. Minston's mettle, anyway."

As the week progressed, Clara was as good as her word. A note arrived at Scrooge's office on Friday afternoon with the guest list and the menu. He made no reply, as he had no opinion on the matter. But he did look across at the closed door of the Tank. Bob and Mrs. Cratchit weren't on the list. Ought he to invite them? Perhaps Clara already had, and they had declined. Either way, Scrooge got the feeling that Mrs. Cratchit hadn't warmed to him yet, despite his recent efforts. Who could blame her? The new year was still young and cold, and there were many past years outweighing it.

In the end, he let inaction decide for him and bid good night to Bob and Peter as they left. He acted like it was any other evening and not one where he was worried he might die of mortification before they returned to the office on Monday. It might be better not to let the Cratchits see what was about to transpire, anyway, if he wanted to maintain any authority around the office.

Of course, the lack of a dinner invitation meant nothing to Bob, who was not used to having friends with time or funds to spare to make such invitations, and besides, there was not much he thought could be better than an evening at home with his family.

Scrooge sat at his desk for a while after the Cratchits left, not doing any work of value. Finally, after about three internal pep talks convincing himself that Ebenezer Scrooge could, in fact, survive a dinner party, he locked up and started his walk home, just as the church bells rang eight o'clock.

Between Clara and Mrs. Minston, Scrooge's front rooms were transformed over the course of the Saturday afternoon. Pretty arrangements of flowers covered the bare surfaces where family portraits or knickknacks would have been placed in any other home. The new furniture that had been acquired so far was supplemented by a few dining chairs carried over from Fred and Clara's. The invigorating smell from the kitchen added the perfect final touch. By the time the guests arrived, Scrooge's rooms had begun to feel like a proper home. Scrooge allowed himself to be carried away by the ladies' enthusiasm, and he even helped lay out the hors d'oeuvres on pretty platters in the parlor.

Clara was a wonderful hostess, keeping the conversation up among everyone in the parlor as they waited to sit down to dinner. There was Clara and Fred and Miss Spencer, who fortunately had no inkling the entire event had been arranged just for her, along with Clara's sister and brother-in-law, Anne and Rupert Huston. The set was rounded out by Mr. Huston's mother, Mrs. Morody, now twice widowed, as she informed everyone almost immediately upon arrival, and her daughter from her second marriage, Lucretia Morody. Clara had invited the latter so that there would be another young single woman for Miss Spencer to socialize with, though right away it became obvious that the two ladies had nothing in common—Miss Spencer found it difficult to discuss much outside of her passion for her work, and Lucretia had never seen the inside of a charitable organization in her life and had no plans to, either.

Lucretia was also unmarried, as her mother managed to state, quite loudly, twice before dinner began. The young Miss Morody was one of those people with strange proportions of features that you had to peer at for rather a long time to determine if she was extraordinarily pretty or extraordinarily ugly: her hair was neither quite brown nor black, her forehead much too tall, her eyes large and set far apart, lips thin, and nose as dainty as could be.

The table the party sat down to about half an hour after their arrival was more heavily laden with food and wine than had ever been in Scrooge's home before. He found himself automatically counting the bottles of wine lined up along the sideboard, ready to refill his guests' glasses, but he shook himself out of the thought. Charity begins at home, he reminded himself.

The guests exclaimed over the food for a few minutes before Mrs. Morody returned to her favorite topic.

"You've never been married, Mr. Scrooge?"

He shook his head, hoping not to encourage this line of conversation.

"Never met the right woman, I assume? That's what bachelors always say."

The image of Belle, his long-ago fiancée, floated to the top of his mind. "Well, now, I wouldn't say that. I just didn't recognize it at the time, I suppose."

Fred glanced at Scrooge and his reddening eyes. "Uncle, why don't you tell everyone about your new plans for the business?"

A sense of relief at the change of topic passed around the table, except, of course, for Mrs. Morody, whose mouth remained in a permanent pout for the rest of the meal.

From the discussion of Scrooge's business, they moved on to Miss Spencer's work and her and Scrooge's upcoming presentation to potential donors.

"I can attend," Fred said, "for support. I can pretend to be a very important investor." His eyes sparkled.

"Nonsense," Scrooge said. "You'll laugh through the whole thing."

Fred lifted his glass. "Such can be summed up my approach to life."

Mrs. Minston peeked her head around the doorway. "Mr. Scrooge!" she hissed in a voice that was perhaps meant to be unobtrusive but caused each member of the party to turn his or her head toward the door.

Scrooge set down his napkin and followed her beckoning finger into the kitchen. On top of the range sat a blackened pudding. "I've burned it, sir. I'm still not quite used to this range and was a bit a short on time trying to get it done . . . and, well, you can see the result."

Scrooge, who had never had a dessert made for him in his life and had never felt the lack of it, struggled to form a response to what had been presented as a dire predicament. He didn't get much out except a jumble of "I" and "you."

Mrs. Minston jumped in to fill the void. "I suppose you'll want to dock my wages, sir?"

"What? No, of course not. Just . . ." He flung his hands into the air. "Figure something out with Clara."

Clara replaced him in the kitchen and soon reemerged in the dining room carrying a tray of strawberries, custard, and slivers of the salvageable interior of the pudding so prettily presented that no one imagined they could have been served anything better.

The guests left soon after dessert. Scrooge sent them all into the world with handshakes and well-wishes. Miss Spencer seemed suitably impressed—or at least not disappointed—so perhaps all the effort had been worth it, Scrooge reasoned.

As soon as the dishes were cleared away, Mrs. Minston left out the back without a goodbye to her employer. Scrooge's good mood deflated. He fretted that she had thought he would be so callous as to dock her wages for something so minor as a burned pudding. She must have heard stories of him from somewhere. He would have to come up with a way to show her his appreciation, as well as how he had changed.

After exiting Scrooge's home, one of the participants in that night's events made her way from there to a not-so-well-to-do flat in a much less well-to-do part of the city. Inside the flat, Michaels and Crane had just finished their own poor supper. Although their business enterprise was flourishing, maintaining their poor, dark lifestyle fit their purposes for now. There was no need to get ahead of themselves. Though, like Crane, Michaels had started to contemplate what life might look like after they achieved their version of success. He would move far from the docks, perhaps get a little place on the edge of the city with a small plot of land. He would buy it in cash, of course, and would not ruin his chances by taking out another mortgage so that he could be taken advantage of by another greedy banker. This line of thought turned his mind back to his favorite topic: furthering their plot for revenge.

"We'll need helpers," Michaels said. "The old bat may recognize us."

"I doubt it," his companion said while working a toothpick between his front teeth. "There's no way he can keep track of all the people whose lives he ruined."

"Still, I think it's better not to reveal ourselves until the end."

"And your sister?"

"She's in place. I've gotten her quite close to Mr. Scrooge." His grin revealed only blackened and missing teeth.

A knock came at the door. "That must be her now to report back to us," Michaels said, then swung open the door to reveal the lady on the landing.

She had brought some remnants of the dinner that had been offered to her. The men nibbled at them while she told her tale of the party, highlighting the awkward moments she had witnessed. Michaels laughed, whereas Crane looked on with a scowl.

"I don't know what you expect me to do," she said when she had finished.

"I'll let you know," Michaels said. "When the time comes, I want him to feel like he has enemies on all sides, like we did all those years ago."

"Hmph. Well, I have to go." She stood and headed to the door. She opened it just as two women—Crane's girl, with her eye mostly healed, and another—were taking the final steps to the flat. She took the women in quickly, their clothing nowhere near appropriate for the winter's night. "Looks like your friends are here," she said to the men in a disapproving tone, then swished out the door around them.

Chapter 6

Mrs. and Miss Morody, both unmarried, called on Ebenezer Scrooge the following Saturday. Unfortunately for Scrooge, he had not yet learned the art of not being at home because no one had ever purposefully sought out his company before. He answered the door before Mrs. Minston could perform that duty. He overcame his momentary surprise at these visitors and showed the two ladies into the parlor.

"How can I help you?" he asked after they had all settled in.

"We were intrigued hearing about your charity work at dinner last week," the mother said.

"So intrigued," Miss Morody echoed.

"My daughter said we simply must go find out how we can help."

"I'm hardly the best person to ask. You would have done better to go see Miss Spencer."

"Oh, but Lucretia also said, 'We must go see that eminent person, Mr. Scrooge, who was so kind to us last week.'"

"Yes, well . . ." Scrooge glanced warily between the two women. He clutched his knees in an attempt to steady himself. After a moment, an idea came to him. He stood and began donning his coat and hat.

The ladies scrambled to their feet, exchanging confused looks.

Once he was wrapped up for a foray outside, Scrooge explained his intent. "The orphanage always needs volunteers and donations. We'll go for a visit. And Miss Spencer may even be there to provide us further guidance." He ushered the two women out the front door. "I hope you don't mind a brisk walk," he said as he stepped purposefully ahead of them. They scurried into position behind him, struggling to keep pace with his long strides. These exertions kept the ladies from annoying him with further questions as they walked.

At the entrance to the orphanage, Scrooge made a show of emptying his pockets into the donation box. Mrs. Morody hurriedly searched through her reticule and motioned for her daughter to do the same. Their search produced only a few coins that clinked dismally at the bottom of the box.

Scrooge pulled the doorbell but charged right inside, recalling his previous unsuccessful attempt at summoning someone to the door. In the foyer, two children sat picking at each other's hair. One child squeezed a small white blob between his thumb and forefinger. Scrooge realized the children were picking lice off each other, like animals at a zoo. He forced himself not to grimace.

"Hello!" Scrooge bellowed to them. "Is Miss Spencer here?"

After a long moment spent looking over their visitors, the children slowly shook their heads.

"No matter." Scrooged turned back toward the ladies. "We can still give ourselves a tour. Perhaps we'll run into Mrs. Thompson. She's the matron of the place."

As they continued into the hallway, Mrs. Morody muttered, "Dreadful creatures."

"Lice?" Scrooge asked. "Yes, a real torture to get rid of once you have them."

A significant glance between the two ladies behind Scrooge's back indicated that lice may not have been the dreadful creatures she was referring to.

Scrooge led them on. They passed a dormitory. Scrooge leaned into the room. "We've just provided all new bedding here." He waved his walking stick around the room in demonstration. "Come on."

They continued silently through the halls, except for Scrooge's occasional greetings to the children they passed. Finally, they came to Mrs. Thompson's office, tucked in the back of the building, as if ashamed anyone should admit working there. For once, the matron was in it.

"Hello, Mrs. Thompson. I've brought you some new visitors. Potential donors."

Mrs. Thompson paused her writing and lifted her pen to indicate behind him, displaying an ink-stained hand. "Your guests don't seem to be enjoying their tour."

Scrooge turned and looked closely at the pair of women for the first time since they had entered the orphanage. Both ladies held their handkerchiefs to their faces, which were exceedingly pale beneath the fabric. "No matter," he said to them, though underneath, he was annoyed that the first guests he brought in should act so poorly. "Not the best fit, then." He turned back. "How are you, Mrs. Thompson?"

"Exceedingly busy."

"Right. Back out, then." He lifted his stick toward the door and led his companions on a reverse march of the halls.

Once they were safely outside, he asked, "Would you like to visit another option for sharing your goodwill?"

"Unfortunately, we have other engagements today," Mrs. Morody said. Her handkerchief fluttered in the breeze as she struggled to fold it and put it back in her reticule. Once she succeeded, she looked up. "We'll find a carriage to take us back."

Scrooge looked up and down the narrow street. "You're not likely to find one around here. But I think there's an omnibus—"

"Thank you for your kindness, but we'll find our own way." She bustled past him, her daughter following close behind.

Once they had lost Scrooge in the crowd, Lucretia said, "Surely you can't expect me to do that again, Mother."

"No, you're right. That was simply unfathomable how he could expect self-respecting ladies to put up with that. But still, he's a very wealthy suitor."

"I would hardly call him a suitor at this point."

"He just doesn't know it yet. We must make him realize."

"How do you suggest we do that?"

"He's a man like any other, I imagine. You will seduce him, and then he'll have to marry you."

"But—"

"No buts. If you do your job right, then there is no risk." She stopped at a corner and peered down the street to their left, which led to a wider panorama at its end. "Here. I think we've nearly made it out of this hellhole." She led her daughter back in the direction of civilization.

Behind them, Scrooge stood in the narrow street, debating what to do. He was so close to the Cratchits', it almost seemed he *ought* to go there. But his appearance would likely only cause the family stress—and elicit another glower in his direction from Mrs. Cratchit.

He decided on a compromise. He wandered down several side streets before he found a small grocer's. He squeezed down one of the tiny aisles and purchased a pound of penny candy. Returning the way he had come—in a roundabout way because he couldn't quite recall the exact direction—he set the bag in front of the Cratchits' door, knocked, and dashed off, easily merging with the rest of the Saturday-afternoon crowd. He grinned the whole way home. "This must be the way Father Christmas feels," he said to himself with a hearty laugh.

A few days later, Scrooge paced in front of the building where he and Miss Spencer would give their presentation in three-quarters of an hour's time. The audience would be no bigger than fifty, but his stomach still recoiled at the thought of speaking before them. Surely some of them would know of his life up to this point. And if any of them should make comments similar to those on that note he found at his door on New Year's Eve . . .

He stopped pacing and his face brightened as Miss Spencer emerged from the crowd. Before he could greet her, a hand clamped onto his shoulder from behind and spun him around into a hug. Once Scrooge extricated himself from the embrace, he said, "You actually came."

"Of course I did," Fred said. "I want to support you in every endeavor."

Before Scrooge could mumble an answer, Miss Spencer reached them. The trio exchanged brief pleasantries before going inside. Backstage, Fred's cheerful chatter occupied them until he had to take his seat in the audience. As soon as Fred left, Scrooge started pacing again.

Miss Spencer laid a hand on his arm as he marched past her. It was the suddenness of her touch, rather than any strength of grip on her part, that halted him.

"It will be fine," she told him. "Just speak with authority and people will listen to anything you have to say."

Thinking back on all the rubbish he had spouted with authority over the course of his life, he mumbled, "That's what I'm afraid of." Then, their moment in the spotlight arrived. A man appeared and directed them toward the stage before Miss Spencer could ask Scrooge to explain. They waited in the wings in silence as a man from one of the organizations Miss Spencer worked with finished giving a lengthy, praise-filled biography of her from the podium. His mention of Scrooge was brief and perfunctory. Scrooge couldn't blame the man, as Scrooge had yet to prove himself in this arena.

The introduction over, Miss Spencer spoke first, describing her charitable projects with an ease sure to coax donations out of pockets. When she returned to the wings, she gave Scrooge an encouraging smile before he walked onto the stage. To keep his confidence up through the speech, he imagined the audience members were his old classmates who had ignored him so mercilessly, and he was finally showing them what's what. He would leave the emotional appeals to Miss Spencer—she was so good at it—and he would focus on his strengths: logic, business, and return on investment, though of course, now with a charitable bent. Scrooge's remarks were delivered gruffly but, he hoped, with authority, as Miss Spencer had wished. The applause after his closing was polite rather than enthusiastic, but he hoped he had hit his mark.

At the reception afterward in the lobby of the theater, many pledges of donations were made, though few monies were delivered on the spot. This, Miss Spencer assured Scrooge, was normal. Donation boxes like the one lingering out front at the orphanage were for smaller amounts and for lesser donors. Here, they worked on promises and agreements.

Eventually, Miss Spencer joined a lively conversation on one side of the room, leaving Scrooge on his own amid all the strangers.

"Must be nice to have done so well in business to be able to give your services away for free," one man holding a glass of brandy said as he walked by Scrooge without stopping for an answer.

Scrooge was still trying to interpret that remark—was it snide or supportive?—when another man stopped and held out his hand for Scrooge to shake, then produced his business card. He was very short and wore a very green coat. He brought to mind a shiny garden beetle.

Scrooge forced himself not to smile at this internal observation and turned the proffered card over in his hand. The name Mr. Lauriston was scrawled across the card in delicate lettering. "You're a solicitor."

"Indeed. If any of your poorer clients need legal services or paperwork drawn up, feel free to send them my way."

"A wonderful offer. We could create a whole support system for these people."

Mr. Lauriston nodded and started to walk away. At the last instant, Scrooge fished into his pocket and pulled out his own business card. Lauriston took it with a little wave as he continued across the room.

This time, Scrooge did not attempt to hide his smile. Perhaps the world really was better than he had thought for so long. And perhaps he could actually make a difference in it.

"Making any good connections?" Fred asked as he walked over, carrying a plate towering with delicate hors d'oeuvres, which he offered to his uncle. Scrooge shook his head firmly. He was still a simple man who preferred a simple diet, and if he couldn't immediately identify a dish as animal, vegetable, or mineral, he wasn't interested. Fred popped a small dough ball stuffed with something green into his mouth. The look on his face as he chewed showed he wasn't thrilled by the taste. "Wonderful speech, by the way," he said. "I have to say, I'm glad you made it through without mentioning any ghosts."

"Is that why you're here? To monitor what I'm saying?" Scrooge's stomach flip-flopped, making him even less likely to accept any of Fred's well-intentioned but dubious snacks.

Scrooge had indeed made it through the whole day without a thought of the spirits, even as he opined over his charitable interests that were a direct result of the spirits' visit. Was that a good thing, or was he doing a disservice to the beings who had enlightened him? He wasn't sure, and he never liked being unsure. As soon as Fred had fully given up on his platter of food, Scrooge dragged him toward the front door, insisting he had experienced quite enough of this rubbish. He had to stop himself from adding "Bah, humbug" at the end.

A few weeks later, a thin, paper-wrapped parcel arrived at Scrooge's residence that brought thoughts of the spirits roaring back to him. By this time, it was late February, and the new year was already starting to feel old. He had begun implementing his resolutions in earnest, but he often found the effort draining as he adapted to his new life.

Dr. Norman's name was scrawled in one corner of the plain brown wrapping paper, giving Scrooge a clue as to what might be inside. He unwrapped the parcel as he ate the dinner Mrs. Minston had left for him, untying the string, then carefully unfolding the paper between bites of potato. Inside, he found a short letter from Dr. Norman enclosing a volume of a medical journal that included the paper Dr. Norman had written about his interviews with Scrooge and others. It took Scrooge three times as long to finish his meal as it normally did, as he became absorbed in hearing the stories of others who had been blessed with the same experience as him. He felt less alone, knowing that there were others like him out there. His burden also lightened with the knowledge that he was not the only one who had been chosen and given such a momentous charge.

However, these anecdotes were only the first part of the paper and were presented without commentary. Once he finished reading the anecdotes and moved on to the analysis in the next section, it became clear that Dr. Norman didn't share Scrooge's perspective. The doctor had talked to people who, like Scrooge, believed they were visited by angels, ghosts, or God himself. Dr. Norman was a man of science first and foremost, and he described these visits as a type of mania in which adherents could live completely normal lives while remaining convinced of the visitation. He stated that the resumption of regular daily activities was crucial for those afflicted. A forced stay in a mental hospital tended to deepen and solidify the belief because the patients had nothing to think about except the vision they had received and how they were persecuted for it by being committed. This seemed like a rather liberal viewpoint—and certainly one Scrooge himself would not have ascribed to in the previous chapter of his life. However, to hold it, one had to accept these people were mentally ill, which Scrooge wholeheartedly did not.

Scrooge scoffed and dropped the journal on the table beside his plate. Clearly, Dr. Norman didn't believe anything he had been told because he hadn't experienced it himself. While Scrooge appreciated the suggestion that he didn't deserve to be in an insane asylum, the idea that such an extreme action could be taken against him had never crossed his mind.

Even so, Scrooge didn't regret giving the interview. Because he had been chosen by the spirits to be saved, it was his duty to share his story so that someone else could turn his life around and avoid the most terrible of fates. If that made him appear a maniac to the rest of the world, then so be it. He had never been a man easily swayed by the views of others.

Still, he regarded the pages dubiously one more time before clearing away his plate. To contemplate that some might think him insane . . . But no, they would never come for him. He was Ebenezer Scrooge, for goodness' sake. He had money, and that still meant something.

Across the city in a well-appointed flat perched high above the mere peons stuck living at ground level, another man read the same article but had a very different reaction. The vignette in the article that most incensed him was the one of the well-to-do businessman. That such a clearly unstable person should still be allowed to take hardworking citizens' money into his care was unthinkable.

The man who experienced this reaction was one Dr. Burnhope. In his line of work, he had a professional interest in keeping those with mental disorders off the streets. This had turned into a fiduciary interest, as these things often do. He had spent many years working at asylums across the country and had done a great deal of good. However, it had given him too much faith in the strength and correctness of these institutions. The suggestion that these types of people were better left alone to live their daily lives seemed to him a dangerous proposition. The idea had to be stamped out.

Dr. Burnhope circled the author's name. It shouldn't be too difficult to find out how to contact this Dr. Norman. They both treated diseases of the mind, so they were practically colleagues, after all. He also had contacts at other medical journals and at the Royal Academy that he could call on to support his position. He would make sure that such nonsense was not allowed to be published again.

Chapter 7

Scrooge's worries over how others perceived his mental health passed quickly, and he moved forward on his new path. Just as February was ticking over into March, Miss Spencer again sat in Scrooge's office. This time, she helped him arrange his charitable donations, setting up regular payments to his top causes. Such an arrangement was very businesslike. Scrooge approved.

Once they had gone through the list, Scrooge said, "Maybe something can be done for Mrs. Minston's family."

Miss Spencer looked up absently from her notes. "Who?"

"You know, my housekeeper. The one who burned the pudding."

"Oh. Was that what all that fuss was about? Well, are her family very badly off?"

Scrooge frowned. "They must be."

Miss Spencer shifted in her seat. "Simply because she is a housekeeper, you mean." Seeing Scrooge's uncertainty, she continued. "I think, probably, you've still not seen what true destitution looks like. Those who are elderly or infirm or unemployed. That said, I can add the Minstons to the list of recipients for our food rounds." She held her pen ready. "Where do they live?"

"I'm not sure exactly."

She sighed, but her smile was good-humored. "Find out and let me know."

"Yes, yes, of course." Scrooge had watched her in admiration throughout her visit. She was so confident in her purpose. And she had needed no ghostly visit to turn her onto the correct path. A thought flashed through his mind of what it might be like to have such a woman at his side. The idea struck him so forcefully, he embarked on a coughing fit. With her usual immediacy of purpose, Miss Spencer quickly stood and poured him a glass of water from a pitcher in the corner. As Scrooge took it, their fingertips brushed. He was, it could be argued, not so old. He was grateful to have the glass to drink from as a shield while he considered such an uncomfortable thought. No, it was absurd. Absolutely absurd.

It was made even more so by the forthrightness of her next declaration, after he had recovered himself, of course. "Are you busy now? I can take you on a tour of a workhouse nearby." Clearly, she still saw him as a project in progress.

"A workhouse?" Scrooge spluttered, as if he had never heard of such a thing.

"Yes. I assume you've never been to one, even though you've probably sent many people there?" She lowered her head and blushed slightly. "Sorry, I didn't mean it so harshly. Sometimes I can be a bit too direct."

"No. You are absolutely right. I should go see it, even if it is uncomfortable."

They bundled themselves into their coats and left without a word to Bob as to their destination. After a walk that seemed much too short to Scrooge because it showed the need that had been at his doorstep all along, they arrived at the workhouse door. There was a short line of people waiting at the entrance. Miss Spencer pushed past them with a few "Good mornings" and an "Excuse me" or two thrown in. Scrooge couldn't meet the gazes of those they passed, but from the corner of his eye, he saw them look him up and down with scorn. He himself, Ebenezer Scrooge, the well-off scion of business, worthy of these people's scorn. The world really was upside down from what he had once thought it was.

Once they entered the building, Miss Spencer greeted the attendant registering those in line. As each person checked in, men went into a room on the left, and the women entered a room on the right. Each person looked more exhausted and bedraggled than the next. One young woman, her hand on a boy's shoulder, caught Scrooge's eye, but he quickly looked away.

Miss Spencer narrated what he was seeing, in a voice he thought a bit too loud and obvious to those she was describing. He cringed, not wanting to draw any more attention to himself than was absolutely necessary.

"Everyone is stripped and evaluated in those rooms," she said. "The children will be separated from their mothers, of course, and everyone, including the children, will work picking oakum from now until tomorrow morning in exchange for having a bed and a meal tonight."

Scrooge watched the young woman and boy disappear into the next room. He thought back on his own childhood, when he had felt so abandoned by his family in that dreadful school. Imagine if he had instead ended up in a place like this . . . Perhaps his own lot in life had not been so bad after all. In an effort to justify this system he had so long supported, he asked, "These women, are they . . ."

"Prostitutes?" Miss Spencer supplied. "Most of them are not, though many of the people who are supposed to help them assume they are." She looked pointedly at Scrooge. "Poverty, you see, is not a moral failing."

"Right." He gripped his hands together behind his back.

"They won't be released until nine or ten o'clock tomorrow morning. As a man of business, you know that at that late hour, work for the day has already begun. So these people must decide whether a bed for tonight is worth giving up a day's wages tomorrow. It's a self-perpetuating cycle that is very difficult to escape."

"I can see how that could be the case."

Miss Spencer watched him carefully for a moment. Scrooge knew he had to be very pale, and the only thing keeping him from trembling was the tight hold of his hands on each other. She gently gripped his elbow, which was still held close against his side. "I think that's enough for today. Let's get you back, shall we?" Relief washed over him. He did not look behind him as they walked away.

Miss Spencer dropped him off at the office door, saying she had other appointments to keep. Scrooge burst inside. Bob was carrying an account book from Scrooge's office across to the Tank. He jumped in surprise at Scrooge's sudden, forceful entrance. "Is everything all right, sir?" he asked.

"Oh, Bob!" Scrooge choked out. "Everything I've done." He shook his head and said much more quietly, "Everything I've done."

When he got home that evening, Scrooge cornered Mrs. Minston in the kitchen. Or, rather, he tried to get her attention from the doorway, but over the clatter of dishes and her own dizzying speed of movement, she didn't notice him, and he followed her meekly around for several seconds until, on a return trip from the pantry, she turned and saw him. Her hand jumped to her heart. The pan she held in her other hand trembled but didn't fall.

"Mr. Scrooge! What in the world are you doing?"

"I wanted to talk to you."

"Wanted to scare me to death is more like." She pushed past him and turned her attention to the stove.

"I wanted to ask—you know Miss Spencer—"

"She's coming to dinner again, is she?"

"No. That's not it." He shook his head. "She has many charitable endeavors, and I was wondering if your family could make use of any."

Mrs. Minston set down a spoon she had been using to stir the contents of a pot and turned to face him, wiping her hands on her apron. "You think we're in need of charity?"

"I just wanted to offer . . ."

"We may not have a big, fancy house like this, but we're not so bad off as you may think. We do all right." The spoon reappeared, and she jabbed it toward Scrooge to emphasize her words. "Now if there's nothing else, I'd like to get back to my work."

"Right. Sorry. Thank you." Scrooge scurried out of the room, cowed by the force of her response, which he saw now that Miss Spencer had tried to warn him about. Perhaps, he reasoned, the spirits hadn't intended him to help absolutely everyone. No, that wasn't quite right. Perhaps not everyone needed his help. Or there were bigger changes that needed to be made. He had to see both the big picture and the individual stories, just like Miss Spencer did. He had a lot still to learn from her, and he was determined to continue to do so.

Across the city, Mrs. Cratchit was not so easily startled by noise and the movement of bodies in her kitchen. That Sunday night, just like every evening, she prepared dinner in the midst of chaos. The meal never suffered for it—not that her family would have dared mention it if it had.

Bob, though quiet and demure at the office, was not afraid to boom over his family at home. Especially tonight, with Martha home on her weekly half day, he was bursting with saved-up stories to share. As they tucked into their simple meal of salted fish and potatoes, he said, "You will never guess what Mr. Scrooge did this week."

His wife groaned.

"What?" Tiny Tim asked excitedly.

"It's nothing bad," Bob said to his wife. "It's quite remarkable, really." He paused for dramatic effect, a grin nearly bursting off his face as if it couldn't be contained much longer. "He visited a workhouse."

Belinda wrinkled her nose. "Why on earth would he do that?"

"To see what they're like." He scooped another forkful of food into his mouth. "He has this new friend who is deeply involved in charity work around the city and has introduced him to a lot of things."

"Who is this friend? Is he legitimate?" Mrs. Cratchit asked.

"My dear, I never thought I would see the day you'd be concerned for my employer's welfare," he teased. "It's a woman, actually. A Miss Spencer."

"She's unmarried?" Martha asked. "How does she support all this charity, then?"

"I assume she has some independent means. But she doesn't dress richly. From what I've seen of her, she's a very nice young lady with a good heart."

"After his money, I assume," Mrs. Cratchit said.

"Really, my dear."

Mrs. Cratchit pursed her lips and returned her focus to her plate but didn't apologize.

Martha's eyes sparkled in the candlelight at the thought of a young woman living on her own and doing good works. It sounded remarkable, much more so than the story of a young woman from a poor family taking her first position in service at the age of fourteen. Some days, Martha already felt old even though she was a mere seventeen. "She sounds wonderful," Martha said. "I would love to meet her."

Bob shrugged. "That could probably be arranged."

"I want to meet her, too!" Tiny Tim shouted from his corner of the table. His mother shushed him, warned him not to get himself too worked up.

"We can all meet her," Bob said.

"Just make sure she doesn't try to throw all her charity on us," Mrs. Cratchit said. "We're doing just fine."

Bob watched her closely for several minutes, but she refused to catch his eye. What she had said gave him the perfect segue to announce a subject he had been aching to bring up for weeks. Bob tapped the handle of his knife on the table to get his family's attention again. It took a few moments for the individual conversations to die down, but eventually, all seven faces turned toward him.

"Just as you say, my dear, we are doing just fine. More than fine! Now that I've been made partner and had my income raised, and now that Peter has joined me there as well, I feel confident our family is entering a new era. And we should take advantage of it."

"Whatever are you saying, Bob?" Mrs. Cratchit asked as she struggled to hold little Charles's head still long enough to wipe some gravy off his face.

"We should move house. Nothing extravagant, just something a little bigger and nicer."

"Oh, yes! Please, mama!" Peter and Belinda shouted. Tiny Tim beamed and rapped the handle of his own knife against the tabletop.

Martha said nothing. The idea of her family moving up in the world without her—possibly even leaving her behind—burned her cheeks red. But she had been brought up well and knew it was better to say nothing at all rather than dampen the others' excitement.

"It's something to consider. But let's not get too far ahead of ourselves and take on more commitments than we can afford," Mrs. Cratchit said.

"Of course not. Like I said, nothing extravagant. There are many grades of quality between this and extravagant." He waited expectantly for a response, but his wife simply nodded and returned her attention to her meal. "Well, I'll look into it then, shall I?"

"Mm-hm," was all she said. Bob watched her a moment longer, then gave up and changed the subject.

After the children cleared the table and Martha was getting them ready for bed, the parents washed the dishes alone. Mrs. Cratchit took the opportunity to make her real views on Bob's proposal known.

"I wish you had talked to me about it first, instead of bringing it up in front of the children. You know they get excited."

"Why shouldn't they get excited? This is an exciting time to be a Cratchit."

She laughed and shook her head. Her red, chapped hands continued to scrub the plate. "Still."

Bob grabbed her shoulders and turned her to face him. Water dripped from the plate to their shoes. "I understand why you're hesitant. But I'm asking you to trust me. I haven't led us wrong yet, have I?"

She turned back to the wash basin. "Don't pretend like you had some grand plan, that you knew Mr. Scrooge would change like this. But I suppose there's no harm in looking at what's out there—that's reasonable, mind."

Bob kissed both her cheeks in jubilation. "Thank you. This could mean so much for the children—a more healthful environment for Tim, better prospects, maybe a good match for Martha."

"Bob Cratchit, you'll be the death of me." But never was a sentence more tenderly said.

The next day, Fred called on Scrooge at the office. He did this with regularity, and while he was always jovial during these visits, he was, in effect, checking in on his uncle. Just as he had done so unrelentingly for all those past years, trying to convince his uncle to join him for Christmas or some other event. The change in his uncle did not mean Fred worried about him any less; in fact, it had brought up all sorts of new reasons to worry. Scrooge had not as yet grasped the many hours his nephew spent unraveling his own concerned thoughts about Scrooge.

But this visit was particularly innocuous, causing Fred no further worry, and therefore he kept it rather short. On his way out, Fred stopped to chat with Bob in the Tank. "How's life as a partner?" he asked from the doorway.

"Much the same." Bob glanced at Peter, then back at Fred. In a lower voice, he added, "But we are thinking of moving someplace nicer."

"Wonderful! I know the perfect place. A house has just become available across the street from us. I know the owner well—I'm sure she would rent it to you if I recommend you. It's nothing too fancy—two up, two down."

Bob stared wide-eyed as if the existence of a house with four whole rooms had never before occurred to him. "Thank you, but a house in your neighborhood is too much for us, I think."

"Nonsense. At least come see it." He broke off, laughing at Peter's enthusiastic nodding on the other side of the small room.

Bob followed Fred's gaze to his overeager son. He suddenly thought his wife might have been right not to get the children excited about things before they actually happened. He couldn't dare say no to Fred now. "I suppose there's no harm in looking. But don't get your heart set on anything, Peter."

Bob and Peter headed toward Fred's home after work the next evening. Peter was about as excited as he had ever been about anything. He exclaimed at everything they passed on their walk—each horse, every doorway—even though there was nothing remarkable about them other than he had not seen these specific specimens before. The only thing that temporarily quieted him was the sight of Mrs. Cratchit, Fred, and Clara waiting for them on the street in front of the house to let, one of a long row of connected homes. He raced ahead of Bob and practically bowled into his mother. "Try to be a bit calmer in the house, please," she admonished him. Peter scurried to the front of the group, eager to be the first inside. Fred set a hand gently on his shoulder.

"I don't know, Bob," Mrs. Cratchit said as Fred knocked on the door. "This seems too rich for the likes of us."

"Stop saying that!" Fred demanded, though his tone was far from angry. "These are modern times. People move up—and down—in the world."

Mrs. Cratchit frowned. "That's what I'm afraid of," she muttered.

Before Fred could exhort her again, the door opened to reveal a cheerful lady who greeted everyone with hugs. She had the sort of warm smile that brought to each one's mind the memory of a beloved teacher, nurse, or governess. Fred went through introductions as she led them all into the entryway.

The hall was narrow and dark, and the six of them nearly filled it. But to the Cratchits, it felt immense. Peter seemed suddenly overcome, and he allowed his mother to press him against her side as he took everything in.

The landlady showed them the parlor and kitchen, the group shuffling in tight synchronization behind her like a set of ducklings swimming close by their mother. Behind the stairs, they nearly ran into a giant, ancient armoire taller than the men. The landlady rapped it with her knuckles. "Part furnished," she said, "because I'm never going to be able to move this thing out."

"It's lovely," Mrs. Cratchit said, running a finger along the carved wood.

"Upstairs!" the landlady announced.

The staircase was only wide enough to let one person scrape by at a time, so the group took up the whole length of the stairs. By the time Fred, at the end of the line, had squeezed up, the two rooms there had already been shown.

"Back down!" At the landlady's command, the whole spectacle began in reverse. Once her feet hit the last step, she said, "I forgot the garden!" She led them back past the armoire again and out a narrow door at the back.

A stone wall encircled a small yard. At last, the group was able to have a little elbow room.

"Rare to have a garden around here," the landlady said. "It's not much, but enough to grow a few herbs or vegetables if you like."

"Oh, yes!" Mrs. Cratchit exclaimed into the silence that followed. Peter launched himself onto the packed earth and ran laps around the perimeter of the yard with his arms out like bird wings. Fred laughed and joined him. The space was so tight that they both stopped after several laps and had to steady themselves from the resulting dizziness.

Bob grinned and laid hold of his wife's elbow. He had watched her reactions closely, and though she was not overly demonstrative—life had taught her this was often a negative quality—he knew what she was feeling. "My dear, I think you might be in love," he teased.

Mrs. Cratchit blushed. "Still, it's probably too much."

"Not for a friend of my Fred's." The landlady edged closer to the Cratchits, and they began discussing numbers. Clara hovered nearby, laughing at the boys' antics and pretending not to be a part of the conversation happening next to her.

When the landlady had made her final verdict, the Cratchits shared a long look across her large bosom. Finally, Mrs. Cratchit sighed and broke the gaze.

"Well, then," Bob said, his chest puffed out with as much pride as if he had just been declared emperor of Japan, "I think it's settled." He added a little clap of his hands for emphasis.

The landlady doled out a new round of hugs. Back out front a few minutes later, Bob stayed and looked up at the building's facade until his wife tugged him away. Peter chattered all the way home, often launching himself ahead in his eagerness to get home and tell the others, then having to wait for his stodgy old parents to catch up.

"Mr. Scrooge!" Peter called as he entered the office in a whir of excitement the next morning. "Guess what! We have a new house. A nice house."

Scrooge came into the foyer from his office. He patted the boy's head and saw immediately by the boy's frown that he had erred. Despite Peter's childlike overenthusiasm, he clearly saw himself as a young man and had no wish to be treated like a child, especially in his place of employment. Scrooge let him scurry off to his desk without further questioning.

"What's this about a new house?" he asked Bob, who was still in the foyer unwrapping himself from his long scarf.

"Fred helped us find a place. It's right across the street from them. We visited it after work yesterday."

"No one told me about that." Scrooge frowned, but determined to be happy for his employee. "Your prospects are changing now that I've made you a partner, eh?"

The flatness of Bob's "Yes, Mr. Scrooge" made the older man bristle. In that moment, Scrooge felt between them all the years he had not made Bob anything and, in fact, had done his best to ensure the Cratchit prospects remained small. He had little to congratulate himself for. "If you need a loan for any expenses—new furniture, clothes, rent—just let me know." Even as the words came out, Scrooge regretted them. He was overcompensating again.

"Thanks, but that won't be necessary. I'll need a day off, though, to move. I can have Peter come in so that you still have some help."

Scrooge glanced into the Tank at Peter hunched over his work. "No, I'm sure I can manage for one day. The lad is clearly excited. I wouldn't want him to miss out on anything on my account."

"It's a big event for all of us. I just hope . . . well, that nothing comes along to shatter it."

"Nonsense. You're simply getting what has been owed to you all these years."

Bob gazed at him for a beat too long. "Life disabused me of the notion of fairness a long time ago, sir." He turned and went into the Tank, leaving Scrooge to consider that he was the one, or perhaps one of many, who had forced such an idea from Bob Cratchit's heart. And once the idea had left a heart, he knew it would never return. It was something that money could never replace or restore. There was a void of his own making swirling around Scrooge, and he was unsure he would ever escape it.

Chapter 8

On a cold, dark late afternoon in early March, Scrooge sat in front of the fire in his bedroom in the same armchair he had met Jacob's ghost in. He had just returned home from work. Outside, the snow-covered street was muffled. Bangs and thuds came from downstairs as Mrs. Minston finished her last tasks for the day. Scrooge had avoided engaging her in conversation since their last embarrassing encounter, and now too much time had gone by for him to easily talk with her again. Secreted away in a bubble of his own making, he felt that he, like his old partner, was set aside in another world not quite accessible to humans except under extraordinary circumstances.

He almost wished for another spiritual visit just to break the aloneness.

He was still ruminating over this when a knock came at the front door. It so surprised him that he waited for it to come a second time to make sure it had really happened. As he made his way downstairs, he reasoned that a spirit was unlikely to knock. Indeed, the apparition waiting for him in the foyer was entirely human.

"A visitor for you, sir," Mrs. Minston said. She pursed her lips in annoyance as if debating whether to say something else. After a short pause, she said, "I could have come up to inform you."

These blasted social protocols again. "Yes, well, as you can see, that wasn't necessary. Thank you, Mrs. Minston."

The woman so addressed disappeared into the kitchen.

The visitor had watched the little interlude in interest. Now that it was over, he addressed Scrooge. "Hello, I'm Dr. Burnhope. I hope I'm not disturbing you. May I come in?"

Scrooge noted the man was already very decidedly inside, but Scrooge reasoned he meant to be invited in to sit. "Of course. We can sit in the parlor."

"Thank you kindly." The man was short and balding but very finely dressed. As he removed his overcoat in the front hall, Scrooge admired the intricate pattern of gold threads on his waistcoat. Scrooge waved him into the parlor, and the doctor settled into a loveseat while Scrooge lit the lamps and put a few coals on the fire. Fortunately, Mrs. Minston did not reappear to remonstrate him for taking care of these tasks without her assistance.

"I hope you don't mind me calling on you unannounced," Dr. Burnhope began once Scrooge had sat across from him. "Dr. Norman and I are colleagues, and he gave me your address. I know your conversation with him was supposed to be anonymous, but you see, I also have an interest in this area. Though my interest is a little different from Dr. Norman's."

"How so?"

"I'm compiling stories of spiritual encounters into a book. There are often common threads through them. Through proper, scientific analysis, we can learn a lot about the other world."

Scrooge sat up straighter. "You're a believer? Have you had an encounter yourself?"

"I haven't had the pleasure. But please, tell me more about yours." He pulled out a notebook and pencil and took copious notes while Scrooge eagerly told his story.

Once Scrooge had finished, Dr. Burnhope asked, "And since this encounter, you have continued your regular life, conducting business and all that?"

"Yes, of course. Though the focus of my business dealings has shifted because of what the spirits showed me."

Dr. Burnhope sniffed and made a mark on his notepad. "Have you been to see a doctor about the visit?"

"Yes, my nephew made me. But the doctor found me to be in excellent health."

"But you haven't been to see anyone about your state of mind?"

"No. Why would I?" The hints about what could happen to those with doubtful mental faculties mentioned in Dr. Norman's article resurfaced in Scrooge's mind. His stomach gurgled in unease.

The doctor sniffed again and shook his head. "People often get taken for observation of their mental capacity without their consent."

"That sounds simply barbaric."

That comment didn't warrant even a sniff, just a tightening of the line of Dr. Burnhope's thin lips.

"Though, of course, there are many acts of barbarism perpetrated in London every day, as I have recently become aware," Scrooge said, trying to reengage his interviewer's interest.

He didn't succeed.

"Thank you so much for your time, Mr. Scrooge." Dr. Burnhope stood and made his way to the parlor door. "I can show myself out." The parlor door clicked neatly closed behind him, leaving Scrooge once again alone with his thoughts.

On his way out, Dr. Burnhope met Mrs. Minston, who was dusting a perfectly clean-looking table in the front hall. "Might I see you out, sir?" she asked as he passed. He indicated that she should lead the way, and they both stepped into the courtyard. Mrs. Minston closed the house door behind them. "I couldn't help but overhear some of what you said to my boss," she said. "He may not see it, but I think your motives are not quite as good as you made them out to be."

"I assure you my motives are unimpeachable. But it's good of you to stand up for him."

"I never said that was what I was doing."

Dr. Burnhope regarded her with a sly smile. "Is there something you would like to add about the situation?"

"I would, sir. The truth is, he isn't the changed man everyone is praising. The only thing that's changed is he's always talking about how he's special because these ghosts visited him. But he's still just as condescending as he always was, I gather. He doesn't know anything about the common people. My opinion, sir, is he's just a senile old man like any other."

Dr. Burnhope finished jotting down what she had said. "Thank you. Your statements have been very helpful." He held out the little notebook. "Would you mind signing this page?" Mrs. Minston took it, signed, and added the date for good measure. The doctor thanked her again and disappeared into the night.

Fred came by the office the next day to admire the new sign that had finally been installed announcing the new business name of Scrooge and Cratchit. In contrast to the bare cast-iron sign that had hung in front of the building for so many years, Scrooge had splurged to have this one painted, with red trim around gold lettering. It was oddly festive. It stood out brilliantly when Scrooge admired it from the street in the dim, foggy morning, but in the brighter light of afternoon, he was beginning to think he had been too garish in his selections. He was pleased, then, when Fred appeared and assured him otherwise. Fred was never less than effusive in his praise, whether the subject was a friend's fine choice of wife or what he had consumed for breakfast that morning. In the past, that quality of his nephew's had irritated Scrooge to no end, but now that the praise was turned on him, he was grateful for it.

The old Scrooge and Marley sign leaned against the wall in Scrooge's office. It felt sacrilegious to throw it away, especially given what Marley had engaged the spirit world to do for his old friend. Scrooge was considering taking the old sign home and hanging it in his little office room there as a memento so that it wouldn't entirely be lost.

Unaware of Scrooge's desire to keep the relic, Fred kicked at it gently with his toe as he talked to his uncle. Scrooge bristled at such disregard for his property but said nothing because he couldn't stand the thought of losing his nephew's goodwill, even for a moment, over something so silly. Instead, in hopes of removing his nephew's attention from the sign, Scrooge determined to share the previous day's events.

"You'll never believe the visitor I had last night," Scrooge said.

"Dear God, Uncle, don't tell me it was another spirit."

"No, it wasn't, though I don't approve of your tone. It was a doctor who is actually a believer. Unlike you, it would seem."

Fred reined his toe back in and swung around to face Scrooge. "And what did he want?"

"He's compiling stories of spiritual visits into a book—"

"And you told him your story again, did you?"

"Of course I did."

Fred leaned forward and rested his hands on the edge of the desk. "You have no idea who this person is or what his real motivations are."

"Why wouldn't he be who he says he is? And what bad motivations could he have?"

"There are plenty of possibilities, I'm sure. You must stop speaking so freely about the spirits. People may start to doubt your mental faculties."

"You have too little faith in your fellow humanity."

"And you've switched from too little to too much. Everything in moderation. Promise me if anyone else like that comes by, you will ask them to return when I'm there."

Scrooge frowned and tapped his fingertips on the desktop. After a moment, he said, "Fine. I promise."

Fred walked around the desk and squeezed his uncle's shoulder. "Thank you. All I've wanted is to take care of you, you know."

Scrooge nodded, tears pricking his eyes at the thought of such familial devotion to him who so little deserved it. He patted Fred's hand awkwardly.

Fred pulled away and started toward the door but paused in front of the sign again. "You know," he said, "I have half a mind to take this old thing and hang it up in my house as a sort of souvenir. It would be a shame to throw it out. What do you think?"

"That sounds like just the thing." Scrooge stood. He picked up the sign, felt its hefty weight, then handed it to Fred. His nephew would be a much better steward of this history than he would himself. Scrooge would see it whenever he went to visit Fred and Clara, a reminder of everything he had lost and all the wondrous things he had gained as a result.

With the odd parcel under his arm, Fred wove back home through the streets of London. Had he known to pay attention, about halfway through his walk, he would have seen a trio of men gathered on a corner. The subject of their conspiracy would have very much interested Fred, but as it was, he passed them without catching a word of their conversation, so we will have to listen in without him. The discerning reader will recognize the tall man and his companion in the large hat as our friends Michaels and Crane.

"This seems like a setup," the man as yet unknown to us said doubtfully.

"It is a setup," Michaels said. "But not for you, for Ebenezer Scrooge." All three shifted position as a surge of people passed through the street corner. "Look, Archie, you know me."

"Yes, and I know what Mr. Scrooge did to you. I worry it may have . . . unhinged you. At least when it comes to that particular man."

The story was visible for all passersby to see, had they cared to look. Archie Parker, the old friend, by no means a rich man, but neatly dressed in clothes that at least hinted at the latest fashion. His companion, swathed in patched garments at least a decade out of date. Something had happened to drive their fortunes apart. Crane was even grubbier and cast a watchful eye over everything.

"Forget about me," Michaels continued. "Think about all the other lives this man has ruined and has no remorse for."

"I've heard—"

"I don't care what you heard." He shook his head so fiercely, his hat nearly flew off his head, and he had to clamp it down with one dirty hand. "He can't be let off just because he's put on a show of changing. Go see him, at least. Ask him if he remembers me or any of the other men he so carelessly sent to debtors' prison. I guarantee you he won't."

Archie regarded Michaels for a moment. "Fine. I'll go meet him tomorrow and see what I think. If he's been as careless with other men's welfare as you say, then I suppose he does need to be punished somehow."

"Good. And look, if you don't want to do it, ask one of your employees. We'll give them money to make the weekly payments, and they'll get to keep the part of the loan they don't pay back. It's not a bad deal. Hell, we could use as many of your employees as you can get for us."

Archie tapped his walking stick on the ground as if sounding out his thoughts. "I might do. I'm sure someone will be desperate enough to join you. And they should come see you in that case?"

Crane broke his silence. "I'll come find you. I manage the recruits."

Archie regarded him with a look and a short laugh that indicated he found the whole proceeding rather ridiculous. "Right. Well, good luck, I suppose." He nodded to the two men and hurried off into the crowd.

In turn, Michaels nodded to Crane. "I have another appointment to keep."

Crane responded with a pointed look and a glance at his pocket watch that showed he knew exactly what the appointment was and that Crane did not see its purpose.

But Michaels would not be swayed, and his feet carried him to the Covent Garden market. Once there, he picked a corner and rocked carelessly back and forth on his heels, scanning the crowd until they landed upon his target: a woman in a purple skirt teetering toward her forties. She carried a basket as she walked slowly among the stalls—a potato peeked over the edge, balanced on a loaf of bread.

Eliza was still pretty, though she looked tired. He could see the dark circles under her eyes, even from twenty feet away. But what woman didn't look tired by that age, he mused, with three children to take care of and more in the ground? Not to mention everything that Michaels himself had put her through.

When he had first gotten out of prison, he had gone to see her, still holding out hope that he could reclaim his old life. She had made it very clear that he wasn't welcome. She had a new man now—Dave, a big, lumbering fellow who worked at a printer's, a position where he might have a chance to improve his standing in the world. Still, Michaels liked to come check on her now and again to make sure Dave was keeping her well. She always looked fine, always filling her basket with groceries with no hesitation as to her ability to pay. Once he had even seen her buy a handful of violets from a particularly persistent and dirty little girl. He occasionally sensed that she saw him watching her, but she never made any attempt to approach him. He mattered that little to her now.

This new life was better for her and for their children. What would he have to show them? Opium dens and late-night pubs? He grunted loud enough that a woman walking by dodged him.

With nowhere else to direct his ire, his thoughts returned to Scrooge. Michaels knew he would never be taken seriously if he tried to pass himself off as a respectable businessman in need of assistance. The scent of his class and criminality would give him away immediately. That was why he needed help—and Archie fit the profile perfectly. And if he were being truthful with himself, he didn't want to see this new front everyone said Scrooge was putting on. It would only make him angrier. It was always the same—second chances given only to the rich. Somebody had to pay for all that had happened to him and to others. Michaels was sure he would be the one to take down Mr. Ebenezer Scrooge. Nothing would sway him from that purpose. He left Eliza behind and walked toward the docks.

Hard at work the next day, the focus of Michaels's ire received a different variety of visitor than the one Michaels hoped to send him. Miss Lucretia Morody appeared in the doorway to Scrooge's office in a low-cut dress and an elaborate hairstyle that made one doubt there was much going on in the head it towered over. He leaped up in his surprise and walked to the door, hoping to keep her in the public spaces of the office. But she would not be moved and held her ground like a standing stone in the doorway. With Scrooge in front of her, she presented him a basket of baked goods.

Scrooge didn't even lift the cloth covering the basket to see what was inside; the scent of warm burned sugar told him of the contents. "Peter!" Scrooge yelled over her shoulder in the direction of the Tank. When Peter's head peeked around the doorframe of Scrooge's office, the older man waved him in. "Here, take these in for you and your father to enjoy."

With an exclamation of thanks, Peter carried the basket across the hall.

Miss Morody's face was sour and her voice flat. "You're so generous."

While Scrooge stumbled over an answer, she turned and shut the office door. Scrooge backed up against the desk with as much fear on his face as if he had been left alone in a room with a bear rather than a young woman.

His attacker sidled up to him and laid a pale hand on his cheek. "You know, I've always appreciated older men." Her other hand moved to his chest. "It must be so lonely in that big house all by yourself." She looked up at him but brought her head back level quickly as the high construction of her hair threatened to throw her off-balance. "I would love to keep you company some evening—"

Her next word was a scream as Scrooge flailed his arms and legs to escape, knocking her down onto her bottom in the process.

His assailant thus temporarily preoccupied, he rushed from the room and into the Tank, slamming the door behind him.

"What on earth has happened?" Bob asked. He had jumped up from his seat at the sound of the scream and was standing next to his desk. "You look like you've just found a snake."

"I think I have, quite literally." He pressed his ear to the door. After a moment, heels tapped in the hall, and the front door creaked on its hinges. Scrooge opened the door a crack to make sure she was gone. It was at this juncture that the front door swung open, and a moderately well-to-do man walked in. He peered at the sliver of face peering back at him.

"Mr. Scrooge?"

Scrooge opened the door and presented himself rigidly in the hall. "Yes, my apologies. We thought we had seen a snake in the foyer."

The visitor cast his gaze around the floor and looked pointedly at Scrooge when nothing appeared.

Scrooge cleared his throat. "Must have been mistaken. How can I help?"

The man extended his hand. "Archie Parker. I'm here about a loan."

Chapter 9

Archie settled into the chair in front of Scrooge's desk. "I have a small business. Manufacturing. I just need something to tide me over to make sure I can pay everyone next week."

Scrooge pulled out his account book and dipped a pen in the inkwell. "We can provide very good terms."

"I was surprised to hear about your change in approach, given your history."

Scrooge's pen halted in midair. He smiled tightly. "I've made some changes to our priorities."

"An old friend of mine lost his house to you a few years ago. Gregory Michaels?"

"I'm afraid I don't recall."

Archie raised one eyebrow. "You don't remember the name of a man whose life you ruined?"

"There were too many, unfortunately. If your friend needs assistance now, let me know how I can help. A good loan, no collateral. Free business consulting, too."

"I'll pass on the message." But something in his expression had shifted, a slight sneer that should have warned Scrooge, had he more experience caring about others' emotions, that Mr. Parker was not dealing with him on the up-and-up.

The men agreed on the loan terms quite quickly because Scrooge was eager to appear the opposite of his old self and was perhaps a touch too generous. Bob drew up the document and doled out the money.

"I may send some of my employees over if they need help," Archie said before he left.

"Yes, please do," Scrooge said, shaking his hand. "I'd like to be of service to as many people as possible."

Archie curled up one side of his mouth in an unconvincing smile before he turned and walked out.

Archie had barely left when Fred came in and threw a newspaper onto Scrooge's desk. Fred pointed to the paper. "Read it."

"The whole thing? Now?"

Fred opened the paper and folded it so that the offending page was showing, then handed it back to his uncle. Scrooge took several minutes to read it, letting no reaction cross his face. Then he slowly set the paper down.

"This is that man you talked to, isn't it? You see what comes of your constant talk to people you don't know?" Fred asked.

Scrooge glanced down at the signature line of the letter to the editor even though he knew what it said. "Dr. Burnhope. Yes. You already yelled at me about it as well."

Fred ignored his uncle's response. "You have got to stop talking to everyone you meet about the blasted spirits! This letter, about a businessman with delusions of a spiritual visit, who is only allowed his freedom because of his wealth—people will know it's you. And there could be consequences. I will try to help you as best I can, but you also have to help yourself." He sat and stared Scrooge down. "Promise me you will stop. Please. I can't lose you just as soon as I've found you."

Scrooge sighed. He hated to make such a promise, but he also couldn't risk losing Fred. "I promise."

Fred held Scrooge's hands in both of his and kissed them. Then he got up and left, taking the newspaper with him, without even a hello to the two Cratchits. For a long moment after Fred left, Scrooge stared at his blessed hands, imagining all the kisses he had missed from this boy over the years and all the ways he could reclaim them.

Dr. Burnhope's editorial hung over Scrooge throughout the weekend. He hadn't meant to put himself—or God forbid, Fred, who would stand by him until the end—at risk. He had only wanted to tell his story. And the good doctor was right, in a way. Who was Scrooge to be able to move on as if nothing had happened, as if he had never done anything wrong?

He contemplated these things as he ate cold leftovers for Sunday lunch at his usual spot in front of his bedroom fireplace. He watched the flames flicker as he tried to resolve this conundrum. He had to prove to everyone that he was all right. That he could continue his business obligations as normal.

To a certain extent, he had avoided doing that. He had yet to face his usual business associates. If he were honest with himself, he was scared of being judged in just the way Dr. Burnhope had judged him. To prove that he was not who Dr. Burnhope said he was, Scrooge would have to make a stand.

He crossed his knife and fork on his plate and leaned his chin on one hand. Yes, on Monday, he would have to face himself, once and for all.

Thus it happened that on Monday, Scrooge was determined to conduct the business he had been putting off since Christmas. He had to go to the 'Change. While charity was all well and good, he still had to keep himself in funds—so that he could continue to help others, of course. There was only so much business he could conduct with Peter as an intermediary.

As he walked to the 'Change, he resolved not to trade in debt as he so often had in the past. Acting as a debt collector was a line of work too cruel for his new outlook.

As he neared the old familiar corner, he second-guessed every foot he put forward and fought the urge to turn back, so he developed an odd hitch in his step. He stopped and peered ahead through the crowd. He glimpsed three top hats nodding together. It had to be them: the men he thought had respected him as a businessman but the spirits had shown him would have no sympathy for him when he died. How could he talk to them now as if his knowledge of them were still only temporal?

He took a deep breath and set his feet in steady forward motion. He had determined to simply tip his hat at these men as he passed, but they refused to let that happen.

"Ebenezer!" a voice called.

Scrooge turned to see the stout man waving him over. Scrooge found he couldn't recall any of the men's names, which might explain why they thought so little of him. So he simply approached, tipped his hat again, and wished them a good day.

"We haven't seen you around here in months," the stout man said.

"We saw your advert in the paper. Quite curious," another added.

"I've simply taken a new approach to business."

"What, an approach to the poorhouse?"

Scrooge ignored the laughter that went around the little circle. "I find I am already wealthy enough. Good day, gentleman."

As he walked away, Scrooge fumed over the hypocrisy of these men—to make fun of him for not focusing on making money but also to condemn him for it when that was what he did. Distracted by his anger—tinged, he hated to admit, with embarrassment, an emotion he was becoming much too familiar with—he didn't do as well as he normally did inside the 'Change, but he still walked out with some new securities that would likely do all right. He had at least made his first return, so his future visits should be easier. He had shown that he was still a competent businessman, at least, and that he still belonged in this world.

Fortunately, the men were no longer gathered outside. They were probably off to their daily lunch appointment—which, Scrooge realized, in all their years as colleagues, he had never been invited to.

From across the street, Dr. Burnhope watched Scrooge with increasing ire. That this man was allowed to go about conducting business, even entering one of the hallowed institutions of London, while Burnhope's own mother had been taken so brutally away from her children all those years ago for much less reason . . . well, it just wasn't right.

He had noticed the odd, halting way Scrooge had walked toward the 'Change, as if he were having an argument with his own legs. The men Scrooge had talked to at least knew something was off. Dr. Burnhope had sensed their derision even from twenty feet away.

The doctor's stomach growled as Scrooge disappeared into the crowd. That was enough of following him around today, then. Time for a spot of lunch. He had seen what he needed to. Ebenezer Scrooge was not well. Since Dr. Burnhope's editorial had not moved anyone else into action, he would have to take charge. As one of the leading medical men in this great city, Dr. Burnhope would make sure all the mentally ill were treated equally—with no exceptions made just because the afflicted was rich. Starting with Mr. Ebenezer Scrooge.

Chapter 10

During the same weekend that Scrooge had spent contemplating his predicament, the Cratchits had moved to their new abode. For Bob and his wife, leaving the space they had raised their family in was briefly bittersweet, but it was quickly forgotten in the excitement about the comparative luxury of their new home. When Martha arrived on Sunday for her half day, she was very quiet as she toured the rooms, reacting very little to her siblings' chatter. No one pressed her for her thoughts. Sometimes, as Mrs. Cratchit had been known to say, a person's thoughts were meant only for themself.

However, Mrs. Cratchit had little time for philosophizing as she worked to get the family settled in. On their first Tuesday afternoon in the house, Mrs. Cratchit was scrubbing the floors—which the little ones had already managed to muddy with their play in the minuscule yard—when the doorbell rang.

The woman standing on the front step didn't speak right away. She took in Mrs. Cratchit's soapy hands and the damp spots on her apron, standing in stark contrast to the visitor's deep-red dress and lace-trimmed shawl. "Are you the lady of the house?" she asked finally, with a look that bordered on concern for Mrs. Cratchit's well-being. When Mrs. Cratchit replied in the affirmative, the woman adjusted her smile. "I'm Mrs. Heron. From next door." She indicated her head in that direction. "I just wanted to come say hello." She extended a neatly gloved hand with her calling card.

"That's very kind of you." A thud came from somewhere in the house, followed by a slew of giggles, momentarily distracting Mrs. Cratchit.

"Perhaps you and your husband would like to come over for dinner on Friday night?"

Mrs. Cratchit repeated the same line about her neighbor being very kind.

"Your children are all small, I believe? They were such a rambunctious ... pleasure ... to watch as you all were moving in. But it would be so lovely if there were another young person to keep my son company during the party."

"I do have an older daughter, but she is only here on Sundays for her half day."

"Ah, yes. I had assumed that was your maid I saw coming and going." She thought for a moment. "I don't suppose she could get time off work?"

Another thud.

"I'm sorry, I must go see what the children are doing. But thank you for the invitation. I will have to ask my husband."

Mrs. Heron rattled off a few more details before Mrs. Cratchit could close the door. As she ran upstairs to check on the children, Mrs. Heron's card slipped from her hand and drifted from the stairs onto the wet floor below.

With all there is to do in a bustling household, Mrs. Cratchit had nary a thought to spare about the visit until she was going up the stairs to bed that evening, exhausted, with Bob following behind her.

"What's this?" he asked a bit too loudly, picking Mrs. Heron's calling card off the floor.

His wife hissed at him to be quiet, the thought of waking the children always foremost in her mind. She yanked the card from his grasp as if revoking his control of the conversation. Back in their room, she described the visit in the forceful murmur she had perfected during the long years of their many-offspring'd marriage.

"I don't know that I want to associate with such a pretentious woman," she concluded.

"I think we should go to be friendly. If nothing else, we can show her that hardworking people can be acceptable members of society." He grinned.

"Stop it. You better not make fun of her to her face." She began to unlace her dress as they prepared for bed. "I don't know how she imagines Martha could go. Even if she could get the evening off, it hardly seems worth it to use up her employer's goodwill for something as silly as a dinner party."

"It could be a good opportunity for her. If they have an eligible bachelor for a son . . ."

"I don't like where you're going with that." She slid into bed beside her husband. "Anyway, who's going to watch the children while we're off enjoying society?"

Bob shrugged. "Maybe Fred and Clara would do it."

Mrs. Cratchit responded with a sniff. Then she put out the candle, lay down, and was snoring before Bob could construct the remainder of his argument.

AFTER THE SPIRITS COME

Mr. and Mrs. Cratchit caught Fred and Clara at home the next evening to make their request. As it happened, Fred and Clara had their own engagement for Friday evening. After a fair amount of persuasion, Mrs. Cratchit agreed to plan B: to ask Scrooge, who was almost guaranteed to be free. Peter was quickly dispatched with a note for said gentleman.

"The Herons are good enough people," Fred said while they waited. "Yes, Mrs. Heron thinks highly of herself. She has a second cousin or something who's a baronet."

"I'm sure she'll tell you all about it," Clara broke in with a laugh.

"The son is a decent fellow. In case you—or Martha—were especially interested in him." Fred wiggled his eyebrows suggestively.

Mrs. Cratchit frowned and looked meaningfully at her husband. "She did seem particularly interested in Martha."

"Exactly," Fred replied.

"Though the fact that she's been watching us so closely strikes me as a bit odd."

"She has nothing else to do," Fred said. "She refuses to work, obviously, so nothing that happens in the neighborhood slips by her nose. Which is not always a bad thing. A few years ago, there was a spate of robberies in the neighborhood, and who do you think held the fatal clue to help identify the culprit?"

Mrs. Cratchit made a sour face. She didn't quite know how to respond to this implication that their new neighborhood had its own ills.

Clara smoothed her skirt over her lap as a physical indicator that she was about to change the subject. "I also wanted to ask," she said, "if you intend to take advantage of the school." When Mrs. Cratchit's blank expression told her she didn't know anything about it, Clara continued. "There's a good school down the street. They take day students and sometimes offer scholarships. The cost is reasonable, even if you do have to pay. You should consider sending your little ones there."

"I've already taught them their letters. I don't think they need much more than that."

"I'm sure you've done an excellent job," Fred said, eager to make up for his earlier faux pas. "But the world is changing. With a good education, their prospects for employment will be much greater."

Clara leaned forward in her chair in her eagerness to jump back into the conversation. "You should ask the Herons about recommending you when you're at dinner on Friday. Mrs. Heron never likes to admit it, but their son attended that school, and he turned out very well. I think they've made some donations in the past, so their recommendation could carry weight."

While Mrs. Cratchit chewed her lip, considering this possibility, Peter returned with an affirmative reply from Scrooge. Mrs. Cratchit seemed, if anything, more apprehensive after this result.

"Look," Clara said softly, "three months ago, I wouldn't have recommended him. But he really is a changed man."

"Still," Mrs. Cratchit said, fixing her gaze on her oldest son, "Peter, you had better really be in charge. I expect you to keep an eye on things—and on him."

Peter straightened and clasped his hands behind his back, as if he had just been conferred a noble title instead of his mother's trust. "Yes, Mother, I most certainly shall," he declared. The adults smothered their smiles at his overseriousness.

All in all, though, it was settled. The coming Friday loomed large in all of their minds, though each for different reasons. No one mentioned it for the remainder of the week, not wanting to risk upsetting the uneasy agreement they had reached.

And so it happened that Scrooge was left with five of the six Cratchit children on Friday evening, albeit with their parents right next door. Scrooge and the children had gathered in the parlor to say goodbye to Mr. and Mrs. Cratchit, and now that they were gone, the children watched Scrooge expectantly. He wasn't sure what to do next. He so wanted the evening to be a success, and not just from the parents' point of view. He already entertained visions of the Cratchit children asking for his presence at every opportunity. He could become an adopted uncle to them, in time.

But all that was far from this moment. Now, there was silence as Scrooge and the children stared at each other in an initial standoff. Scrooge pulled at his collar nervously. Peter, at least, was there to help him, Scrooge reasoned. He was old enough to work, so surely he was old enough to help with the children. Belinda hovered over Tiny Tim, who still leaned on his crutch, although his color looked much better since beginning the regimen of Dr. Norman's care and advice. She looked ready to protect and defend her brother at a moment's notice.

A scuffle in the corner drew Scrooge's attention to the two little ones. Charles poked his sister in the ribs once Scrooge's gaze was on them. With a gulp, the sister took up her brother's unspoken dare. "Let's play a game," she said.

"What game shall we play?"

"Elephants!" Charles shouted, then covered his mouth with a hand to show he recognized his transgression in not using his inside voice.

"You're the elephant," Sarah added.

After a moment's hesitation, Scrooge decided he had to follow their wishes or risk a revolt. His knees popped as he got down on all fours, but once his knees and hands hit the rug, the awkward position was oddly freeing. He laughed as first Charles, then Sarah, climbed on his back for a ride around the room. He even threw in a few movements of his arm in place of a trunk for good measure, though it took a lot of persuading from the children before he accompanied the movement with the appropriate noise. Scrooge briefly worried that he had damaged his reputation as Peter's employer, but one look at the glee on the oldest boy's face told him he needn't worry.

Meanwhile, next door, the mood was decidedly more reserved. The three Cratchits were arranged along one side of the Herons' dining room table, with Mr. Heron at the head and Mrs. Heron and their son, Steven, seated across from the Cratchits. The Herons' home was not much bigger than the Cratchits', but the Herons were determined that every bit of space would be used. They had stuffed the dining room with knickknacks and covered every inch of the walls in paintings, giving a claustrophobic feel to the proceedings.

The Cratchits had donned their best clothes, some articles freshly turned out to make them appear newer than they were. Without her usual plain cap, Martha's fair hair made a luminescent appearance that would have been the envy of many a society lady. Steven Heron snuck a number of sideways glances at her while their parents did most of the talking.

The group covered the usual topics: employment (Mr. Heron owned a small import-export business) and family (the Cratchits were hazy on this, whereas Mrs. Heron's baronet made several appearances). Mr. Heron said little. Mostly, he looked around at the others and laughed at their comments, his laughter broken occasionally by an unnecessary attempt to smooth down the dozen or so remaining hairs carefully plastered against the top of his head. He had a shy way of peering out of the corner of his eye rather than looking at anyone directly, which likely stemmed from the forcefulness of his wife's rule over him.

Eventually, Bob relaxed enough to mention the school Clara had told them about. "We are thinking about sending our younger children there," he explained.

Across from him, Martha dropped her fork so quickly, it clattered onto the edge of her plate and tumbled to the floor. Once she had retrieved it, she asked, in increasingly incensed tones, "They're going to go to school? Whatever for? I never went to school, and I support myself just fine."

Bob blushed at his daughter's admission of that in company. Of all things, he did not want his family to be thought uneducated. He was a professional man, and Peter was well on his way to a business career as well.

To smooth over the awkward moment, Mrs. Cratchit said, "We were told by the Williamsons that you have some connections at the school."

Mrs. Heron looked pleased at this talk of her well-connectedness. "Why, yes, we do, in fact. We could almost certainly make an introduction. Couldn't we?" she asked her husband, who simply nodded. Mute agreement seemed to be his favorite strategy in dealing with his wife.

After dinner, they adjourned to the parlor for coffee. The two married couples gathered in conversation, leaving the two young people to secret themselves in a corner. Though they were only six feet or so away from the others, the amount of furniture one was required to navigate between the two points made it feel like they were in their own little fortress.

"You know, Miss Cratchit, you seem more mature than most girls your age," Steven said.

"That comes from not having lived a life of leisure, as I assume most of the girls you know have."

"Oh? You mean—"

The rest of his sentence was cut off by a shrill scream coming from the other side of the wall—which meant from the Cratchits' own parlor.

It took less than a minute for everyone to reach the Cratchits' front step and start banging on the door. Belinda answered, looking flustered, her neat ringlets now astray.

Bob pushed his way in, trailed by everyone else. "What's happened?" He stopped abruptly at the parlor door, causing a backup behind him and more than a few bumped elbows.

Scrooge lay on his back on the floor, his eyes glassy and unfocused. Peter knelt by him, trying to shake him awake. Eventually, a small moan escaped from Scrooge's lips.

"Someone get a doctor," Bob instructed.

"I'll go," Steven volunteered and dashed off from his place at the rear of the pack.

"He fainted," Peter said.

His father knelt beside Peter and eased him out of the way. "Yes, I can see that. It's all right."

Scrooge, whose skin was dreadfully pale, began to move his head and look around, but it took a few more minutes before recognition began to dawn in his eyes. He tried to sit up, but Bob gently pushed him back down. "Wait until the doctor gets here." Scrooge didn't resist.

It was a long, nervous wait, but eventually, Steven returned with a doctor following close behind him, carrying the requisite black bag. By this time, Scrooge had mostly regained his faculties, but he was still lying prone on his back on the floor due to everyone's remonstrances anytime he attempted to right himself. He did not look happy about it.

After a convoluted explanation of events from the others, the doctor checked Scrooge's eyes, his pulse, and his breathing, then pronounced him out of danger. A simple fainting spell, caused perhaps by not enough supper but more likely by stress coupled with the excitement of the evening. "A rest cure," the doctor said. Seeing Bob's quizzical look, he patted Bob's arm. "He needs a holiday."

Chapter 11

After all the excitement that evening, Martha decided to stay the night at her family's house. Even though nothing had happened to the children, Mrs. Cratchit was shaken and even more adverse than usual to hearing the name Ebenezer Scrooge. Martha got her mother into bed, then did her best to calm the children, but she still guessed no one would sleep much that night.

However, when Martha awoke long before dawn the next morning, the house was silent except for Bob's snores, which could be heard quite distinctly throughout all four rooms of the house. She dressed quickly and hurried out so that she wouldn't miss her morning chores at the Werthers'. She emerged into a world draped with heavy fog. It felt as if she might be the only person on earth, and the thought sent a delicious thrill down her spine.

The illusion was soon shattered. After making it a few yards down the street, she heard the tap of footsteps behind her. She turned but couldn't see anyone through the fog. It was far from the first time she had navigated London in the dark, but there was something disconcerting about the disembodied sound in a neighborhood she was not yet overly familiar with. Besides herself and her mysterious follower, there was no one else about.

The steps quickened, and her heart sped up to match. She clutched at her skirts, holding them up in case she had to run from the increasingly frantic taps. Just as she thought she might have to, a form emerged from the fog.

"I thought that might be you," Steven Heron said, lifting his hat to her.

Martha stopped walking and dropped her hold on her dress. "You gave me a fright trying to find out."

"Sorry, I didn't think."

She started walking again, and he fell in beside her. Seeing she wouldn't shake him so easily, she asked, "What are you doing out so early?"

"I have some business in Oxford today, so I'm catching the early train. What is a young lady like you doing out alone this early?"

Martha paused for a step to frown at him, then plunged ahead. "I'm headed to work."

Steven matched her increased pace. "You don't have to run off. I'm not shocked. My mother did say she suspected . . ." He trailed off at a sharp glance from his companion. "I'm not like my mother. I think it's wonderful that your father is making his way up in the world. And it must be good for you, too."

"I get to keep more of my wages. For now, at least."

"Do you expect circumstances to change?"

"I don't entirely trust my father's employer's change of heart will continue. But we'll see."

"That's our fainter, Mr. Scrooge, isn't it? I've heard about him. Seems a bit of an odd duck." There was silence for a few moments. "Don't let my mother intimidate you. As much as she likes to talk of her baronet, we are far from that world. I went to the day school myself, just like your siblings will."

Martha frowned at the mention of her younger siblings' futures shining brighter than her own. She stopped at the next intersection. "You're going that way to the train station, I assume?"

He glanced down the street he was meant to take. "Yes, but I can walk you a bit farther if you wish."

"I'll be fine."

Steven bowed, but she had already hurried off.

There was already plenty of activity in the courtyard when Martha arrived back at the Werthers'. Deliverymen dodged each other as they carried their wares through the small space. Martha stepped lightly around several of them. One, however, did not get out of her way. In fact, he rolled his barrel of beer right into her path.

"And where are you coming from, Miss Cratchit?" Ian asked with a teasing grin. "Shouldn't you be safe inside and starting your chores at this time?"

"That's what I'm trying to do." She took a step to the side to try to make it around the barrel, but the coachman, Thomas, walked by carrying harnesses for the carriage horses, inadvertently blocking her path. She gave up on trying to escape.

"Come now, I hope everything is all right at home? Is that where you were?"

"Yes." She paused, then took advantage of a calm moment to step around the barrel and closer to him.

"That's all? If I didn't know better, I'd say you've been avoiding me these last couple of months. Kitty always says you're busy whenever I come round. I hope I haven't offended you in some way."

She looked up at him. He was disarming with the way his wry smile twinkled both on his lips and in his eyes. She suddenly felt guilty for all the times she had told Kitty to give him those messages. In an attempt to make amends, she said quietly, "I told them my brother was ill, so they let me go. But there was actually a dinner party with our new neighbors..."

"How naughty, Miss Cratchit. I didn't think there were many dinner parties happening in Camden Town."

Martha shook her head. "We moved to Bloomsbury recently. Or my family did, at least."

"That's quite a move up in the world."

"Yes, and the mother was simply awful. The son wasn't too bad, though."

"The son?" Ian asked with an arched eyebrow. "Personally, I'd feel out of place in the likes of Bloomsbury," Ian said. "I'm working-class, through and through. Nothing wrong with it, either. I'm finishing up my apprenticeship at the brewery later this year, and I'll be making a good living after that."

"Your family must be pleased." Her voice, however, did not indicate that she was impressed. This sort of braggadocio did not appeal to her.

"I don't have much of one to speak of—a family, I mean. Father and Mother have been dead for years. I have a brother in the navy. Lord knows where he is right now."

"I'm sorry to hear that. I see now how you have so much time to spend hanging around an establishment where you don't even work."

"I like to meet people." He grinned. "I've enjoyed meeting you."

Kitty leaned out of the back door. "Martha, they're asking for you!" she called.

"I have to go."

Ian grabbed her elbow as she stepped away. The touch was gentle, not jarring. "What about our Sunday get-together? You've been putting me off for a long time."

Martha hesitated. Ian was a conundrum. There were things about him that rubbed her the wrong way, but the things that were nice about him . . . "I suppose since I just saw my family last night, I can see you tomorrow instead of going home."

"I can't wait." Ian grinned and let her go.

That Sunday afternoon, Martha assured her colleagues that her brother was in fact fine and had pulled through his illness, so there was no need for her to return home again so soon. Once they were satisfied on this point, she met Ian in the courtyard, which she knew would escape no one's notice. He was wearing a fine brown bowler hat; she was in her best dress. Despite herself, her stomach fluttered with excitement at the rare outing. She took his arm, and he led her with purpose down the street.

They took an omnibus down to the National Gallery, where Ian paid their entry. "Have you ever been?" he asked as they walked into the first grand room.

Martha shook her head. Her attention was already captivated by the paintings on the walls, though they seemed to her awfully dark and disconnected from real life. Who were these people gazing out at her from the canvases, who had not a care in the world and plenty of time to laze around with angels and fairies?

The next room was landscapes, and these drew her in. She had never been to the countryside, and it amazed her to think that all those rolling hills and winding streams existed not so far away.

"I've tried my hand at a bit of art myself," Ian said, breaking the long silence.

"Really?" she asked, pulling her gaze away from the paintings for an instant.

He smiled. "I can show you sometime. I'm not half-bad, I don't think. Sketches, though. I don't have all these fancy paints."

"I'd like to see them." She blushed under his pleased gaze. After they had walked a few more steps, she asked, "Did you ever try to pursue it?"

"Of course not. People like us, we have to worry about putting food on the table first and foremost. These artists . . . they live in another world, I think."

"You're probably right."

"Besides, there's nothing wrong with having a secret talent to share with a pretty lady."

Martha laughed and blushed again. Ian squeezed her hand.

After the gallery, they went to a small café nearby, where they shared a pot of tea and a scone. It seemed like an extravagance to Martha, but Ian assured her it was fine. She had put him off so long, he'd had plenty of time to save up, he joked.

They walked back to the Werthers' as the sun set, choosing to skip the omnibus and take their time. Outside the courtyard entrance to the house, Ian bent down and kissed her hand. His lips lingered there for a second while he looked intently at her. He must have seen something in her face to encourage him because at the last instant, he threw down her hand and dove in for a kiss on the cheek. He pulled away quickly, and Martha put her hand up to her cheek automatically, but the gesture was tender rather than upset. She held her palm there, over the spot he had touched, until he had walked away and disappeared.

Chapter 12

Embarrassed by what had happened at the Cratchits', and with his babysitting career cut off before it had begun, Scrooge temporarily returned to his old habit of going nowhere but home and the office. Fortunately, after asking Scrooge about his health on the following Monday and receiving a curt reply, Bob picked up on the sensitivity of the topic and did not mention the incident again. Besides, Bob overheard Fred remonstrating Scrooge about the fainting episode frequently enough over the next few days to understand there was nothing Bob could add.

About a week into Scrooge's self-imposed exile, Fred wore Scrooge down about consulting a doctor. He won by citing Scrooge's own willingness to talk to doctors who randomly showed up on his doorstep as the reason why he should have no qualms about visiting an actual medical man known to his family. Scrooge let Fred drag him to see Dr. Smelton, the man who had planted the seed in Fred's mind after Christmas that all the changes in his uncle's life may have resulted from an apoplexy rather than a good old-fashioned change of heart.

It was the former condition that Dr. Smelton examined Scrooge for. He poked and prodded and moved fingers and a candle flame in front of Scrooge's eyes without saying anything for a quarter of an hour. At the end, he put his hands on his hips and stood back for a moment, surveying Scrooge.

"I don't see anything wrong with him." The doctor frowned, as if this lack of disease disappointed him.

"But the apoplexy?" Fred asked.

Dr. Smelton shook his head. "If there was one, I certainly don't see any ill effects of it. And the fainting was probably a temporary, unrelated condition. It could be, Mr. Scrooge, that you are proof that an old dog can learn new tricks."

He laughed, but Scrooge did not join the merriment. He simply stood and straightened his shirtsleeves. "Now that we've established I'm not in eminent danger of death, can we go?"

"Of course. Thank you, Dr. Smelton." Fred reached up a hand to lay on his uncle's back, but Scrooge charged ahead. Fred shrugged and followed him.

Back out on the street, Scrooge slowed to let his nephew catch him up. "Are you satisfied now?" he asked.

"Yes, Uncle. Aren't you pleased to know you're in fine health?"

Scrooge sniffed haughtily. "I never had any doubt of it."

"Of course you didn't."

Scrooge thought back to the suggestion the doctor at the Cratchits' had made. "And that means I'm not in need of a holiday, either." Such a dereliction of his workaday duty had never before occurred to him, and it was hard to adjust to the notion that he might now be the type of person who would do such a thing.

Fred bellowed a laugh. "Good God, Uncle. People *want* holidays; they don't need them."

Scrooge shifted his shoulders uncomfortably. "Still," was all he could find to say.

Despite this good report on his health, Scrooge continued to mostly sequester himself at home for another couple of weeks. Eventually, even though his solitude had never bothered him before, he began to feel the lack of society. He suggested at one of Fred and Clara's visits to his home that he have another dinner party. This time, he would make the guest list, and he made it vehemently clear that the Morodys had been removed.

"What's your problem with Mrs. and Miss Morody?" Clara asked. "They may be ridiculous, but they're harmless."

"Harmless? That young woman attacked me in my office!"

Fred choked as he tried to contain his laughter. "Attacked, Uncle? Please, define that term for us."

"She came into my office, completely uninvited, and I don't know, tried to . . . she got much too close for comfort."

"Both her and her mother are unmarried, you know." Clara laughed.

"Yes, maybe the older lady is more to your taste," Fred added. "I'm sure three times lucky must apply to husbands."

Clara let out a little shriek of laughter at her husband's comment, then covered her mouth with a hand to muffle the rest of it.

"You both are terrible," Scrooge said, though a smile tugged at the corners of his mouth. "I don't know why I spend time with you."

"Bah! Humbug!" Fred said with a dramatic flourish, sending Clara into more fits of giggles.

Once the young people had settled down, Scrooge continued with the rest of his plan. "I think not inviting the Cratchits last time was an oversight. If Bob is supposed to be my business partner, then he and his family should be treated as such."

Fred and Clara exchanged uncertain glances. "You know they will have to find someone to watch the children . . ."

"When I say the Cratchits, I mean all of them. Why not? We'll do it on a Sunday when their oldest is home. That way, they can enjoy their time as a family without having to worry about making dinner and all that." He paused and smiled. "I just won't be giving any elephant rides this time."

"I wish so badly I had seen that," Fred said.

Scrooge shrugged. "Bob mentioned that his children wanted to meet Miss Spencer, so it will be a good way to make the introduction."

The young couple acquiesced to the plan and prepared to leave. Once they were at the door in their coats, they exchanged a more serious look.

"For God's sake, what is it now?" Scrooge asked.

"We just wondered . . ." Fred began.

"This Sunday's Easter, you know," Clara added.

"Would you like to accompany us to church?" Fred's words came out in a rush, as if they had been held back by a dam and now flooded out. "In the morning. Then we can have the dinner party in the evening."

Scrooge frowned. "It's been many years since I was last in a church."

"I think they'll still let you in." Clara smiled.

"It will be good for you to think about where these spirits of yours came from."

The frown remained plastered across Scrooge's face. Fred hardly ever mentioned the spirits unprompted, and Scrooge wasn't sure how much he was being manipulated by Fred calling upon them now. But there was some sense in his nephew's words. "All right,

I'll go." He tried on a weak smile. "Let's hope I won't be smote with hellfire as soon as I enter."

Clara gripped her husband's arm and grinned at him at this result. Fred kept his reaction measured. He put his hand on the doorknob but didn't turn it. "You've changed a lot about your life, Uncle. I'm proud of you for that. Don't be afraid of more change." He grinned, opened the door for his wife, and followed her out.

When the door closed behind them, Scrooge was still frowning. After a moment, he smiled, but he quickly slammed the door on whatever thought had led to such a reaction. His characteristic scowl returned to its rightful place.

Outside, Clara squeezed her husband's arm in happiness at the success of their invitation.

"You know," Fred said, "I believe I have won our little bet from New Year's. That Uncle would stay the course until Easter."

"So you have. And you will be happy to learn I do not intend to extend it. I believe your uncle to be quite cured," she said with another squeeze. The pair practically skipped home through a world that seemed to have everything right in it.

Scrooge dressed in his Sunday best—which, to be fair, was the same black three-piece suit and white shirt he wore every day. His clothes were plain, simple, and practical, just like him. As he adjusted his collar in the mirror, he wondered if a touch of color wouldn't make him look younger. Perhaps he could ask Clara to help dress him as well as his house. Fred always wore a brightly patterned waistcoat or something equally ridiculous, and Scrooge couldn't imagine a man picking out something like that of his own volition.

A knock at the front door interrupted his reverie. He went downstairs to meet Fred and Clara. On the front step, Clara presented him with a pretty pink flower. Was it a rose, perhaps? It had been so long since he had given any thought to flowers. Clara pinned it to the lapel of his coat.

"Honestly, Uncle, I don't think I've ever seen someone look so pleased about an Easter flower," Fred said.

Scrooge realized he was beaming. "Well," he said, but he could find no words to follow it to encapsulate his thoughts.

"Onward!" Fred declared, pointing through the tiny, awkward square in front of the house and out to the street. His companions followed agreeably in that direction.

A crowd milled in front of the church, and the three attached themselves to the fringes of it.

"Why is no one going in?" Scrooge asked.

"They are going in, Uncle," Fred said gently. "They are just taking their time about it."

Scrooge watched as two brightly bonneted women did indeed disappear through the doorway of the church, and then the next group in line stopped to talk with the minister.

"Hullo! Fred!" a voice arrived before the young man it belonged to pushed through the crowd. He greeted both Fred and Clara with a hug and a kiss on the cheek.

Once they had exchanged pleasantries, Fred set a hand on Scrooge's shoulder. "My uncle, Mr. Ebenezer Scrooge."

The look of surprise on the young man's face showed he knew something of this relative and would have been less surprised to hear Mr. Scrooge had visited the moon.

"How do you do," Scrooge said simply, saving the man from having to scramble for something innocuous to say. The young man simply bowed and dove back into the crowd.

Eventually, with slow, shuffling steps, they made it inside the church. They slid into a pew that really only held room for two more, but seeing how many people still had to find seats, the entire row worked together to squeeze in three. Scrooge had no idea how they would deal with having to stand up and sit back down again. They would end up in each other's laps.

"When was the last time you were in a church, Uncle?" Clara asked.

"Goodness. I was a boy. We had to go every Sunday when I was in school, of course. I hated it."

"There are no stern schoolmasters here, so I hope you will feel differently this time."

Scrooge smiled but did not reply. After several more minutes, the service began. As the ministers walked down the aisle carrying an imposing golden cross, Scrooge gulped and kept an uneasy eye on its progress to the altar. He had never been one to believe in God smiting someone, but in this room, he had an inkling it might be possible.

As they went through the old, familiar order of service—the same hymns as when he was a boy, even now—and laughed with their pewmates each time they had to squeeze back into their seats, he relaxed. The sermon was bright and happy and left no room for the possibility of smiting. By the time they got toward the front of the endless communion line, Scrooge's stomach was rumbling. Had the entire morning passed already? Finally, his turn to kneel at the communion table arrived. Even after such a long wait, he did not feel prepared. At the last moment, he crossed his arms over his chest to receive the blessing only. He didn't yet feel worthy of taking communion. He would work on that and return. The spirits' plan for him, he felt now, was about more than just business. Here, he could help save his soul, too. Back at the pew for the last bit of the service, he asked silently for a sign. Something to show him he was doing right by Marley, the spirits, and all those he had harmed over the years.

Back out in the sunshine, Fred remarked, "That wasn't so bad," and accented it with a clap on Scrooge's back. Scrooge wasn't sure whether to nod or shake his head to this, but Fred wasn't waiting for a response. "You can get yourself home? We'll see you for the big event this evening." He leaned in close and said in a stage whisper, "I hope you know what you've gotten yourself into." He winked and turned away, taking Clara's arm as they sauntered off.

Within ten minutes of the Cratchits' arrival that evening, Scrooge had had his foot stepped on by little Charles, had exclaimed at a glass of punch spilled on the new rug by an anonymous assailant, and had broken up a tussle between the children that nearly knocked over Tiny Tim in all the excitement.

Scrooge relished it. There was more life in his house in those ten minutes than had existed all the years he had lived there, and all the years Marley had before him, put together. Scrooge shushed Bob's profuse apologies and told him to sit on the couch and relax with a drink. Belinda had done her hair up and stood as tall as she could, desperate to be seen as one of the women. She ignored her younger siblings and attached herself to Clara, happily discussing the latest fashions and the pretty way Clara had twisted up her hair. Clara accepted her company with good grace, pleased that the young woman found her so intriguing. Peter, oddly enough, seemed rather taken with Scrooge and engaged him in a conversation on a few points of clarification on some letters he had copied the week before.

"I hope you think my penmanship is all right, Mr. Scrooge," he said. "I've learned the best I could."

"Your penmanship has been wonderful," Scrooge said. He leaned in conspiratorially. "Much better than your father's was when he first started working for me."

Peter giggled and glanced at Bob with a newfound personal pride gracing his countenance.

Shortly thereafter, Miss Spencer arrived. The entrance of this intriguing new person caught the children's attention and corralled their energy for the time being. With the same tenderness of care Scrooge had seen in her first at the orphanage and then at the workhouse, Miss Spencer sufficiently petted each child in turn, asking them questions and actually listening to the answers.

Only after she had made these rounds did she turn her attention to the grown-ups. Martha lingered awkwardly by the fireplace, not quite fitting into the adults' conversation or the children's. She busied herself by sipping her punch in between helping Mrs. Minston lay out the hors d'oeuvres along the sideboard. The tasks of orderliness and preparation comforted her. But when Miss Spencer's gaze lit upon her, Martha's eyes brightened, and she held her punch glass a little tighter as her newfound idol approached.

"This seems like the perfect spot for us ladies to hang our hats," Miss Spencer said as she slid into position next to Martha, her back to the fireplace, her gaze taking in the rest of the crowded and noisy room. When Martha didn't respond, she continued, "I hope you won't regret spending your day off with us lot."

"Oh no," Martha said with a little lurch forward, enough that a few drops of punch spilled over the edge of her glass and onto her finger. She wiped her hand on the side of her skirt. "I've been wanting to meet you, actually."

"Me? Why?"

"I've never met a woman of independent means before. I mean, without a husband."

Miss Spencer grinned. "Husbands are overrated, I think. You're a live-in maid, I believe?"

Martha mumbled a response, the eagerness gone from her face.

Miss Spencer set a finger under Martha's chin, lifting until the girl's eyes met her own. "Don't ever be ashamed to work for a living. I may not get paid for it, but I work hard every day. And trust me, life in a crowded boarding house is probably not as romantic as you imagine."

"But still . . . it sounds wonderful."

Miss Spencer sipped her punch before answering. "I've been very lucky. Well, lucky and not. I probably would rather still have the relatives living who left me their inheritances, but I have tried my best to do well by their bequests."

"I'm sorry."

"Just remember, everyone you see is suffering in some way or other. We're none of us immune." The empathy in her gaze kept the sentiment from sounding trite. Martha opened her mouth to respond, but at that instant, Mrs. Minston called them in for dinner. Miss Spencer smiled at Martha before taking her place in line at the dining room door. Martha hung back to wrangle the little ones into position. She walked close by Tiny Tim, who insisted on walking in without his crutch. His steps were slow and jerky, but he looked so proud that everyone watched him without judgment. No one was quite sure if it was a trick of the light or if there were tears in the corners of Bob's eyes as he watched his son.

The first part of the meal was spent expounding on Tim's improvement, then moved on to the school enrollment of Sarah, Charles, and Tim. Charles, in particular, seemed unconvinced that the classroom was where he needed to be and showed this displeasure by spooning some mashed potatoes into his sister's hair. While Mrs. Cratchit rushed to rectify the situation, Miss Spencer distracted the others by giving an update on her latest charity work.

"I want to help, too," Tim declared.

Miss Spencer swiveled to face him, not realizing he had been paying attention to her rather than the noise of his siblings. "That's very kind of you, Tim. Perhaps I could give you a little task to do at home. Making bandages for the charity hospital or something of the sort."

"Yes, please." He grinned around a mouthful of food. Newly freed from the situation with Charles and Sarah, Mrs. Cratchit tapped Tim's shoulder and hissed at him to keep his mouth closed. As she took her seat, she looked apologetically at Scrooge, who seemed nonplussed.

"I talked to Mr. Steven Heron the other day," Fred said. "He wouldn't stop going on about Miss Martha."

"Really?" Bob asked, leaning forward to look down the table at his daughter.

Martha's reddened cheeks resulted from anger rather than embarrassment, as evidenced by her forceful tone. "I've only talked to him twice in my life. I don't know why he feels like he can go around talking about me to other people."

"I'm sure he meant no harm by it," Fred said meekly. He was used to people accepting his teasing with good cheer, and Martha's response took the wind out of his sails.

"I don't think it's a bad idea to take the opportunity to get to know him," Bob said.

Martha sighed. Miss Spencer watched her carefully, then ventured, "Martha should certainly decide for herself. Perhaps there is someone else she is taking the opportunity to get to know?"

"Who?" Mrs. Cratchit asked sharply, as if Martha herself had said it.

"I've been out a few times with a young man I met through work."

"Oh, boy!" Tiny Tim shouted. "Martha's got a beau!"

Martha leaned her forehead in her hand, blocking her face from the rest of the company as her fork scraped her plate.

"All right, let's leave her alone now," Mrs. Cratchit admonished, though she didn't take her gaze off her daughter. "But I do want to hear more about this later."

Martha made no reply. Tiny Tim giggled until his mother shushed him again.

The rest of the meal managed to be accomplished with little fanfare. The Cratchits gathered to leave soon after. At the door, Scrooge said, "Thanks for coming, Bob. And if you need to come in a bit late tomorrow morning, that's fine."

"Thank you, sir." Bob nodded before following his family out.

Miss Spencer delayed Martha a moment. She folded Martha's palm around a small slip of paper. "Feel free to write or call whenever you need," she said. "I'm always happy to offer advice to another woman."

Martha smiled and held the scrap of paper as if it were gold. "Thank you," she said. Miss Spencer followed her out.

Fred and Clara hung back with their uncle. "That was nice," Clara said. The two men agreed wholeheartedly.

"Will we be having a lot more of these dinners with us couples?" Fred asked as he helped his wife with her coat. He pulled an overly serious face as he looked at his uncle.

"What are you talking about?"

"Us and the Cratchits. You and Miss Spencer. She seems to like you."

"Don't be absurd. Besides, there was also a large number of children present, in case you didn't notice."

"She's rather pretty," Clara added, ignoring Scrooge's remark.

"What do I care about pretty?"

"Fine. She's kind, then," Clara said. "The children seemed to love her."

"Bah. Humbug. Get out of my house." But the last was said with a tenderness that belied the words themselves.

"Good night, Uncle," Fred said with a bow. Clara followed him with a smile and a little wave back at Scrooge.

Chapter 13

The new, charitable aspects of Scrooge's business had gotten off to a slow start. Archie Parker, so far, was the only business owner who had come to take advantage of a loan. In the subsequent weeks, Scrooge had heard nothing from him, except for a few small payments on the loan. He was beginning to think Archie had not seen as much benefit in Scrooge and Cratchit's services as Scrooge had hoped. However, things changed the week after Scrooge's latest dinner party. Over the course of a few days, three men who worked for Archie Parker took out loans, in addition to several who claimed no relation to that establishment. Once, with two men at the office at the same time, Scrooge let Bob negotiate the loan terms of one on his own; when Bob knocked at Scrooge's office door to get a signature, Scrooge said without looking up, "Bob, your signature is as good as mine." He kept his head down to avoid seeing Bob's reaction. He hoped it was one of pride rather than feeling condescended to. Scrooge was learning he often had trouble distinguishing when he would elicit the latter rather than the former.

Then, on a Thursday afternoon, Archie Parker returned to partake of Scrooge's business advice. He dropped two heavy account books onto Scrooge's desk. "I hope you are still offering that free business consulting you mentioned the last time I was here. Because I have to warn you, these are probably a bit of a mess," he said.

Scrooge pushed aside his own ledger and pulled Archie's toward him. "The most important thing," he said as he opened the topmost, "is to establish a system." He flipped through a few pages. "I assume that since you needed a loan to cover payroll, business isn't going so well."

"Not really, no. I made some purchases based on the belief that there was money left in the accounts, which, well, there wasn't."

Scrooge was flipping more furiously through the pages. "My God. Half these sums are wrong. Who did this?"

"A clerk I used to have. I've only just begun to realize how much damage he actually did to the business."

Scrooge closed his eyes and pinched the bridge of his nose. "You didn't test him when you hired him or even check his work?"

"I'm afraid not. He came with an excellent reference." Archie's face was oddly open and pleasant. Had Scrooge been in the same situation, he would have been red with shame.

"As the owner of the business, it is imperative that you always know exactly what's going on and that you trust your employees completely. Just as they trust you for their livelihood." Scrooge bit the inside of his cheek as he made this last statement, a sharp sting of pain reminding him how little he had taken that into account until a few months before. "But no matter. We'll get this cleaned up. Then, at least, we will know the reality of the situation." He pushed one book toward Archie and drew the other to himself to begin correcting the sums.

The gas lamps were long lit along the street by the time the two men finished. Ink stained their fingers. A few of the dark splotches had even made it to Scrooge's forehead, where he had tried to rub the ache out of it.

Archie languidly gathered the books. He wrapped his arms around the thick volumes and leaned forward with them over the desk, like a dog protecting her newborn pups. "I'm sorry to have taken up so much of your time."

"No, no. I want to help. And the time was sorely needed." He waved a hand vaguely at the books. Then he pulled out his pocket watch and frowned. So many hours wasted. No, not wasted, he admonished himself. He may have just helped Archie save his business.

Archie caught the frown and paused before leaning in farther. "How much do I owe you for your time?" His breath came out close to Scrooge's face, and Scrooge flinched at the warm, rough scent of it. Without moving, Archie continued, "Surely I owe you something."

In a fit of pique, Scrooge recanted his advertisement of free services. Surely what he had done tonight was above and beyond. "If you are able, any sort of donation would be nice."

"Of course." Archie straightened and shifted the books to his left arm so that he could dive his free hand into his trouser pocket. It emerged with a handful of coins. He set them neatly on the edge of the desk. He bowed. "Thank you so much. I'm sure we'll continue to be in touch about the loan. I'll make more payments when I can."

"Yes, yes." Scrooge waved him away. When Scrooge was alone in the silent building, he stared at the pile of coins for a long time before reaching over and picking them up. He felt their negligible weight in his hand. A pittance—for him, anyway. He shouldn't have asked for anything. This trifle was worse than nothing—receiving nothing wouldn't have cost him his dignity, at least. Tears pricked his eyes. He clenched the coins in his fist so tightly, their edges dug into his palm. This love of money was rooted deep within him. He was afraid he wouldn't be able to cut it out in time to save himself from the fate so terribly predicted for him.

He would have to do better.

And he would have to stop being so goddamn emotional. He had never cried in his adult life before this year, and now it seemed like his eyes always threatened rain.

As Scrooge wiped his eyes, he was surprised to hear the bell over the front door tinkle. Visitors rarely arrived at such a late hour. "Hello?" he called.

A man appeared in the doorway. In the dim lamplight, it could have been an unsettling visit, but there was something about the man that made Scrooge relax immediately.

"Can I help you?"

"Sorry to call so late," the man said. "But I saw you were still in here working away and thought there might be a good man inside."

He turned his head slightly, and in the flickering lamplight, for a mere instant, Scrooge was sure he was looking at Jacob Marley. But in the next transition of shadow and light, he was just as sure he wasn't. The nose was all wrong, and the eyes.

"No bother," Scrooge said.

"I'm taking donations for the poor." He held out a small wooden box. "Might you have some change to spare?"

Scrooge rolled the coins from Mr. Parker around in his palm. "Yes, actually, I have some here." He reached out his hand and dropped the coins into the proffered box. Relief washed over him as soon as the money was out of his possession.

"Thank you. Sometimes the littlest donations mean more than the biggest."

The statement seared into Scrooge's soul. How had the man known just what to say to him in that moment? Was this the sign he had asked for?

The man turned and walked out. As he turned the corner into the hall, Scrooge swore he saw Marley's little pigtail tied at the base of his neck. It appeared for an instant, and just as quickly, it was gone.

The next day, after his embarrassment had sufficiently passed at how his time with Archie had ended, Scrooge remembered the encouraging words of the odd visitor and resolved to try again. He wrote a note to Archie and had Peter deliver it. If there was so much confusion over basic things like account books, then there were probably many other issues that needed resolving in the business. Scrooge was determined to help sort it all out.

Peter returned carrying Mr. Parker's reply. The same employee who had kept the books had also drawn up contracts with suppliers that Archie suspected were not correct. Could Scrooge recommend anyone?

Scrooge smiled. Indeed he could. He opened a little box where he filed away business cards and sorted through them until he found the one he was looking for: Mr. Lauriston, solicitor. He wrote a letter explaining the situation and had Peter carry it off as well. Bob frowned as Peter left again, but Scrooge could tell the boy enjoyed getting out of the tiny, stuffy office. It was the odd time of year when the morning cold required the coal stove to be lit, but even after it was put out as the day warmed up, the excess heat still lingered through the afternoon, and only a sharp breeze through an open window had any hope of keeping the room comfortable.

Peter returned with an affirmative reply and a promise that Mr. Lauriston would connect with Archie Parker. Scrooge, feeling especially pleased with himself, did something he had never done before in his life. He left work early and went for a stroll in the park. Out in the sunshine, he felt it glorious to be alive.

Martha left the Werthers' and headed in a different direction than she normally took when embarking on her Sunday half day. She had arranged to meet Miss Spencer at her boarding house and had looked forward to the visit all week. Spring had just emerged, with round buds tipping the tree branches, and it mirrored Martha's feeling of having just come out into the world of fresh and untested adulthood.

The streets in Miss Spencer's neighborhood were broad and clean. The people walking them seemed genteel but only just so. Unlike many London neighborhoods that dealt in extremes, Miss Spencer seemed to have hit on an area where people did not have too little or too much but just the right amount.

It was with this pleasant observation that Martha arrived at Miss Spencer's front door. She pulled the bell and delighted at the loud ring that echoed inside—one that she did not have to answer. The matron led her into the front parlor, where Miss Spencer greeted Martha and beckoned her to a sofa along one wall. Across the room, two young ladies giggled at the pianoforte. Through a door left discreetly ajar, Martha glimpsed a young woman with her head leaned forward to catch the whisperings of a not-very-handsome young man.

"I'm so glad we could finally get together," Miss Spencer said.

Martha turned from her survey of the room to her companion and thanked her profusely.

"There's no need for that," Miss Spencer said with a soft smile. "I have so enjoyed getting to know your family. Tim really is a joy. He's been so eager to help."

"I appreciate you finding him something to do. I think we are all still adjusting to the fact that he's doing so much better. I'm afraid my mother keeps him indoors with her too much still."

"Well, we can all relate to that, can't we? Keeping the things we are most at risk of losing close to us."

Martha tilted her head to consider the comment. Since Miss Spencer had said it, Martha was inclined to think it very wise, but as she examined the words, they did not seem to be saying much at all. She settled on a more literal response. "Fortunately, we are in much less danger of losing Tiny Tim than we were six months ago. He has made such an improvement."

"So I hear. Soon the epithet 'tiny' may be ironic rather than true."

Martha paused as the two young ladies from the pianoforte swept past them and out of the room. "What about you?" she asked after they had gone. "Do you have any family?"

"Some aunts I see now and again. A distant cousin out in the country who looks me up when he is in London." She smiled. "You're lucky to have such a big family that is so close."

"Yes, we are, rather. But still"—she cast her gaze around the room again—"it must be wonderful to be able to live here on your own."

"It's probably not nearly as romantic as you think. But I do like it. Though you have your own independence, with your position."

Martha made a sour face to show it wasn't the same.

"You can work your way up," Miss Spencer said enthusiastically, pressing her point. But Martha noted Miss Spencer's smooth hands that never did any work they did not want to do. It was easy for a woman like her to say such things.

"Most maids just work until they find a husband."

"Marriage may offer many benefits, but independence is rarely one of them."

Martha thought of Ian. She hadn't considered what would happen if they did marry, but she would certainly have to leave her position. Then she would spend her life as a brewer's wife. Was that what she wanted? The possibility was distant enough that she wasn't sure. Realizing Miss Spencer was waiting for her to speak whatever was clearly on her mind, she said, "Would you ever consider marriage, Miss Spencer? Or have you?"

"Absolutely not," she said quickly, but her cheeks flamed red. "I would never. Let's have tea, shall we?" She turned and rang a bell sitting on the end table behind her. The matron came in, and Miss Spencer asked for tea. Martha envied Miss Spencer's surety of being on the other end of that bell. Martha feared she would be on the receiving end of it for her entire life.

Once the tea tray appeared, Martha asked, "You spend a lot of time with Mr. Scrooge. Do you really think he is a changed man?"

"I never knew him before except by reputation. But he seems very sincere. He genuinely wants to help, although he has a lot to learn about how the world works. Am I to take that to mean you don't think he's changed?"

"I don't know. Maybe he has. But it galls me that Father and everyone else can forgive him so quickly, just because he's been kind for a few months."

Miss Spencer lightly touched the back of Martha's hand. "My advice is never to look down on kindness no matter where you find it. It's rare enough as it is."

The bell at the front door rang, and a moment later, the matron appeared in the parlor. "You have another guest, Miss Spencer." She extended her hand, and Mr. Scrooge entered the room.

Miss Spencer stood and directed him to a seat nearby. Martha set down her teacup and glowered at the new arrival.

"Ah, Martha," he said once he was seated. "So good to see you getting to know Miss Spencer. She is quite the font of wisdom, isn't she?"

Miss Spencer waved a hand to shush him. The matron returned with an extra teacup, and Miss Spencer filled it for him.

"Well, this is perfect. What did you say your employer does? Manufacturing, isn't it?" he asked Martha.

She nodded.

"What sort?"

"I don't know really."

He put a hand to his ear to indicate she should speak up.

"I don't know anything about his business."

"Hmph." He crossed his wrists over the top of his walking stick and regarded Miss Spencer. Then he launched into a story about a man who had come to the office for help sorting out his business. And a ghost had appeared . . . ? Martha couldn't keep the story straight, but Miss Spencer listened adeptly and prodded him along. "And that solicitor I met at the presentation we gave is going to help him as well," he finished.

"How wonderful," Miss Spencer said. "Making connections between people is such a useful skill."

Scrooge beamed for a moment under her praise, then turned his attention back to Martha. "Anyway, all that is to say, the reason I asked after your employer's business is that if he is in manufacturing just as Mr. Parker is, and he seems rather successful, then perhaps he could also offer some advice—and connections, as you say, Miss Spencer—to Mr. Parker. Perhaps you could ask him about his interest in helping those less fortunate."

"That would hardly be my place. I rarely even see Mr. Werther."

"Quite right. I'll write him a letter instead. Could you carry it to him?"

Miss Spencer nodded at Martha encouragingly.

"Yes, I suppose that won't hurt anything."

"Wonderful!" He threw his hands up in the air in excitement, causing his walking stick to fall against the coffee table and nearly upset the teapot.

Once Miss Spencer had righted everything, she went and got him some writing materials, so the last bit of Martha's visit with her dear Miss Spencer was spent watching Mr. Scrooge write a letter, with their hostess occasionally offering advice.

When he was done, he handed Martha the letter, and she stood to go.

"You don't have to go now, child. It can wait," he said, as if Martha's desire to leave could only be because she wanted to help him so badly.

"It's getting dark. I best get back," she said through clenched teeth. She leaned over and gave Miss Spencer a peck on the cheek. She nodded curtly at Mr. Scrooge and swished out into the night.

Scrooge found himself in a place he never thought he would be: in a rather crowded, very noisy coffee shop being served that new-fangled drink rather than a good old pint of ale or cup of tea. Unsurprisingly, the proprietor was an American. His accent grated against Scrooge's ears as he rang up Scrooge's order and poured the beverage, keeping up an innocuous line of chat all the while.

Freed from the American by the next customer in line, Scrooge made his way to a table by the window so that Mr. Werther could spot him when he came in. The meeting place had been Mr. Werther's idea, and as Scrooge sipped the bitter drink, he considered what such a selection might tell him about the man. He must like to be seen, Scrooge reasoned, particularly in places where new trends were establishing themselves. This was supported by the little Scrooge knew of Mr. Werther from the Cratchits. Mr. Werther kept a coach-and-four and lived in a large house on a square. While Scrooge considered himself to be the same class of man as Mr. Werther, Scrooge preferred not to be seen—though that was changing—and he preferred the traditional to the new.

Perhaps that came from age, Scrooge considered as a large man in a red silk waistcoat entered and, after a moment's looking around, headed full tilt for Scrooge's table. He was fortyish, easily a decade Scrooge's junior. The two men shook hands, and Scrooge waited while his companion purchased his own beverage.

As he sat down across from Scrooge, Mr. Werther said, "I've heard some very interesting stories about you."

Scrooge smiled wanly. A few months ago, such a declaration would have embarrassed him, but by now, he had come to expect it. It was his penance, in a way, to be constantly reminded of what he once was. "I haven't heard quite so many about you," he said in response.

"I'm sure you've heard something, or you wouldn't have reached out to me."

Scrooge inclined his head in acknowledgment of this fact. "I am always ready to meet another man of business. Although I haven't yet been able to determine exactly what it is you manufacture."

"Parts for steam engines."

"But not the whole engine?" Scrooge asked with a hint of sarcasm.

"No, then you'd have to hire people who know how to build the damn things, and your profits would plummet."

Scrooge stopped and considered for a moment. The profit-making part of him appreciated Mr. Werther's point of view. He decided it would still be all right to lead with that part of himself in a meeting such as this. "I also hear you've been rather successful."

"I do all right, I do all right." He took a long look around the room, as if trying to identify everyone in it. This review complete, he fixed his attention back on Scrooge. "You are a businessman's businessman, am I right?"

"Yes, we trade in loans, lines of credit, that sort of thing."

"Debt and mortgages, too?"

"Not so much anymore. We have been refocusing our operations."

"So I hear, so I hear. And what do you want with me?"

Scrooge straightened, ready to deliver his pitch. "I'm putting together a roster of sorts. Of businessmen and other professionals who, due to their own success, are willing to donate some of their services to smaller business owners who would not normally be able to access such services."

"Donate? You called me in here to talk about giving things away? That's the biggest load of horseshit I ever heard. You realize that's the opposite of business, right?"

Scrooge did not let himself be swayed by this response. "I think it will help all of us if more businesses in our metropolis are successful. If we raise everybody up—"

"Horseshit."

Scrooge was beginning to realize that Mr. Werther liked to repeat himself.

"Business is about competition," Mr. Werther continued. "And I am sure as hell not going to give you something for free when we have never engaged in business together before."

"It would not be for me, but I take your point. How about, as a gesture of good faith, we enter into a small business agreement? I could secure you a loan, if that is needed."

Mr. Werther leaned back in his chair and regarded Scrooge. "I need to build a new warehouse."

"That sounds like an expensive endeavor."

"And build up my inventory, so I need to invest in more raw materials."

"Even more so."

"What could you do for me in that way?"

"For that amount and those ongoing projects, a line of credit would probably be more applicable? Say, ten thousand pounds at eight percent?"

"That's awfully generous."

"Like I said, a gesture of good faith."

"How long?"

"Eighteen months to start?"

Mr. Werther relaxed, leaned forward quickly, and stuck his hand out. He grinned. "You've got yourself a deal, Mr. Scrooge." He downed the rest of his coffee and left without another word.

Scrooge smiled to himself. That had gone rather well. Now back to the office to draw up the paperwork. A new client was never a bad thing, even if Mr. Werther didn't end up joining Scrooge's "roster." Bob would be pleased. Scrooge left his coffee behind, barely touched.

Bob was not as pleased as Scrooge had hoped. "You realize this could be a delicate situation?" he asked after Scrooge had told him the plan.

"How so?"

Bob closed the door to Scrooge's office to keep their conversation from Peter. "Martha's position could be at stake. If this deal goes sour, he may take it out on her."

Scrooge frowned. "Surely he wouldn't."

"Why not? He thinks nothing of her." He paused. "I think this is another situation in which you have been too trusting."

"Have you been talking to Fred?" Scrooge asked sharply.

"No, I—"

"Listen, if she loses her position because of me, I will continue to pay her salary. How does that sound?"

"I think she would rather have the work."

Scrooge rubbed his forehead. "Then I will pay her salary while I find her another position, damn it . . . I'm sorry, Bob . . ."

"It's all right, sir. You have a headache, perhaps."

"Yes, that's it," Scrooge said, glad to have the out. "I will do my best for you and your family. You have my word."

"Yes, Mr. Scrooge." Bob left without the little bow to which Scrooge had become accustomed. Scrooge feared something had been tarnished. Was he dragging the Cratchits into his own mess? He hoped to God he was not.

Chapter 14

The next few weeks passed uneventfully—or rather, with only those events that marked the highs and lows of each passing day. Mr. Werther was not immediately ready to draw down his money, though he sent Scrooge occasional updates about the bids he received for his new warehouse. Scrooge, in turn, provided a letter of commitment as proof to others involved in the project that it would move forward. Things seemed to be going swimmingly, so to Scrooge, at least, the threat of a great clash between Bob's interests and Mr. Werther's had been much diminished. Bob had not confronted Scrooge again, and Scrooge was glad of it. Though he tried to push it down, part of him still felt that he was the boss and his decisions should not be questioned. He was kind to Bob during this period but perhaps a little cold, not intimating much about his life. Scrooge did not have to ask Bob about his family life, as Peter volunteered almost all information freely, even to the point of sharing details of a stomach bug Belinda contracted that made Bob hush him fiercely and turned Scrooge a bit green.

During this time, Fred embarked on a new mission. His success in getting his uncle to see a doctor and attend church empowered him to attempt something even more audacious. In this, too, he finally wore Scrooge down. One morning, Scrooge announced to Bob that he would be going on a seaside holiday—the first one Scrooge had ever indulged in. Though the passing days had occasionally revealed hints that summer was around the corner, this particular morning was disagreeable, wrapping everything in a chill fog and making the prospect of Scrooge taking a trip to the sea at any point in the near future even more ludicrous. But Bob gave no hints of his thoughts on his partner's suitability for such an enterprise.

"Fred and Clara convinced me to join them," Scrooge explained as the two men stood in the foyer between Scrooge's office and the Tank. "We leave in a fortnight. Though I still think everyone is overreacting to that episode at your house and that blasted doctor who tried to make it sound like I was ill."

"Everyone should enjoy a holiday once in a while," said Bob, who had never taken one in his life, though for very different reasons than Scrooge.

"Bah," Scrooge said, but he did not follow it up with his characteristic "humbug." Someday, the once-familiar phrase might disappear from his vocabulary completely.

Overhearing this exchange, Peter asked, "Father, can we go on a holiday? I want to see the ocean, too!"

Scrooge opened his mouth to respond, but Bob shot him a sharp look.

"No, Peter," Bob said. "Maybe one day, but for now, that is simply too extravagant." Bob walked into the Tank and closed the door behind him.

Scrooge watched the door for a moment, surprised at being cut off in this way. He couldn't remember the door to the Tank ever closing, and indeed, the squeal of the hinges hinted at how long it had been since they had last been called to movement. But it was best for him to leave the family discussion to the family. If he offered funds for a trip, he should do it to Bob privately and not in front of Peter. Scrooge was at least beginning to understand those dynamics. But he also sensed that Bob might not take kindly to anything else that smacked of charity. Scrooge returned to his office and closed his own door. The two men worked in their separate cocoons for the remainder of the day. Scrooge resolved to leave well enough alone. Best that only one of the partners became a gadabout anyway, Scrooge thought with a smile, pleased to find the gadabout was him.

Neither Bob nor Scrooge was used to giving in to his emotions, and their work together continued pleasantly enough as Scrooge's trip neared. Peter made no further mention of the Cratchits enjoying such an event. Scrooge guessed Bob had given him a good talking-to at home. Indeed, Peter kept his head down and did his work well, mostly leaving Scrooge alone. Scrooge thought he would make a fine man of business one day. And leaving him to Bob's guidance in such matters was probably for the best.

The Friday before Scrooge was due to leave dawned bright and clear, though still holding a touch of a damp, late spring chill. To finalize matters before Scrooge's absence, both Scrooge and Bob arrived at the office early, Bob with a sleepy-looking Peter in tow.

The two men spent most of the morning in Scrooge's office, poring over the books. Ostensibly, Scrooge was preparing Bob to take over all operations for the coming week, though in reality, Bob already knew every detail. It had been a while since they had held an in-depth check-in such as this, and Scrooge relished seeing Bob's growing confidence in monitoring and reporting to him on the business. Scrooge had begun considering the future and had decided that even though he had pushed off the idea of a holiday at first, this week away was actually quite propitious. It would be a good opportunity to see how Bob could handle the business himself, should Scrooge decide to direct his focus elsewhere in the future. He had begun to chafe at being tied to his desk every day and hoped he might be able to join Miss Spencer in more of her charitable activities.

"I think we have a couple of problems developing," Bob said, drawing Scrooge's attention back to the present moment. Bob ran his finger down the page of the account book to locate the suspect entries. "This man here is a month late on his payments, and he hasn't responded to the letters we sent. And this one here is only a few days late, but I suspect he's headed in the same direction."

"They're small loans," Scrooge said, willing himself not to look too concerned.

"Yes, but if it indicates a trend in this new loan policy . . ."

Scrooge drew the book toward him and peered at their names. "They're both Archie's men, aren't they? Why don't you go talk to him next week and see what he can do?"

"You're still going away?"

"Is there any reason why I shouldn't?"

Bob gulped. "No, sir."

"Good. I should be able to leave the other partner in charge for a week."

"Of course, sir. It's just that, with my attentions diverted elsewhere, Peter will have to take on more responsibility. Perhaps a small raise would be in order?"

"How small?"

"A couple of shillings a week."

Even though Scrooge had just been considering how well Peter was doing, he couldn't shake the need to negotiate. Never take the first offer, he had always told himself. "One shilling for now. Then we'll see how he does."

"Yes, sir. Thank you."

They went through a few final items of business. When they were done, Bob gathered up the books, bowed, and backed out of the room, as if he had been in the presence of a king. Scrooge laughed to himself a little at that thought. Bob had surely never admired Scrooge in the way Scrooge had liked to imagine in the past, and now . . . well, probably not now, either, as Scrooge was showing himself to be awkward in almost every aspect of his new life.

Scrooge surveyed his desk, trying to recall anything else he needed to take care of before he left. "Ah, yes," he said to himself as he pulled out a blank sheet of paper and tapped his pen in the inkwell. He needed to check in with Mr. Lauriston. He hadn't heard anything about how the work was going with Mr. Parker. Scrooge penned a short letter, then called Peter in, intending to ask him to carry it over. But it was already late in the day, and if Peter had looked sleepy at their early start that morning, he looked positively browbeaten now, his face practically disappearing within the confines of his starched collar. Scrooge relented. "Here," he said. "Put this in the post for me in the morning." He was unlikely to get a response this late in the day, anyway. He'd deal with it when he returned.

Once Peter left, Scrooge sighed and pushed his chair back from his desk. He had expected that their new loan terms were so strong that no one would struggle to pay the loans back. But with this unforeseen hiccup in the rollout of their new loan policy, there would be a lot to deal with when he returned. He couldn't expect Bob to take care of everything. Scrooge would have to learn to tidy his own messes sometimes.

But leaving Bob in charge of his messes was exactly what Scrooge was about to do for the next week. It was a responsibility Bob was able to push out of his mind while in the midst of the constant rush that was his family, but that evening, Mrs. Cratchit caught a characteristic furrow of his brow during a rare quiet moment as they were getting ready for bed.

"What's on your mind, then?" she asked. "I know there's something."

"It's just that he's never been away before."

"And what, you'll miss him while he's gone?"

Bob shook his head. "No. It's, well . . ." After a moment's hesitation, he told his wife a bit about the changes Scrooge had instituted in the business and the concerns that were just starting to appear in Bob's mind.

Mrs. Cratchit sat poised on the edge of the bed, ready to expound her opinion the instant her husband finished. When he did, she said, "When you told me about him engaging Mr. Werther in business, you made it seem as if there was no chance it could fail." Her voice was not angry. Instead, she sounded as if she had known all along that was not entirely the truth.

Bob grimaced as he put on his nightcap. "I don't think—it's just that I didn't want you to worry."

Mrs. Cratchit took in a deep breath. "You know how I feel about him. The man deserves to go out of business and get a taste of his own medicine. I wouldn't mind seeing him take a stint in the poorhouse, either."

"But—"

She held up a finger. "Let me finish. I don't know how that man thinks he can suddenly make up for fifty years of bad behavior. But since I don't want you to lose your situation, then I suppose you must help him. But maybe you should help him just enough so that he must exit the business and leave you as the sole partner. Then you can set things to rights. And make sure your daughter keeps her position."

Bob sat open-mouthed at the audacity of his wife's plan. "I couldn't . . ."

"Why are you men always so weak?" She stood and started to pull down the bedclothes but stopped mid-yank. "Another thing—you've been spending far too much time at work lately. You mustn't let it take over your life. You mustn't become like *him*."

"I would never—"

"Come to bed, Bob," she said.

He did as he was told without another word of protest. But the furrow on his brow persisted, telling his wife that he was deep in consideration of what she had said.

Chapter 15

"I can't remember the last time I left London," Scrooge said as the coach rumbled out of that city. That wasn't entirely true, as he knew it must have been before he partnered with Marley and they set up their business as young men, but the sentiment held. He thought back on the long years he had wasted moving between his office and his house with no deviation. The thought made him shudder.

"I'm glad we could be the ones to accompany you, Uncle," Fred said.

"I think it's going to be a beautiful day," Scrooge said after a look out the window. The sun was rising through the horizon and even brought a little warmth. Scrooge took off his hat and gloves and set them on his lap.

Scrooge had never taken so much pleasure in a coach journey in his life. The company was good, the scenery novel, and the people they passed along the way! He watched intently out the window, particularly enjoying the scenes of children running alongside the coach as they trundled along.

They were a good distance out of London before he noticed how quiet his normally giggly niece and nephew were being. He shifted his attention away from the window and to the interior of the coach. Fred closely watched his wife, while Clara herself looked pale and uncomfortable, occasionally bringing one lace-gloved hand gently to her lips.

"What's going on with you two, then? You've hardly said a word."

Fred kept his gaze on Clara. "She's just feeling a bit under the weather."

"Oh, no! Why didn't you say? We could have delayed the trip."

"No, no. This is the best time for us to go." Husband and wife shared a long glance during which several nods of the head and furrowed eyebrows were exchanged. "The truth is," Fred said once the silent discussion was complete, "Clara is with child." Fred could hold back his beaming smile no longer. Clara turned from pale to a bit pink under the proud gazes of the two men.

"How wonderful! I am to be a great-uncle."

"Yes, so you see, this is to be our last holiday for quite a while, probably."

"Of course it is. I am so glad for you." Scrooge squeezed both his companions' hands and left Fred and Clara to continue their silent communing without interruption. He returned to his people watching out the window, though he no longer consciously registered the scenes passing before him.

Instead, he turned this new idea over and over in his mind. Just as he was finally starting to learn how to be the uncle he should have been all along, the spirits threw him a new challenge. He would relish the opportunity to start fresh with this child, unencumbered by the weight of the past. At the same time, his relationship with his niece and nephew would almost certainly change. They would be busier and wouldn't be available to escort him around and plan his dinner parties and other extravagances for him. And how close of a relationship was a great-uncle, anyway? Though with both of Fred's parents long departed, perhaps Scrooge could take on more of a grandfatherly role. The thought comforted him momentarily, before he felt a surge of guilt at feeling grateful that his dear sister was no longer among them.

"Are you all right, Uncle?"

Scrooge shook himself out of his reverie. "Yes, of course." He touched his cheek gingerly, aware that he felt flushed and was probably siren red. He loosened his cravat and suddenly felt silly wearing it. Did one wear cravats on holiday? "It's just a bit warm in here."

"Of course, Uncle." But the look Fred directed at him made Scrooge feel his young nephew saw right through him, to the quivering, scared man he was at his core as his long-held defenses were torn down one by one.

After stopping at their hotel in Brighton and allowing Clara a half hour's rest on a stationary object, the trio went for a walk along the chain pier. Scrooge was overwhelmed by the noise around them. It was the same *amount* of noise as in London, but it was an entirely different set of sounds. This wasn't the noise of business and duty, but of happiness. All around him were shouts and laughter and friendly chatter. He couldn't help but smile.

They stopped at a few shops along the pier but found nothing they couldn't live without, though they did indulge in glasses of lemonade. At the end of the pier, they laughed as the wind whirled bits of seafoam around them.

Scrooge was gazing over the sea and imagining what lay beyond it when a familiar voice popped up behind him. "Mr. Scrooge, Mr. Williamson, Mrs. Williamson."

The three so mentioned caught each other's eyes as the joy drained out of their faces.

As the elder statesman of the group, Scrooge led the charge and turned toward the voice first. "Mrs. Morody. Miss Morody," he said to their new companions.

"Fancy seeing you lot here!" Mrs. Morody exclaimed.

"My sister didn't mention you were coming here also," Clara said.

"Oh, I assure you I had no idea myself until a few days ago. It's such a small, funny world, isn't it?"

"Quite," Fred said, with a wink at his wife and uncle.

Mrs. Morody led them through a series of questions about where they were staying and what they were doing and what they thought of the weather and how the ride was from London. Once her questions were exhausted, she swept the group right along into a long description of all the times she had been to Brighton "before she was widowed twice."

Throughout her mother's monologue, Miss Morody watched Scrooge through the same fluttering eyelashes she had used on him before. This time, at least, her hair was not so precariously piled on top of her head. Scrooge tried to avoid her gaze but couldn't help darting the occasional uncomfortable glance in her direction to check what she was doing, as if she were a wild animal approaching too close in the woods.

When Mrs. Morody finally paused for breath, her daughter took her chance. "Perhaps you'd like to go for a walk along the pier, Mr. Scrooge."

"No, thank you." He felt the lack of a proper excuse at the end of the sentence, but he was no good at coming up with one on such short notice.

"Come now," Mrs. Morody said. "What man wouldn't want to walk with a young lady as pretty as my Lucretia?"

"I have no desire to be alone with Miss Morody, especially after her behavior last time we met."

Mrs. Morody's eyes narrowed, and she seemed poised for attack. "Don't you think you might share some responsibility—"

"I would advise you not to make baseless accusations against my uncle, Mrs. Morody," Fred cut in.

"I was simply trying to protect my daughter's reputation." Getting no reaction to this comment, she smoothed the front of her dress and continued. "Well, perhaps we can meet again while we're all here."

"We'll let you know," Fred said.

After a brief hesitation, Mrs. Morody turned away and motioned for her daughter to follow.

When the two women were out of earshot, the remaining three formed a tight circle.

"I am so sorry," Clara said. "I never should have invited them to that dinner party. My sister tried to warn me, but of course, her husband loved the idea. I see now he was eager to foist them on someone else."

Scrooge looked at his nephew. "No joke you want to make?"

"For once, no. I've never seen a lady so blatant in her designs."

"I'll talk to my sister. Maybe she and her husband can make Mrs. Morody see sense." Clara looked off in the direction the women had gone. "I do feel sorry for Lucretia, though, being so manipulated by her mother."

"Bah! Humbug! She isn't a child. That girl knows perfectly well what she's doing."

Fred started walking slowly back down the pier, and his companions fell in beside him. They didn't speak as they walked. Scrooge kept his eyes roving the crowd to make sure the Morodys didn't reappear and catch them by surprise.

At the point where the pier met the shore, the vista widened, and Scrooge relaxed, seeing the dreaded ladies weren't there. He motioned to a bench on the beach, and the three sat hip to hip with Fred in the center.

"You know they won't be the last to make an attempt on you," Fred said.

"Honestly, Fred, you don't have to make it sound like someone is trying to kill him."

Scrooge ignored Clara's comment. "Why me? I've lived the last thirty years of my life without drawing the attention of a single woman."

"To be fair, you looked like you wanted to murder everyone you met during those thirty years—or at least send them off to the poorhouse," Fred said. "Now that you've reentered the world with a smile on your face, women think there's hope."

"Hope of what, for God's sake?"

"Hope of capturing a rich—and kind—man. But mostly rich." He finished this off with another of his characteristic winks.

"So now, after all this, I'm just supposed to accept that people are solely motivated by money? Hogwash. Besides, I'm too old for this nonsense."

"Are you really so old, Uncle?" Clara asked. "There have been even more confirmed bachelors than you who have given in."

Fred added, "You don't have to accept marriage for money. There are people who aren't so motivated. Would you consider one of those ladies?"

A small black dog ran up and yapped at their toes until a boy came and scooped him up.

"Beautiful dog!" Scrooge called after the boy. Then, to his companions, he said, "Perhaps I should get a dog. What do you think?"

"Yes, get a dog if you want. But don't change the subject."

"Fred, you are driving at something I know I will not like."

"What else is new? That's never stopped me before. Look, you have to know who I'm talking about."

Scrooge shook his head firmly. He watched the crowd instead of meeting Fred's gaze.

Clara leaned forward so that she could see Scrooge on the other side of her husband. "We may not be able to spend as much time with you once the baby comes. We want to make sure you have some companionship."

"That's what the dog is for."

Fred and Clara shared a long look and decided to give up for now. "Let's go eat," Clara said. "I'm starving."

Fred and Scrooge bathed in the sea while Clara stayed on the shore and sketched. The purported reason was that she did not want to bathe by herself in the women's area of the beach, but based on the disapproving look Fred gave his wife when the activity had been proposed the day before, Scrooge guessed that his nephew had vetoed the idea due to his wife's condition. And he was quite right to do so, Scrooge thought as he and Fred walked toward the row of bathing machines lining the shore. It would be a silly thing to lose a child over.

Scrooge had agreed to the idea of himself sea bathing without argument, but secretly, he wasn't sure it was something he should engage in. For a man of his age to be out practically in his underclothes. And what if he should catch a chill . . . ? He shook his head. He had come all this way. He must participate in the holiday to its fullest. To do otherwise would be insulting to his nephew. And the spirits. So he made no complaints as he and Fred entered bathing machines next to each other.

Scrooge's heart clenched in the small space. The machine was tall, narrow, and wooden—far too reminiscent of a coffin for his taste. There was hardly room to change without knocking his elbows against the walls. He was relieved to step out of it and into the water a few minutes later. He drew a breath in sharply at the shock of the cold. He and Fred had waited until the afternoon so that the water would be as warm as possible, but it was still England in May, and the word *warm* was not one he would use to describe his current state.

He hardly had time to collect himself when a spray of water splashed his face. He looked over and saw Fred splash him again. "It will feel better if you immerse yourself in the water all at once," Fred called. He disappeared under the calm surface of the water to demonstrate and popped back up quickly.

Scrooge stood submerged only up to his chest, his arms lifted above the water to keep as much of himself as possible away from the cold. *Another area of life in which one must not do things by halves,* he thought, and followed Fred's example.

He reappeared a moment later, coughing and spluttering. He pushed his wet hair back away from his face. His eyes stung, and his mouth tasted nothing but salt. It was glorious. He laughed and splashed Fred.

The action of his hand slapping gentle waves transported him back to a moment in time he had not thought about in forty years. In the memory, he was a boy, before he had been sent away to that awful school. They were at a beach somewhere, and she was grinning. Fan had the prettiest smile. He had almost forgotten that about her. That must have been the last time he was in the sea.

He moved in an awkward sideways paddle closer to Fred.

"Is that your attempt at swimming, Uncle?" Fred teased.

"I'm doing my best, never having had a lesson in my life."

"I can show you, if you like."

Rather than responding directly, Scrooge asked, "Did your mother ever take you to the sea as a boy?"

Fred looked a bit surprised. Fan was rarely mentioned between them. Fred learned years before that any mention of Fred's mother shut Scrooge down even faster than a suggestion of Christmas cheer. "Yes, several times. Why?"

"She invited me along once when you were small. Only I wish now I had gone."

"There's no point in worrying over that now. We made it here together at last, didn't we? Now let me show you a basic stroke before you drown yourself."

The two laughed, swam, and teased each other for the next hour. By the end of it, Scrooge could make a passable attempt at swimming twenty feet or so along the shallows. Fred clapped and encouraged as if Scrooge were the child and he the father. Beside them, a corpulent man clearly taking his three medicinal sea dips very seriously viewed them with derision. The occasional apology from Fred and Scrooge did nothing to wipe the frown from his face.

"Try to enjoy yourself," Scrooge said to him as he and Fred walked back to the bathing machines. "Think of all those people back in London who will never get the chance to be here."

The man's eyes widened in surprise, but Scrooge didn't wait for a response. He knew nothing he could say to the man would affect him until he had his own life-changing experience. Scrooge fervently hoped the spirits would bring it to the man soon, as Scrooge wanted everyone to be well and free from their own misconceptions of what life should be.

Dressed and back on the shore, Scrooge said, "I feel like a boy here. Or at least, what I imagine it feels like to be a boy, as I'm not sure I ever really got to be one." He squeezed the last of the sea water out of the ends of his hair as they walked.

"Better late than never," Fred said, steering them toward the bench where Clara waited. "Though to be honest, Uncle, I can't picture you as a boy at all."

"Like I said, I wasn't much of one . . ." He trailed off. Out of the corner of his eye, he glimpsed a face he recognized. He stopped. At first, he thought it was an apparition created by the thoughts of the long-ago past swirling in his mind. As she neared, though, the way her lace collar fluttered in the wind and her boots kicked up the sand proved she was a physical being. Fred said something, but Scrooge couldn't interpret the sounds. He kept his gaze fixed on her until he was certain. Yes, it was that face. The face he had only seen in youth in real life but that the Ghost of Christmas Past had shown him surrounded by her family around a warm hearth in her middle age. On Christmas Eve, he had thought it cruel to show him such a thing, but maybe the spirits were preparing him for just this moment. How would he have recognized her otherwise after so much time had passed?

It was her.

It was Belle.

"Uncle, are you all right? Here, come sit." Fred guided Scrooge by the elbow to the bench.

Scrooge was torn between allowing Fred to lead him and running down the beach after Belle. But in the end, it was easier to stay put. What on earth would he say to her anyway? Nothing could erase the decades or the decisions he had made.

Clara stood as they approached. "Is he all right? He looks so pale."

Fred navigated Scrooge into a seat, then kneeled in front of him. "He was fine in the water—"

"I'm fine now." Scrooge rubbed his forehead, coming to himself. "Don't make such a fuss." He looked over his nephew's head, watching the woman who had so shaken him walk farther away, arm in arm with her husband. She was older than the last scene he had glimpsed of her, but it was definitely her. He couldn't mistake the dimple in her left cheek or the way she tilted her head to look at her husband when she talked—the same way she had looked at him so long ago.

Fred followed his gaze. "Who's that?"

"Nobody."

"It's clearly somebody."

Scrooge looked after her again as she grew smaller in the distance. "It's Belle."

Fred looked confused for a moment as he searched for the meaning of the name. Finally, it hit him. "Your old fiancée?" He glanced back at the couple, but they were no longer in sight. He returned his focus to his uncle. "But how can you know that? You haven't seen her in thirty years."

"The spirits showed her to me back on Christmas Eve. It's her."

The two young people exchanged concerned glances. Clara shut her sketchbook and stood. "Why don't we head back to the hotel? I think we could all use a rest after all this sun." The walk back was tense, broken only by Fred and Clara's forced chatter about what had happened in the hour they were apart. Scrooge said nothing, lost in his own thoughts and regrets.

AFTER THE SPIRITS COME

At the hotel, Scrooge shut himself in his room, leaving Fred and Clara to have what he knew would be a worried conversation about him. Why couldn't people believe anything that wasn't right in front of their noses? Especially Fred, who was so eager to believe in the magic of Christmas and the goodness of people. Never mind that prior to his own visitations, Scrooge had been exactly the same—worse, even.

He sat at the small desk pushed against one wall. Though Belle had lived in his thoughts all this time, seeing her in the flesh was different. It solidified all the years he had wasted chasing money instead of love. Tears welled in his eyes. He attempted to dab them away, but then they came in full force, and he had no control over them anymore. When he had finally run dry, he stared out the window at the gathering dark. The street outside his window became a land of shadows, ghosts darting between the dim dollops of light from the streetlamps. He felt like that in his life: walking through the darkness, trying to find his way, his journey punctuated with brief flashes of bright hope. Some days, like today, the stretches of darkness seemed too much to bear.

Fred and Clara knocked to take him to dinner, but he insisted he was not hungry and did not want to go out. They exchanged the same concerned glances they had shared earlier, but he could not bother to placate them. He was an old man, and old men should be allowed to stew in their own histories for a while. Fred and Clara said they would send up his supper, but when the food arrived an hour later, Scrooge took no more than three bites.

That night, Scrooge dreamed. He was again in the presence of the silent specter of Christmas future. They stood on a barely familiar street. The spirit pointed him to the same window through which he had seen Belle and her family with the Ghost of Christmas Past. The scene was much the same, except the children were gone. They must be grown now, Scrooge thought, if this was the future. Belle and her husband looked the same as they had that morning on the beach.

"I saw Ebenezer Scrooge in his office again today," Belle said. "After all that talk in the papers about how he has changed, he was still alone. It's obvious he still doesn't know how to live."

The room grew smoky for no reason Scrooge could see. Belle and her husband didn't notice. It suddenly angered him that he didn't know this mysterious man's name, the man who had been able to give Belle everything Scrooge could not. Soon, Scrooge could hardly see them through the smoke. The flue was probably backed up, Scrooge thought. He coughed. Wait—if he wasn't actually in the room, how could he be affected by the smoke? During his past visitations, he had simply been watching visions move around him. He couldn't feel the cold or warmth of any of them. He glanced at the black, towering form beside him. Unsurprisingly, the specter offered him no answers.

Scrooge woke in a sweat. It was still dark, and his eyes took a moment to adjust to the low light. He took a few deep, cleansing breaths. His mind whirred. How was one to tell the difference between a dream and a visitation? But the spirits wouldn't deign to visit him twice—and this time just to show him that one scene. And so odd about the smoke. It had to be a dream. Yes, definitely. A dream and nothing more.

He couldn't help ruminating over dream-Belle's words. Would he always be alone in a certain sense? He had cemented many relationships in the past months, but would he always be missing out on something by lacking that most important type of love, the ones poets wrote about—romantic love?

He lay awake for over an hour with these thoughts rushing through his mind. Eventually, they exhausted him, and he fell into a restless doze.

He awoke for good when the first sunbeams peeked into the room. He smiled. The sunbeams felt friendly, like they had come to check on him. But after a few minutes of early-morning quiet, last night's thoughts tugged at the edges of his consciousness, trying to drag him back to that dark place. To keep them away, he urgently needed to do something. He had to act to change his situation, to further deviate from the path of his old life. He thought back to what Fred had hinted at after their recent run-in with the Morodys. Scrooge had known exactly who Fred was talking about and what he was getting at even though Scrooge never would have admitted it out loud. The question remained, Could his blasted nephew be right again? It did not escape Scrooge that if he had listened to Fred years ago as he had begged for his uncle to accept an invitation to Christmas, his life now would be very different.

Determined to force a change, Scrooge got up and, still in his nightgown, went to the desk to write a letter. The words came onto paper in fits and starts, with many crossings-out and squashed-in additions in the draft. But eventually, he ended up with a clean copy.

Dear Miss Spencer,

I am very much enjoying the holiday in Brighton. I have always thought of holidays as a dreadful indulgence, but now I understand why people take them. Somehow things become clearer when one is removed from one's daily life.

It is hard to overstate how much I have learned about the richness of life over the last few months. Lessons I should have by rights learned as a young man have finally become clear to me. In that context, I greatly value your role in my education and your wise guidance on how to best improve the community around me that I have so long neglected. It is my most fervent hope that our partnership long continue, perhaps in its current guise, perhaps in another more kindred.

I have had several opportunities to reflect on my life while here. We ran into an old friend of mine whom I had not seen for many years. Also, I found out I am to be a great-uncle. I feel this is especially a blessing, as I will have the chance to provide the love and care I did not apply to poor Fred as he was growing up. Not that it seems he lacks anything in kindness and humanity due to my lack of guidance. For this, I can only thank my angelic sister.

I write this to say, I hope you have not forgotten me in my short absence, and I hope you remember me kindly.

Sincerely,

Ebenezer Scrooge

P.S. When I return to London, I hope you will find it appropriate to call me Ebenezer.

Before he could second-guess himself, Scrooge dressed and walked down the carved oak stairs to the front desk to leave the letter for the post. From the instant he handed it over until about halfway up the first flight of stairs back to his room, he was certain he had done the right thing that would help him bring more love into his life. As his feet hit the second landing, though, he instead knew he had made a horrible mistake. He was making an old fool of himself. However, inertia overtook him, and he didn't turn back. His thoughts wavered between these two avenues all day—openness versus foolishness.

Fred and Clara noticed his distraction but only asked if he still thought of Belle. He told them, yes, that was it, grateful to offer a simple answer.

Alone in his room again that night, he almost resolved to write another letter recanting the first. But before the pen even touched paper, he saw this would only make things worse. Besides, he had said nothing outright in his letter—though women were so intuitive, he knew Miss Spencer would be able to read between the lines. Just as he had wanted her to originally.

He decided he would leave well enough alone and keep their relationship professional when he returned. He didn't think she was likely to be cruel about it, but still, better to follow her lead.

The next morning dawned much the same as the one before it. To keep himself from becoming too enmeshed in his own thoughts, Scrooge went down early to breakfast, hoping to strike up a conversation with a young waiter who had been friendly to them so far. It had been excellent practice for him on how to be kind to the staff but not condescending—and he thought he had been doing rather well.

He halted at the bottom of the stairs instead of continuing into the restaurant. On the other side of the lobby, conversing with the concierge across the front desk, stood Belle. She was wearing the same blue dress as when he had seen her two days before. So she was not so wealthy, he thought with a little too much pleasure, then quickly chastised himself. He hesitated, then took the first few steps across the foyer.

She finished her conversation and, after tucking a slip of paper into her reticule, she turned. Her gaze landed briefly on Scrooge, then darted back after she had taken one step toward the door. She recognized him.

He finished crossing the distance between them. He removed his hat as he approached. "Belle?"

"Ebenezer," she said. It was not a question.

"How funny to see you here after all this time. How are you?"

"I'm very well. You look well yourself. Much better?"

"Better?"

She blushed and lowered her head. "I have spied you once or twice in your office over the years."

He smiled softly. "It wasn't hard to find me there. I was hardly ever anywhere else. You are here with your family?"

"My husband. And you?"

"My nephew and his wife."

"How nice."

"Look, I wanted to say I'm sorry."

"Really, Ebenezer, there's no need." She touched his arm gently. "It was so long ago." Belle looked over his shoulder.

He turned to see her husband approaching. "Well, it was lovely to see you. Enjoy the rest of your trip."

"You as well." She took her husband's arm, and they walked toward the front door.

Scrooge turned to find Fred and Clara watching him with curiosity from the foot of the stairs. He strode toward them. "How long have you two been gaping there?"

"Was it her?" Clara asked breathlessly. "Was it Belle?"

"Yes. I told you it was."

Fred shook his head in wonder. "I still don't know how you managed to recognize her after all this time."

Scrooge opened his mouth to remind him but stopped. *Fred has seen the proof himself,* he thought, *and he must do with it what he will.* "Shall we go in for breakfast?" he asked instead. The pair agreed, and Scrooge took a turn escorting Clara in on his arm. He couldn't have looked prouder if he had the queen of Sheba at his side.

Speaking with Belle and making some minuscule amends helped Scrooge mostly put his concerns about the fairer sex out of his mind for the rest of the trip, feeling only the occasional twinge of embarrassment when he thought of how he would have to face Miss Spencer when he returned. No reply to his letter arrived, which he knew was for the best. He glimpsed Belle one final time, across the restaurant the last night at dinner. He was tempted to go speak to her but knew it was better to leave it be. They had said all there could be to say to each other.

Fred, Clara, and Scrooge lingered over dinner that night, with Fred and Scrooge sharing a bottle of sherry and getting perhaps a bit too merry. Fred, whose boisterous laughter always drew attention to him, positively boomed through the room with a few drinks under his belt. But the other patrons felt the noise emanated from his good cheer and found no reason to complain.

Back in his room that evening, Scrooge sat on his bed and contemplated his pending return to London. His thoughts were a bit fuzzy from the alcohol, but even after this glorious week away, he couldn't keep them entirely from work. He hadn't admitted it to himself before, but he knew he had a mess to clean up when he returned. He could only hope that Bob had been able to right some of it while he was away. As he readied himself for bed, he muttered to himself, "My God. Who would have ever thought my fortunes would hinge on the likes of Bob Cratchit?"

Chapter 16

Mrs. Minston greeted Scrooge at the front door when he returned home the next afternoon.

"I've got your room all warmed up for you, sir," she said as she helped him off with his coat. "Now, what can I fix you to eat?"

"I don't need much of anything. I can—"

"Don't say it," she cut in. She reprimanded Scrooge whenever she found him nosing around the kitchen, trying not to make trouble for her—when that trouble was in fact her job, and his nosing around often caused her more trouble than his simple request would have. "I'll just prepare you a plate, shall I?"

While she did that, Scrooge went upstairs with his traveling case. He had bought one especially for the trip, seeing as he had never traveled anywhere before in his life. It was a handsome thing of supple dark leather. He admired it as he laid it on the bed. He opened the lid but didn't have much idea what to do with its contents after that. Mrs. Minston had a system for everything now, and Scrooge's attempts to help usually ended up doing the opposite.

Fortunately, she came up shortly and shooed him away. She handed him a plate of bread, cheese, and apple slices. "Let me deal with this," she said.

Scrooge sat in his chair by the fire, the same one he had been sitting in when Jacob Marley came to visit. He ate his simple meal contentedly, cheered by the thought of his special visits.

"How was the trip?" Mrs. Minston asked as she began pulling his clothes out of the case and laying them on the bed.

"We had a lovely time. In fact, I don't think I've ever enjoyed myself quite so much."

"I'm glad to hear it. Did anything interesting happen?"

"Actually, yes." He brushed aside his sadness at the thought of Belle and determined to tell the story just as it was. "We saw my old fiancée walking down the beach with her husband and then at the hotel. I spoke to her briefly."

"Fiancée?" She turned and put her hands on her hips as if she were admonishing him. "I didn't know about that. When was this?"

"Oh, many years ago. Decades, now."

"And you recognized her after all this time?"

Scrooge set down his plate and twisted in his chair so that he could see her, like a boy sharing knowledge of a secret plot. "You see, I've seen her more recently. I had a vision of her when the spirits visited me over Christmas." He paused. "You know—"

"Oh, yes, I've heard." She returned to folding his clothes.

He nodded. "I had another dream of her while I was there, after we had seen her. A dream, I think, and not a vision."

"How does a body tell the difference?"

Scrooge returned his focus to his meal. "I'm not sure."

Mrs. Minston watched his back for a long moment, a troubled look darkening the hollows of her face. Just as she had turned away, Scrooge shouted, "Oh!" He set his plate on the small end table next to his chair, then jumped up. He hovered next to her on his tiptoes, like an eager child. "Look in the case," he said. This not being a very specific direction, several more hand motions and instructions were needed before she unearthed a thin wooden case at the bottom of the valise. She set it on the bed, touching it with only the ends of her fingers, as if afraid it might explode.

"Open it," he said when she took too long.

Finally, she flipped open the lid, revealing a grooming set: a hairbrush, comb, mirror, and a small trinket box, all silver with delicate mother-of-pearl inlay. She sucked in a breath. "It's beautiful." She dragged one finger along the back of the mirror.

"Is it? Clara told me any woman would like it, but I don't know about these things. I know I'm not the easiest man to get along with, and I thought perhaps a small gift would be a better token of friendship than my clumsy attempt to help you before."

She looked up at him and smiled. He sensed something off in the smile, but after an instant, he deduced that, for once, her smile did not contain any judgment of him. "I appreciate it very much," she said. "It really is too nice for me."

"Nonsense. I only hope we can consider ourselves friends now."

"Yes, of course." Her smile vanished. "I—I take back everything I said."

Scrooge beamed. Perhaps he could bring everyone around after all. The unease in her eyes, he thought, must only be regret that this reconciliation hadn't happened earlier. It could be nothing more, he was sure.

For the first time in his life, Scrooge found himself not wanting to go to work. He lay in bed much longer than his usual time. He could already tell through the window that it would be a sunny day. After his joyful vacation, the idea of sitting in his dark counting house on a day like that depressed him.

But it had to be done. He finally rose and prepared quickly for his day, arriving at the office only a quarter of an hour late.

Bob and Peter greeted him, their surprise at his uncharacteristic lateness barely showing on their faces. They went through a typical round of questions about his holiday. Scrooge didn't mention Belle. He didn't want to bring her into the office. It was bad enough he had let talk of her invade his home. He thought back to the promise he had made to Fred about not talking to others about the spirits, and he worried that what he said to Mrs. Minston the night before had broken it.

After the pleasantries were over, Scrooge handed out the presents he had brought back: a small toy for Peter and an ornate pen and inkwell set for Bob. Once these had been accepted, Bob followed Scrooge into his office and shut the door. "We need to talk about the status of those loans," he said.

"Didn't you talk to Archie like I suggested?"

"I did. But he said there's not much he can do since the loans are with the individual employees. Plus, he's having his own difficulties paying back the loan we gave him. No installments have come in since you left. On any of them."

"Have you written to everyone?"

Bob nodded.

"Sent the bailiff, then?"

"No. I wasn't sure we wanted to go that route."

Scrooge thought about it for a moment. "No, you're right. We shouldn't fall back on old habits. We'll just have to devise new tactics."

"I think we should hold off on making any new loans until these are sorted. We have a lot of capital tied up in these loans. I don't want to risk becoming insolvent."

"Well, well, don't you sound like the practical businessman." The words came out harsher than he had intended. "I don't mean that as a slur against you. You're right to be concerned."

"I just think perhaps we were a bit too eager to provide loans to everyone who came in. We may want to consider still offering some more traditional loans at better terms for us—to those who can afford it."

"Why don't you contact some of our previous big clients and see how we can help them now?"

"Good idea, sir. I'll do that." He started toward the door.

"Don't flatter me. I reckon that's what you had a mind to do anyway. You've learned a lot about business from me over the years, Bob. And you were right not to listen to me about anything else."

"Oh, and a letter arrived for you from Mr. Lauriston." He pointed to the folded page on the desk. "I didn't open it since it was addressed to you."

"Right, thank you." Scrooge grumbled to himself after Bob had left, but it was true that he had given no instructions to Bob on dealing with Mr. Lauriston. It seemed Bob had been busy enough as it was.

He unfolded the letter, his frown deepening as he read down the page.

Mr. Parker has wasted more of my time than any client I've ever had—and my clients normally pay me, mind you. I have to say, while I supported the idea of your new business model at that speech you gave, in practice, I must say I am now a skeptic. People do in fact take advantage, or they at least must be vetted better first.

Scrooge tossed down the page. It appeared he had erred once again. How to smooth over the situation? After a moment's thought, he decided he should go to see Archie first. There were two sides to every story, after all, and he wanted to make sure Mr. Lauriston wasn't simply overreacting to Archie's lack of business knowledge. "Bob," he called as he stood. "I'm going out."

The warehouse where Archie Parker worked was close to the docks, but not so close that the stench of the tanneries invaded it. It was noisy and full of life and movement. It took several minutes for Scrooge to find someone who would pause in his business for a second to tell him where to find Archie. Finally, one man pushing a stack of crates on a dolly pointed toward the back. Scrooge headed in that direction. He came to a door and knocked. He had to lean his ear against the door to be able to hear if there was any response, but he concluded that no one inside could hear him in all the racket, and vice versa, so he opened the door without receiving an invitation.

Inside a cramped room half taken up with a desk sat Archie Parker, poring over the newspaper. He glanced up when Scrooge entered the room but made no move to stand.

"Mr. Parker," Scrooge began, shuffling to the small space in front of the desk. "How are you?"

"Quite well," Archie said, setting down the paper and looking a bit more friendly. "You've been away, I heard?"

Scrooge cocked his head, wondering where Archie would have heard this from. Had Bob been going around advertising that fact? "Yes, I've just come back. And while I was away, I received a rather concerning letter from Mr. Lauriston."

Archie nodded slowly. "Yes, I'm not surprised. We didn't get on too well, I'm afraid. But thank you for the recommendation."

Scrooge bristled at Archie's careless attitude. "That recommendation may have cost me my relationship with Mr. Lauriston. Would you care to tell me what happened?"

"I brought him the contracts as we had discussed. They were a mess, which I expected. And I think Mr. Lauriston was frustrated that I wasn't more knowledgeable in this area. And there was the whole issue of whether the contracts could even be changed at this point because they've been signed. Then we had a little spat about the best way to deal with that. I was for litigation, but he refused to do that for free, as it would take up too much of his time. That was where we left it." He shrugged and smiled up at Scrooge.

"I figured it was something of the sort. A misunderstanding. I'll talk to him and see what can be done. If funds are the issue... well, we can figure something out." He beamed, tipped his hat, and walked back out through the fury of the warehouse.

A short while later, he arrived at Mr. Lauriston's place of business. He was made to wait a quarter of an hour before he was led back to the solicitor's office. Scrooge arrived at the door just as a young man decked out in the latest fashions and sporting several gem-encrusted rings left it.

After curt greetings, Scrooge settled into the leather armchair in front of Mr. Lauriston's desk. "I apologize for the delay in responding to you about the situation with Mr. Parker. I've just returned from holiday, you see."

Mr. Lauriston nodded, but his face remained stern.

Scrooge cleared his throat. "I've just been to see Mr. Parker, and he's explained to me a bit more about what happened. I apologize if there was a misunderstanding. And if funds are the issue—"

"Funds are not the issue." He pointed his finger at Scrooge as he talked. "The issue is that Mr. Parker is clearly wasting my time. And your time as well, I assume. Why, I don't know. He gets a kick out of it, maybe. Or he likes to see important people for whom time is money waste both. But there is no way on earth someone actually signed those contracts. And"—he shuffled through some papers until he pulled out and unfolded a page—"I looked into some of the companies that supposedly signed those terrible contracts with him. They don't exist." He laid down the page and tapped it furiously for proof. "It's a sham. I don't want to make any assumptions about what you are doing, but Mr. Parker is running a sham." He leaned heavily back in his seat. "That is what happened."

Scrooge drew the page gingerly toward him with only his index finger and thumb. It was a letter from the business registry office confirming no such places existed. "I see," Scrooge said quietly. "It seems I have been naive. I apologize for taking up your time needlessly." He stood and extended his hand. "I shan't bother you again."

Mr. Lauriston nodded and shook his hand.

Scrooge's head reeled as he left the solicitor's office. What on earth had Archie been playing at? He still didn't want to believe that he had been scammed. There were probably plenty of businesses around the docks that went unregistered. Mr. Lauriston's proof meant nothing. Nothing.

But he still felt his newly bright outlook on humanity darken a bit as he stepped outside. He stood on the sidewalk for several minutes, debating in which direction he should turn: back to the docks or return to the office. He became quite a stumbling block for those trying to traverse the street, but no matter. He would take his time. Eventually, he decided he needed to clear his head and assess the situation before talking to Archie again. For now, he headed back to the office and the familiar safety of his counting house.

Despite his retreat to the safety of his work, the next day, Scrooge's thoughts were stuck in the Parker–Lauriston situation rather than the pages he had laid out on his desk to calculate. He was watching out the window, not actually seeing anything passing before him, and sipping a cup of tea when Miss Spencer walked unannounced into the room. Startled out of his reverie and not mentally prepared to face Miss Spencer after that ridiculous letter he had sent her, Scrooge choked heartily on his tea. It took several minutes to recover himself and catch his breath, with Bob even popping his head in to make sure he was all right.

Scrooge waved everyone off. "I'm fine. It just went down the wrong way," he said when he could speak again. He knew his face was beet red, and he tugged at the collar of his shirt, though what good that would do, he wasn't sure.

Bob frowned but returned to the Tank. Miss Spencer sat facing Scrooge.

"My, I don't think I've ever provoked that kind of a reaction in someone before."

Scrooge smiled, but with the last vestiges of his cough, it turned into a grimace. "I was just startled. I was so involved in my work . . . Bah," he finished weakly.

She paused but determined to forge ahead as she always did. "I have a proposition for you. A new charitable initiative that requires your investment." She went through the details: one of her friends was starting a secretarial school that would offer scholarships to women of low means. It was hoped that the paying students would allow for a return on his donation to the scholarship fund. In this way, it was more of an investment than a pure donation, Miss Spencer explained, which is why she had thought of him first. Scrooge wasn't sure he liked what she was implying about his motives, but he agreed to all of her proposals in the hope she would leave as soon as possible. When he had signed at the last place requested, she began preparing to leave.

"Is there nothing else you wanted to talk about?"

She looked up from arranging the folders in her satchel. "No. Should there be?"

"No, no. Absolutely not."

"Oh, yes," she said, leaving off with the folders. "How was your trip?"

"Lovely."

She waited a beat for more of a response, then swung the satchel onto her shoulder. "Good. Glad to hear it. Until next time, then."

"Actually—" Scrooge stood as he said the word. A thought had just occurred to him, and he suddenly hoped to halt her from leaving.

"Yes?"

He sat back down, and she followed suit, dropping the satchel to the floor with a thud.

"Actually, you are just the person I need to talk to," he said. "I have had some challenges with this new business model, and perhaps you can set me right."

"I will try my best."

He explained, at perhaps too great a length, exactly what had occurred. "You see," he concluded, "I am struggling not to come round to my original vision of humanity that it is a great mass of people not worth a rat's ass." He flinched. "Sorry."

"Oh, come, I'm not so delicate as that." She laid a hand gently over Scrooge's. "You are missing the greater point, which is that even if everyone else is not worth a rat's ass, that does not release you from your duty to improve the lives of those around you. They may neglect their charge, but that does not let you off the hook. Do you see?"

He sighed and relaxed a little. "Yes, yes, I do. Thank you."

"You must keep at it. Just because the first person you helped was not appreciative, that doesn't mean that others won't be." She walked around the desk and motioned for him to stand. When he complied, she wrapped him in a hug. "No one ever said it was easy. We must keep going anyway."

"You're right, of course."

She pulled away and picked up her satchel, giving a little wave behind her as she left.

He stood rooted to the spot for a long moment, trying to hold on to the floral scent that had been floating in her hair.

Scrooge sat back at his desk but didn't return his attention to his work right away. Instead, his mind attempted to piece through what had just happened. She was right about everything she had said; he simply needed to redouble his efforts. More importantly, though, she had made no reference to the letter he had sent her. Perhaps she had never received it. Could the spirits have made a miracle such as that happen? Or maybe she had received it but had recognized it for the absurd nonsense it was. In that case, she was right to pretend it had never happened. Scrooge nodded firmly and dragged his account book back toward him. He told himself he must never think such drivel again—and if he did, for the love of God, he would keep it to himself!

Chapter 17

"Tell me what you've found out," Scrooge said to Bob at their next office huddle a few days later.

"Most of the small loan holders still have not made payments. Mr. Parker has made some payments and is trying to keep up. As for our larger past clients, Weston and Weston said they will be looking for investment in a new building they're constructing. But Baker Smith said . . . well, that they no longer agree with our business philosophy."

"Rubbish! What does that even mean?"

"They don't want to do business with us in the future."

"Yes, Bob. I got that part. I simply meant, what an inane thing to say."

"Right." He handed Scrooge a sheaf of papers. "Here's the prospectus Weston and Weston gave me."

Scrooge perused the first page, then looked at Bob over the top edge of the paper. "All is not lost, Bob. We will figure this new path out."

"Of course, sir."

"The spirits set me on this path, and they will provide for us."

Bob made no response, and his silence was enough to make Scrooge waver. Maybe he had been naive to think his path would be clear and that he would receive no punishment from the physical world at all.

He wavered even further when Mr. Werther appeared later that day and demanded an audience with both partners. They settled into Scrooge's office. Mr. Werther scraped his chair angrily across the floor as he pulled it out to sit. In that instant, Scrooge noticed that their visitor was wearing the same red waistcoat as the last time Scrooge saw him. For all his show, perhaps the man only had one.

"I can tell you're agitated—" Scrooge began.

"You can, can you?" Mr. Werther held up his hand to stop Scrooge from responding. "Let me tell you why." He pointed at both men, Scrooge first, then Bob. "Both of you have been jerking me around. Me and this whole town."

"That's ridiculous," Scrooge said.

"Let me finish. I know a lot of people, and I hear what goes on in this city. I've heard about all these inquiries you've been making around town, threatening the common man who hasn't paid you back. And"—he jabbed a finger in Scrooge's direction for emphasis—"I know Mr. Lauriston personally. We're members of the same club. He's told me all about how much of his time you've wasted."

"I assure you that was all a misunderstanding—"

"That was the same scam you tried to drag me into, helping out these people for free. And I don't want to do business with anybody who jerks me, or my friends, around. I need your line of credit for this project since it is already moving forward, but I don't think our relationship will continue after that." He stood. "Good day, gentleman."

For an instant, Bob watched Mr. Werther retreat, but then he jumped up and chased after him. At the door, he said, "Please, please, Mr. Werther. Don't take any of this out on my Martha. It has nothing to do with her. She needs that position."

Mr. Werther swung the door open so forcefully it nearly knocked Bob over. Mr. Werther merely grunted and strode into the street.

Scrooge heard Bob's plea at the door. After Mr. Werther's departure, he let Bob return to the Tank. Even to offer an apology would be an insult. He had promised Bob he would take care of his family, and already he had failed. Perhaps it had been hubris to embark on such a grand business endeavor after all.

Tormented by such thoughts, he decided to leave early, feeling it was better for Bob to be without his presence for now.

Scrooge was almost to the front door when Bob called him back.

"Sneaking out, are you?" Bob asked. His eyes flashed with anger for an instant but then relaxed into his normal good-humored features, leaving Scrooge wondering how much of the statement was a joke.

"I thought it best . . ." He trailed off as he saw that Bob did not look impressed with this reasoning.

"What is this about Lauriston? What was in that letter he sent you?"

Scrooge glanced at Peter, then inclined his head in the direction of his own office. "Let's talk in there."

Bob hesitated as if he were about to argue but then gave in and followed Scrooge. Scrooge left his coat on while they talked, as if he were not planning on this taking long. He tried to keep his summary of events succinct, but it took several lines of questioning before Bob was satisfied that he had gotten the entire tale out of Scrooge.

"When were you planning on telling me all this?"

"I don't know. I haven't decided what to do."

Bob's mouth stood agape. "*You* haven't decided what to do? What about me while I've been running around trying to collect payments from all these people, even from Mr. Parker himself? What about our new status as partners that you made so much of?"

It was Scrooge's turn to flinch. "I'm sorry, Bob. Truly. I just didn't want to admit that I might have been wrong about it all."

Bob collapsed onto the back of his chair. "All of it?" he asked in disbelief. "You think you were wrong about all of it?"

"Well, no. No." He rubbed his right temple. "Miss Spencer advised—"

"You told Miss Spencer about this before you told me?"

There was no reply Scrooge could make that wouldn't worsen the situation. Silence dragged on for several seconds.

Finally, in a quiet voice, Bob said, "Perhaps it is better if you left early today."

"Yes." Scrooge stood. "Thank you, Bob." He vacated his office, but Bob stayed seated. Scrooge glanced back and saw Bob leaning forward, his elbows propped on his knees, his hands gripping his hair as if he might rip it all out at any moment.

Bob's mind swirled as he locked up that evening, trying to process everything he had learned. He debated whether he should go see Mr. Werther at his home and perhaps warn

Martha what was afoot or if that would only serve to make things worse. With all this going through his thoughts, he didn't notice a man approaching until he spoke.

"Mr. Cratchit, I presume?"

Bob startled at the sudden presence next to him. "Yes." He took the card the man handed him, but his eyes couldn't focus on the printed words and instead darted from the card to the man and back again. The fading sunlight glinted off the gold thread in the man's waistcoat, and Bob, in his current state, found it distracting.

Coming briefly back to himself, he motioned to Peter to continue home. Peter did so reluctantly, dragging his feet and glancing back, hoping to catch a snatch of the adults' conversation, sure it was going to be interesting.

The man must have felt the edge in Bob's demeanor because he continued in an even, soothing voice, "I'm Dr. Burnhope. You may remember I interviewed your employer and wrote a piece about him."

Bob relaxed a bit and tucked the card into his trouser pocket. "Right. The journal article. Sorry, I'd forgotten your name."

Dr. Burnhope smiled, but it was not a smile that brought happiness to mind. "Might I have a moment of your time?"

Bob nodded. The two men fell into a slow walk side by side.

"I wonder if you've noticed any changes in Mr. Scrooge since his presumed experience last year."

"Of course. He truly is a new man."

"So I've heard. But I also wonder, do you have any concerns about him? Any doubts?"

Bob hesitated.

"It would be perfectly natural if you did. You don't have to be afraid of telling me."

"Doubts about what exactly?"

"About his faculties, shall we say. About the appropriateness of his retirement, perhaps."

Again, Bob hesitated. "I think his retirement may be near," he said slowly and carefully. "His interests mostly lie elsewhere nowadays." He peered at his companion. "Have you talked to him again yourself?"

"It's useful to talk to those around the afflicted, as he himself may not realize what's wrong."

"Right."

"I have some treatments that I think may help him adjust, but I need an inside man. Best if he doesn't know to expect what's coming, as I'm sure he thinks he doesn't need any help."

"Of course I'd like to help him in any way I can . . ."

"Excellent. You have my card. I'll be in touch." He set a hand on Bob's shoulder. "We have to think about not only Mr. Scrooge's health and happiness but that of the people around him, too. I want to think of you, Mr. Cratchit, and what is best for you and your family as well."

The doctor veered away across the street, leaving Bob to watch after him for a moment, unsure how to react. He only came to himself when he felt a tug on his arm and saw Peter looking up at him. Clearly, the boy had thought it prudent not to wander too far away from the scene of the action.

"What did he say, Father, huh? Who was that?"

"A doctor," Bob said. "That's all." As they started walking, he mused, "Funny how a poor man cannot get a doctor no matter how hard he tries, but a rich man gets one whether he wants it or not." He shook his head to clear it and launched into a footrace with Peter down to the end of the street. It was the start of the weekend—Scrooge had instituted those since Christmas—and Bob's focus was on his family. Soon, all traces of Scrooge and Dr. Burnhope left his thoughts.

Bob walked cheerfully with Tiny Tim atop his shoulders on the way back from church. The boy had grown much stronger and could get around now without his crutch, but the fun of a ride on Father's shoulders could not be given up so easily. Tim cheered his father on as they maneuvered through the crowd, giving his head a playful pat every now and then as if his father were a prize racehorse. Bob laughed and played along. He slowed, though, as they neared the house. Through a parting in the passersby, he glimpsed Martha talking to Mrs. Heron. Mrs. Heron appeared to be doing all the talking, and a few words were accompanied by an attentive tap on Martha's elbow. Martha looked tense, with one arm crossed over her body to grip the other. Martha's discomfort with their new neighbors was not entirely her fault, Bob reasoned as he watched the awkward scene—his oldest daughter tended to follow her mother's skeptical lead, and lord knows Mrs. Heron had not made the best impression on Mrs. Cratchit.

The two women parted, and Bob resumed his normal pace. "Martha!" he called once he was close enough to be heard over the bustle of the street.

Martha stopped and turned. She crossed her arms over her chest and watched her father approach with flashing eyes. Bob tensed, worried that her annoyance was directed at him because something had happened with Mr. Werther.

"Is everything all right? With work?" he asked.

"Yes, of course," she said. Bob's shoulders slumped in relief, causing Tiny Tim to lean forward and grab at his father's hair to steady himself. "Mrs. Heron was just being a terrible snob, as usual, is all." She reached out for Tiny Tim and gathered the boy in her arms. His toes dangled down to her knees, but no one was ready to admit that he was getting too big for such treatment. Father and daughter climbed their front steps but didn't go in. "Honestly, if she thinks I'm so low class, why doesn't she just leave me alone?"

"Did she say that?"

Sensing a boring adult conversation looming, Tim hopped down and dove inside the house. Bob pulled the door shut behind him.

"Not exactly. But it was implied." Martha scuffed the toe of her boot against the stone step. "She told me Steven can't stop talking about me, and she feels I have potential, so if I quit working, she might support the match. But I never even said I wanted the match. Ste—Mr. Heron is nice enough, but . . ."

"You mentioned before there was someone else."

She nodded. "A nice young man at work. Ian Thatcher. But I wouldn't quit my job for him, either. I know our family is doing better now, but I don't want our fortunes to depend on the whims of Mr. Scrooge. Some savings would give us a cushion if things were to change."

Bob reached out and rubbed his daughter's shoulder sympathetically. "I can see our financial struggles as you were growing up have affected you. I won't presume to tell you which match to pursue. But I don't want you to think that a person shouldn't seek to improve her fortunes."

Martha shook off his touch. "Mother's right. You are becoming just like them."

"She said that?" Bob asked, but Martha had already pushed past him and disappeared inside. He stared at the blank front door for a minute before resolving to go inside and greet his family as if nothing had occurred or changed.

Chapter 18

Life ambled on as normal for the next few weeks. The city moved its many thousands to and fro, some well provided for, others left all alone. London, a benevolent father who simply had many more children than he could ever hope to support. Ebenezer Scrooge served as stepfather as best he could for as many of these residents fallen between the cracks as possible. Scrooge's own fortunes, however, continued to fluctuate. His business was up one day, down the next. But his own happiness was no longer so closely tied to the rise and fall of stocks and bonds as to upset the even keel of his present life. There were no more grand confrontations with his clients, but he offered no more free services, just to be safe. He began to feel that he had gotten over the worst of the rough ground and had regained his footing. His greatest trial, however, lurked nearby, waiting for his next false move.

The tiger lying in wait most imminently was Dr. Burnhope, who pounced on Bob Cratchit a second time as Bob emerged from the office one warm and drizzly evening. Peter had been sent off on an errand to the 'Change late that afternoon and had been told that he could go home straight from there, so Bob did not have to shoo him off as he had the last time. The two men greeted each other, Bob rather coldly. Now that the immediate danger to his family's security had passed (Mr. Werther having made no more threats and Martha's position still secure), Bob's doubts about Scrooge had been mostly assuaged. The two men had been getting along well over the intervening weeks. To keep from rocking the boat any further, Bob had not mentioned Dr. Burnhope's earlier visit and its implications that Scrooge might no longer possess all his faculties. In fact, the doctor had mostly faded from Bob's own mind.

"I've contacted some of my colleagues and made arrangements to provide Mr. Scrooge the help and support he needs," Dr. Burnhope said.

"I'm glad to hear it," Bob said, but he kept walking.

"Perhaps you could set up a time for us to meet, as we had discussed. So I know he will be there when we—I—arrive."

"He rarely leaves the office." Even though it was warm, Bob pulled up his collar to stop the rain from dripping down his neck.

"But when would be a good time for an interview? This Thursday, early afternoon, shall we say?"

Bob stopped and sighed. "Yes, that should be fine."

"You'll be so glad you helped him, trust me, Mr. Cratchit. Your own fortunes won't hurt for it, either."

"Why does everyone think I have so much care for my fortunes?" He shook his head and pushed ahead with a mighty speed. Dr. Burnhope made no move to follow him.

On the following Thursday, Scrooge was in high spirits. "Fred and Clara have asked me to be godfather to their child," he told Scrooge and Peter as they settled in that morning. "I feel like I finally have what I never had—no, never *appreciated*—before. I can't decide whether I'd rather it be a boy or a girl. No, either will do. Either will do."

Bob smiled at his partner's childlike eagerness, a characteristic no one would have ever assigned to Scrooge before Christmas. Surely, there could be nothing *wrong* with him—a change like this benefitted all those around him, even though he had made some missteps along the way. Bob glanced at the clock. He hadn't told Scrooge about the appointment; Bob preferred not to be in the middle and let the two men work it out themselves. He sensed that Dr. Burnhope would be discreet and not mention Bob's part in it. The doctor would decide what was best. Bob could claim no expertise in such a delicate area. He waited for the appointed time with only a little trepidation.

Just as the clocks struck one that afternoon, the bell above the front door tinkled and heavy footsteps echoed through the front hall. By the time Bob got up and made it to the doorway of the Tank, three men were in the entryway, with Dr. Burnhope following an instant behind. Bob noticed, abstractly, that two of the men were constables. Suddenly, he saw that, somehow, he had been tricked, but there was no time to linger over such a thought.

"What's happening here?" Bob asked, but the men bypassed him and turned into Scrooge's office.

"That's the patient," Dr. Burnhope declared.

Bob strained to watch over the constables' shoulders, which were blocking the doorway. The other man, large and muscled, grabbed Scrooge from behind and lifted him from his chair with a smoothness suggesting he had executed similar maneuvers many times before.

"What's the meaning of this?" Scrooge shouted, flustered, as he tried to shake off his captor.

With the help of the doctor, the man wrestled Scrooge into a straitjacket. Both Bob and Scrooge shouted for answers but were ignored. The doctor and his lackey pushed through the hall with Scrooge dragged between them. The constables held Bob back. When Scrooge was outside, a sudden silence fell across the rooms. Seeing the task had been successfully carried out, the constables released their hold on Bob.

Now that the action was over, the younger officer looked a bit apologetic. "There's an order for him to be committed," he said.

"Committed? Where? Where are you taking him?"

The officer shrugged. "We're just here to enforce the order." His companion exited, and he paused in the doorway. "Good day," he said, with a tip of his hat. He closed the door behind him with a gentle click.

Bob stood stunned for a moment until he noticed Peter quivering behind him. That they did such a thing in front of a child! With his own feet locked to the floor, he did the only thing he could think of. "Run and get Fred," he ordered, and Peter rushed out onto the street, glad to be free of the scene.

Once Fred arrived, there was a flurry of exclamations and explanations, until it was fully determined that, actually, nothing much was known. When some sense of order had been restored, Bob began to meekly admit his part in it, though the sentences began in such convoluted fits and starts, it was hard for anyone to understand them. Finally, to offer some justification, Bob held out the card Dr. Burnhope had given him weeks before.

"This is the man you've been talking to? The man who was here?" Fred asked.

Bob nodded.

"You idiot!" Fred tossed the card on the ground, then thought better of relinquishing his one piece of evidence and picked it up again. It also made an effective tool to brandish at Bob as he yelled. "This isn't the doctor who did the research! This is the doctor who wrote that blasted editorial implying he needed to be locked up. And now he's gone and done it." The steam seemed to go out of him, and he rubbed his forehead several times before he spoke again, this time in a much quieter voice. "We have to find out where they've taken him." He turned and looked around Scrooge's empty office as if it might release some answers. "What's the nearest police station to here?"

"I've never had cause to look into it."

"There's one three blocks down and two streets over," Peter piped up.

"Why do you know that?" Bob asked, but Peter's attention was already on Fred's instructions.

"We'll go there first as the most obvious place, then fan out from there."

The three walked out, with young Peter leading the way.

Night had fallen by the time they emerged onto an unfamiliar street for the final time, utterly defeated. After a sunless, wet day, the night was cold, and all three men shivered without their coats. Their string of visits had brought them to the conclusion that every constabulary held two types of officers—one, the first you met upon entering the station, absolutely full of his own stupidity and ignorance, and a second, brought in to support the useless other, who clearly knew everything but refused to tell it. There were no answers to be given, they were told, over and over again.

"We'll have to try new tactics tomorrow," Fred said. "Though I hate to think where he's spending the night."

"Try not to think about it," Bob murmured. Fred took no notice of him.

Wordlessly, Bob and Peter began to drift off toward home, with Fred trailing behind. The drizzle began again, mingling with the tears on both men's cheeks.

Chapter 19

"Have you seen this?" Michaels set the morning newspaper on the table alongside his large brown hat. He had just returned to their shared flat after a night spent drinking, followed by a rendezvous at the room of a lady of the night. One he had never used before, of course. Unlike Crane, he did not like to get too attached.

Crane picked up the paper and perused the page Michaels had opened it to. After a few minutes, he said, "It looks like someone else is doing our work for us."

"No one is going to take this revenge away from me." He pulled out a chair and sat. "That business of his will be destroyed whether he's locked up or not."

"We have to get to his partner, then. What's his name? The one with all the kids."

"Cratchit." Michaels leaned over and rapped on his friend's shoulder. "Mayhap we should pay a visit today, then. They can rot in debtors' prison together just like we did because of them."

"Or we could use him to take down Scrooge and leave him out of it."

"You're too soft, my friend. But I guess Scrooge has made him miserable enough over the years. We'll figure out the best way to leverage him." He stood quickly and had to steady himself on the back of his chair.

Crane raised an eyebrow. "Wouldn't you like to sleep first?"

Michaels rubbed his stubbled chin. His cheeks were red and blotchy from last night's drink. "It wouldn't hurt for us to look somewhat respectable. We'll go in a few hours." He disappeared into his bedroom and was soon snoring loud enough to wake the dead.

Bob returned to the office at first light, but he had no new ideas for how to proceed after their miserable failure the night before. With all that was going on, he had asked Peter to stay at home today, and for once, the boy didn't object to being left out. Perhaps Peter was starting to understand that the career of a clerk was not quite as glamorous as he had imagined. Bob shuffled aimlessly through papers for a quarter of an hour, hoping to find a sign of what to do. Frustrated, he approached Scrooge's office, so empty without its owner's heavy presence. Bob glanced around. His eyes lighted on the edge of a flyer peeking out from the middle of a stack of papers on a corner of the desk. He tugged at it, causing a cascade of papers to descend to the floor. He read the page eagerly, paying no heed to the mess. Thank God Scrooge had saved this flyer as a souvenir of his talk with Miss Spencer. Now Bob knew exactly what to do next.

Bob waited with his hat in hand on the front step of Miss Spencer's boarding house. He hoped he looked suitably respectable and apologetic. Finally, a painfully tall and thin woman answered the door. She peered down her nose at him, as if she couldn't see all the way down to his level.

"I'm sorry to call so early, but I must see Miss Spencer. I assure you it is a matter of some urgency."

"Have you a card?"

"No, but you can tell her it's Mr. Cratchit calling."

"Wait here." With that order, she slammed the door.

Five minutes later, Miss Spencer appeared, with no hat and her hair still in a long braid.

"Have you heard?"

"Yes, I just saw it in the paper. What on earth has happened?"

"They took him. We can't find out where. Dare I hope you have contacts at some of the mental institutions?"

"Yes, I'll start making inquiries right away. Leave it to me." With a nod, she went back inside. Somewhat heartened by her determination and the sense that he had accomplished something, Bob returned to the office in better spirits than he had left it.

When he got there, Fred was pacing the sidewalk. "Where have you been?"

"I've just come from calling on Miss Spencer." Bob unlocked the door and let them in.

"Miss Spencer? Whatever for?" Fred kept up his pacing in the corridor.

"She knows people at these institutions, you see."

For an instant, Fred stopped and looked up. "Oh!" Then his feet carried him along again. "I haven't had such good luck this morning. I went to see the Morodys, thinking they would have some concern. But they've refused any help."

"I'm not surprised. From what I've heard, they've always seemed most concerned about their own interests, if you ask me."

"So now what?"

"I think we may just need to wait. If Miss Spencer or the police find anything out, they'll come here."

"I can't wait here. I'll go home, go back to the police station, something!" Fred rushed past Bob and back outside.

Bob was still processing this abrupt departure a moment later when a messenger arrived with a letter. Bob slid his finger under the seal and sat at his desk in the Tank to read it. He could tell by the first sentence that it was not good news.

Dear Mr. Cratchit,

We, the undersigned, as partners and associates with the firm of Scrooge and Cratchit, lately called Scrooge and Marley, demand an explanation as to the notices we have read in the paper regarding the committing of Mr. Ebenezer Scrooge to an asylum for the insane. If the explanation received is not satisfactory, we reserve the right to cease conducting business with said firm, up to and including taking legal action as needed.

The undersigned were Mr. Werther, Mr. Lauriston, and representatives of two shipping companies that the firm had long done business with that Mr. Werther had clearly corralled into supporting his cause.

Bob rubbed his forehead. The matter had now reached a most delicate point. This was no longer just about rescuing Scrooge or the business; it was also about protecting Bob's livelihood—and that of his family, who were now so entangled in the business of Scrooge and Cratchit. With Scrooge indisposed for the foreseeable future, Bob would have to be the one to figure out a way to salvage the situation.

He was still contemplating the best way to respond to this letter a short time later when he heard the front door open. "We're closed," he called without getting up.

Two men appeared in the doorway. "I think you'll want to hear the kind of business we propose," the shorter man said, doffing a ratty hat as he finished.

"And why is that?"

Michaels stepped into the Tank. "Your situation has changed considerably since yesterday, sir."

"We read about your employer's situation in the paper this morning," Crane chimed in, leaning casually against the doorjamb.

"Now, what we propose," Michaels said, taking a slow amble around the room, "is that we help you take advantage of the situation." When he got no response from Bob, he continued. "We have the ability to get back to you monies on a number of loans you've made recently. But we will only do that if Scrooge is out of the picture. Keep the name outside if you want, like Scrooge did for Marley all those years, but the only person working here today is Mr. Cratchit. You'd be well within your rights to take over, with your partner committed and all."

"I'll have you know I've spent my morning trying to help get him out of that situation."

"As well you might. But that doesn't mean you can't help yourself at the same time. What do you say?"

"You seem to know a lot about me, gentleman. I ought to at least know your names before we engage in business together."

Michaels's eyes narrowed into slits as he peered at Bob. "Mr. Michaels," he said finally. He jabbed a thumb in the direction of his companion. "Mr. Crane."

Bob studied both men's faces. "There is something familiar about both of you. Have you been here before?"

Michaels slung his hat onto his head. "Think about it. This opportunity won't be here forever." He and Crane walked out. Bob hurried to the front step and watched as they took an oddly zigzag path through the crowd, as if afraid they would be followed.

"What an odd interview," he said to himself as he went back inside. "And how did they know about those missing payments?"

Whatever they knew, it was clear there was some sort of net closing in around Scrooge, and Bob wasn't sure if he would be able to keep it from catching him up and dragging him off to unreachable depths. And taking Bob's family with it.

The truth was, there was nary a man in London who was still willing to do business with Ebenezer Scrooge. The founding partner's name was more of a liability than anything else at this point. It would be best if Bob stepped forward and made himself the face of the business, at least for now. He picked up the letter from Mr. Werther, then tossed it back onto the desk. He set his chin on his hand and stared off into a corner of the room.

While he did so, flashes of emotion occasionally crossed his face—a stern frown, a raised eyebrow—providing a silent commentary on the turmoil within.

Finally, he picked up a fresh sheet of paper and dipped his pen in the inkwell. Bob Cratchit was not a man who dashed off a note; he prided himself on the care he took with each loop of a *g* and cross of a *t*. This approach, he was sure, would help him now. He slowly wrote out his thoughts, pausing before each word to make sure it was exactly the right one and that he would have to make no cross-outs. Once he was satisfied, he signed his name in large, curly letters at the bottom of the page. He folded and sealed it, then stepped into the street to find a boy to deliver it.

Fred eventually returned to the office to await any news. Instead of his earlier constant movement, he now looked exhausted. He sat at Peter's usual spot, and at Fred's request, Bob gave him a stack of letters to copy so that he had something to occupy his mind. Bob tried to do much the same, but after several minutes, Fred broke the silence.

"I never thought I'd say this, but I am really starting to dislike people in general."

A short laugh burst from Bob's mouth. "I can't say I blame you, given the circumstances, but you can't let this sour your view of everyone."

A blob of ink dripped on the page in front of him, and Fred put his pen down in frustration. "I went to see Dr. Norman after lunch. Clara suggested it. I haven't wanted to involve her in this too much because of her condition, but she knows how to ask the right questions."

"Dr. Norman is the other one who interviewed Scrooge?"

"Yes, Bob. If you had remembered that in the first place, we wouldn't be in this mess." Fred covered his face with his hands and rubbed his eyes. When he removed his hands, his face looked slightly more relaxed. "I'm sorry. This is not really your fault. Yes, that's Dr. Norman. Clara wondered how Dr. Burnhope got Scrooge's name and deduced he was the most likely conduit. Turns out, he did give up Scrooge's name, thinking Dr. Burnhope was writing some book or other and meant well. Of course, he takes no responsibility now. The most infuriating thing is he seemed the most upset that his article didn't get him an invite to the Royal Society like he had hoped." Fred drummed his fingers on the desktop. "See if I ever invite him to any of my parties ever again," he said to himself.

Eventually, both men settled into their work. After an hour or so, highlighted only by the scratch of pens and the turning of sheets of paper, the front door, now locked after the earlier visitors Bob had encountered, rattled. "Police!" a voice called.

"Finally!" Fred jumped up and rushed to let the officer in. "What's the news?"

The officer gave him a confused look. "Where's Mr. Scrooge?"

"That's what you're supposed to be telling us."

"I'm here to ask him some questions about a complaint we got in today."

Seeing Fred's frustration, Bob stepped in. "Mr. Scrooge was taken forcibly from here yesterday by a doctor and two of your brethren. We've gone to all the police stations around here trying to find out where he's been taken. So, no, he's not here, and it does not give me much faith in your institution that you're here asking us where he is."

"I don't know anything about that. All I know is we have a young lady who has made a very unsavory complaint against him."

"May I ask what young lady?" Bob asked, although the glance he shared with Fred showed he already had a guess as to the answer.

The officer pulled a folded sheet of paper out of his breast pocket and checked it. "A Miss Lucretia Morody."

"Oh, for God's sake," Fred said.

"You know her, then?"

"Yes, and whatever she said is not true."

"Well, if you see Mr. Scrooge again, please send him—"

"Get out!" Fred pointed at the door.

The officer shrugged and left. Bob locked the door behind him. When he returned to the Tank, Fred was already seated back at Peter's small desk, looking close to tears.

"You should go home and get some rest, Fred. I have things in hand here."

Fred turned his wet blue eyes on Bob. "I won't be able to sleep until my uncle is returned to us. And it seems the whole world is against us. How can you be so calm?"

"Panic never helped anyone," Bob said, hoping his voice wouldn't waver as he spoke. It seemed he had to be the sole strength between the pair of them, for now. "We must keep at it."

"You sound like my uncle."

"Well, perhaps he isn't always wrong."

This finally cracked open a smile on Fred's face. He stood and engulfed Bob in a long hug. "Thank you," Fred said as he released his hold on Bob.

"I'll stay here and do what I can."

"Thank you," he repeated, then walked out to the street. His steps seemed heavy and slow, with their usual bounce sucked out of them.

Bob did not have much of a respite after Fred left. Soon, another guest turned up: Mr. Werther, driven to respond personally to Bob's letter of that morning. Without waiting for an invitation, Mr. Werther entered Scrooge's office and sat opposite the grand desk. Bob hesitated. He didn't like to put on that this office was his own, but if he was supposed to be telegraphing that the company was in good hands with only Cratchit, then it would be best not to let on that Bob was not an equal in the firm. So determined, he sat in Scrooge's chair, flinching slightly as his bottom hit the old leather. It was strange to see the room from this side. Everything looked slightly bent out of shape—the desk a little wider, the door a little farther away.

"How can I help you?"

"I came about your letter. You say this whole situation is a misunderstanding, but surely you can see that such a vague explanation cannot feel satisfactory to those of us not in the know."

"I understand. But I assure you that the misunderstanding involving Mr. Scrooge and his detainment is in no way related to the business of this firm. I do not think it ought to cause you to withdraw from your agreement with us."

Mr. Werther looked around the office before responding. Despite its many decades of use, the walls were completely bare and the desk devoid of any hint at the personality of the man who usually occupied it—though such a lack of any such mementos perhaps told more about Scrooge's personality than any could by their presence. "You seem like a good man of business, Mr. Cratchit. In fact, I suspect that you are in charge here more than you would like to admit. Therefore, I believe I can speak for my compatriots in saying that we will do business with you, exclusively. You know I had an agreement with Mr. Scrooge regarding a line of credit for my own business."

"Yes, of course."

"I would like to begin drawing down on those funds."

"I hope you understand that this is not the best moment for us to be releasing new funds."

Mr. Werther leaned forward. "I have been kind with you so far, Mr. Cratchit. But I am a man of business, and I will not let any personal affiliations get in the way of my profits. In that, I think your Mr. Scrooge and I are not so different. So let me tell you this. I have a contract in place to begin building my new warehouse next week. I have tried multiple times in the past couple of weeks to take advantage of this line of credit and have been put off each time by Mr. Scrooge. I will not be put off again. If I can draw down the funds needed for the deposit and the first week's work by Monday, then I will make it worth your while. Being head maid would make quite a salary increase for your Martha."

Bob gulped. This is what he had worried it would come down to. "And how much is required?"

Mr. Werther pulled a slip of paper out of his pocket and read from it. "One hundred seventy-two pounds, four shillings, and ten pence."

Before Bob could answer, Mr. Werther stood and held out his hand. Bob took the slip of paper from his hand, then shook it.

"Remember, I am relying on you, Mr. Cratchit. I don't want this mess with Mr. Scrooge to affect our ability to do business together."

"It won't," Bob said, though he looked slightly surprised that the words had come out of his mouth. What had he just committed himself to?

"Good." Mr. Werther tipped his hat and left. Finally, Bob was alone in the office, truly now the sole proprietor of the business. It was not a position he wished to be in. How could Scrooge have committed them to that large an outlay of capital for Mr. Werther without looking at the books or consulting Bob, his supposed partner? And knowing the precarious point they were at, with so much changing constantly? How the hell was he going to get one hundred and seventy-two pounds in time to meet Mr. Werther's deadline three days away?

Bob looked at the desk and sighed. The change in this office mirrored the change in Scrooge. Before, there had never been a stray paper lying about, never a piece of work left undone until the morning. Now pages were stacked in each corner of the desk. Neatly, mind you, except for the stack Bob had overturned that morning, but still a striking difference from the prior sparseness. A broken pen lay on the floor nearby, not bothered to be cleaned away.

He sighed again. He hated to breach his trust with Scrooge, but he had to find out what had really transpired between Scrooge and Werther. That was the only way he could fix it. He only hoped he wouldn't come across any other surprises in his search of Scrooge's desk. He pulled the first stack of pages toward him and began to read.

Chapter 20

Bob discovered letters among Scrooge's papers that corroborated Mr. Werther's claims of Scrooge putting him off. Bob sighed. That sort of behavior was not like Scrooge at all. He had always promptly paid and eagerly pleased clients—probably because those transactions meant more money would return to him in interest.

Bob stayed late reading hundreds of pages but, fortunately, came across no new revelations. In other transactions, at least, Scrooge seemed his old self. Bob rubbed his tired eyes and locked up. He splurged and took an omnibus home rather than walking. He was so exhausted, however, that he didn't enjoy the indulgence. Fortunately, a wayward pothole jolted him out of his doze just in time to alight at his stop.

The house loomed dark and silent over the street as he approached, his family already abed. After peeking in at the children, he slid under the covers beside his wife. She didn't stir. Bob slept fitfully, and during a long insomniac stretch in the darkest part of the night, he concocted a new plan of attack for resolving his business woes. In the morning, determined to carry out the plan, he left again shortly after breakfast, even though it was a Saturday and since Scrooge's change of heart, business had rarely been conducted on that day. Mrs. Cratchit watched Bob's back doubtfully as he left but did not remonstrate him.

He took long strides to the office, appearing to those he passed as a man of set purpose. And indeed he was, so much so that he often missed offering his usual pleasant greetings to those around him. He had to occupy himself while the search for Scrooge crept along, so next, he turned his mind to the problem of Mr. Michaels and Mr. Crane. He sensed that their vendetta veiled something Bob could exploit to his—or the company's—benefit. There was a very real possibility now that Scrooge would not return—though Bob would never admit that out loud—and Bob needed to make sure that he salvaged what his partner had failed to rebuild.

Back at the office, he left off with Scrooge's papers and instead pored through the business's record books. By the time he found the entries he wanted, the city had fully woken around him. The loud bray of a horse followed by a vulgar shout outside brought him back to reality. Michaels and Crane hadn't been clever enough not to use their real names. Or they had been too certain that Bob would be on their side. Now, the facts stood clearly before him, unarguably sealed in ink. Both men defaulted on their mortgages years ago, losing their homes and entering debtors' prison. Two men with a very large axe to grind with the firm of Scrooge and Marley. But Bob would show them Scrooge and Cratchit would not be cowed by mere financial concerns. The pair had given Bob one crucial clue during their meeting: that they had some connection to the men who had defaulted on their loans taken out since the new year. Bob would start there and interlock the puzzle pieces as he went.

Bob personally visited each man who owed back payments under the new loan program. He refined his approach as he went along, hitting on the right mix of threats of debtors' prison and promises that Scrooge and Cratchit would forgive the future balance due if they paid what they were behind on so far and relinquished their deal with the two men pulling the strings. In this way, he gleaned a lot about Michaels and Crane's plan. The loan holders had participated because they kept the payments they received from Michaels and Crane instead of paying off the loan. Many now saw they had been caught and, to keep their own noses clean, gave up what funds they had not yet spent. Several men also admitted they relished sticking it to a man like Scrooge.

Bob couldn't say he blamed them. At each house, he saw much the same story. Squalid, one- or two-room dwellings, a mess of children, occasionally a wife who directed Bob to a loud and backbreaking worksite by the docks, sometimes one or two opium pipes peeking out from a drawer or the bedclothes. All situations that might make men more concerned for money than for what was right.

The last man he visited was one of Archie Parker's employees. As Bob prepared to leave with his money box, the man asked, "How come you asked so much about the Michaels and Crane fellows and not Mr. Parker?"

Bob dropped the box back onto the table. He couldn't take another twist in this story. "Is Mr. Parker involved, too?"

"I would assume so. He and Mr. Michaels were great friends for many years, before Mr. Michaels lost it all."

After a moment's surprise, Bob said, "Damn, there really is a conspiracy, isn't there? Thank you for your time. And the information." He went out, fuming. He would have to plan a special visit to Mr. Parker to let him know exactly what Bob Cratchit thought of him.

When Bob returned to the office, Miss Spencer was leaning against the front door. Bob was surprised at her haggard appearance. A rash of pimples marred one pale cheek, and dark circles weighed down her normally bright eyes. Perhaps she was more worried about Scrooge than she admitted. Could it be possible . . . ? No. He pushed the thought quickly away. There were much more important things to ponder than Miss Spencer's attachments.

"Have you found him?" he asked.

She only shook her head and moved out of the way so that he could unlock the door.

Once inside, he set the cash box and account book on his desk. "No one will admit to having him?"

"That may be the case. But they also may just not know. The records kept by these places are abhorrent. Plenty of people disappear into the system." Seeing Bob's startled expression, she added, "Sorry. I didn't mean to frighten you."

"No, it's not your fault. We're not having any better luck, either."

"I'm sure we'll find him. I'll keep thinking of more avenues we could use. Keep me updated, and vice versa."

"Of course." Bob bowed, expecting her to leave.

She hesitated. "How are Fred and Clara doing with all of this?"

"I'm surprised Fred's not here, actually. He's been running around like a chicken with its head cut off ever since it happened. Not that I blame him, of course."

"Have you seen Clara?" Miss Spencer asked.

Bob shook his head. Surely, he shouldn't feel guilty about not being more attentive to Scrooge's family the last few days. He had been about Scrooge's business, after all. But he imagined the genuine concern in Miss Spencer's voice covered a touch of reproach.

"Perhaps I'll pay a call on them, then," she said. "You seem busy here."

"I'm sure they'll appreciate knowing you're on the case."

She glanced down at the cash box Bob had brought in with him. "Everything running smoothly here?"

Bob flushed. "Yes, of course."

"Good." She smiled and walked out, seeming somewhat restored to her usual perky self.

Once she was gone, Bob sat at his desk in the Tank with a great flourish of his coattails. He lifted the lid on the cash box and began counting. He had logged each man's payment carefully in the account book so that there was a record of everything. He was not, he told himself, attempting anything underhanded.

Nonetheless, his heart fell when the total came to only one hundred forty-seven pounds. He was short. His determination wavered for a moment, but then he stood and pulled out his keys. He stepped quickly to the safe in Scrooge's office, where the petty cash was kept. He counted out the remainder that was needed. This, too, he logged in the small notebook kept in the safe. He added the bills and coins to his existing stack in the cash box. One hundred seventy-two pounds, four shillings, and ten pence. It was time to pay a visit to Mr. Werther.

As it was getting on toward evening, and was a Saturday to boot, Bob made his way to Mr. Werther's home rather than his office. When Bob arrived at the square, he halted on the sidewalk, torn between where to enter. As the maid's father, he would never have dared use the front door. But as a man of business—a man essential to Mr. Werther's new venture, he reminded himself to bolster his confidence—he could not dare knock at the back. It would make him appear too subservient. He had just set on this plan and taken a few determined steps toward the front of the house when Martha's voice called, "Father?"

He turned. She was just outside the Werthers' courtyard, having seen her father passing. He hesitated. He had hoped she wouldn't end up being part of this. Plastering a smile on his face, he walked over and hugged her. Then he headed off her inevitable question. "I'm just here to discuss a small matter of business with Mr. Werther. Nothing of any consequence. We have a bit of business with him, helping to fund his new warehouse."

"Oh." It was clear by her glazed look that she had no inkling of what Mr. Werther's business did. She gave her head a clearing shake. "I didn't know. You never said."

"I didn't want you to feel awkward about it, that's all."

"And at this hour?"

"Tight deadlines in business, you see. Nothing more." He was relieved when a tall, lanky man appeared behind Martha with a questioning look on his perfectly cheekboned face. "Who's this?"

Martha turned to look at the man and blushed. "This is Ian."

"Ah. Your young man."

Behind her, Ian grinned at this description. He stuck out his hand for Bob to shake.

"He just stops by of an evening sometimes," Martha explained.

"I see." Bob allowed himself a wink in Ian's direction, which, if it was possible, made Ian's grin even bigger. "Well, I must go. I'll see you tomorrow, won't I?"

"Yes, of course."

"Ian is welcome to accompany you if you wish."

The corners of his daughter's mouth twitched up and down for several seconds, as if she were trying to force her smile into a frown. "We'll see," she finally said.

"I must be on my way," Bob said. "Nice to meet you, Ian." With that, he walked around to the front of the house and rang the bell.

The butler who answered the door looked so serious Bob almost burst out laughing. The man must think himself the Raj of India or some such nonsense. Bob gathered himself enough to ask, "Is Mr. Werther in?"

"May I ask who's calling?"

"Mr. Cratchit."

"Cratchit?" He looked surprised, and Bob could tell he had caught at the familiar name.

"A business matter. He's expecting me."

The butler gave him a disapproving look for a moment before stepping aside and waving him in. Bob followed him into the back parlor—a Cratchit wasn't good enough for the front parlor, it seemed—where the butler told Bob to wait.

After a few minutes, Mr. Werther burst into the room. Bob had a hard time believing Mr. Werther ever entered a room any other way. From the doorway, which his large frame almost filled, he said loudly, "Mr. Cratchit. I didn't expect to see you again so soon."

Bob stood and shook his hand. "I have your money, as we discussed. I assumed you wanted it as soon as possible so that you can get started straightaway on Monday."

"Very good of you." He took the envelope from Bob and leafed through the bills. "Interesting that you were able to get it so quickly when your Mr. Scrooge couldn't," he said.

"The business has strong cash flow, I assure you. Mr. Scrooge is a busy man. Perhaps he had the money but hadn't the time." Bob had never strung together so many lies, white or otherwise, into one speech before, and his cheeks flushed slightly at his own audacity.

Mr. Werther's face showed he didn't believe a word of it. "Well, I'm glad you were able to take care of it for me, at least. I appreciate it."

"I hope we will continue to do business together in the future."

Mr. Werther nodded. He let Bob squirm for a moment before he said, as if he had just remembered, "Oh, you must be wondering what this means for your Martha. The maid."

Bob felt the inclusion of the last two words was meant to needle him. A reminder of who he was—a maid's father. He didn't respond. He refused to be pulled in.

"I'll meet with my team on Monday. If all seems in order, I'll talk to Martha about her promotion."

"Thank you, sir." He started to walk out.

Mr. Werther called after him, "Any word on Mr. Scrooge.?"

"None yet, sir." He bowed and exited, passing the dour butler in the foyer, who made no move to open the front door for Bob. Back out on the square, Bob's hand shook as he scratched at one eyebrow. The day's string of confrontations had worn him out, mentally more than physically. He went straight home, determined not to waste a single thought on business again until Monday, a sentiment with which his wife would have wholeheartedly agreed, had he shared it with her.

Bob did not check in on Fred and Clara when he arrived home, preferring to put the whole situation temporarily out of his mind. But had he visited, he would have encountered the Williamsons deep in conversation with Miss Spencer, the three devising their own campaign that would come dangerously close to running counter to Bob's own.

Chapter 21

Martha and Ian left the Werthers' and began the walk to the Cratchits' for Martha's regular Sunday half day. This alone was not unusual. In recent weeks, Ian had accompanied Martha on her walk, splitting off to go his own way once they reached the top of her street. After her father's sudden appearance and dinner invitation the previous evening, uneasy anticipation colored the air. Martha hadn't planned on introducing anyone in her family to Ian yet. The knowledge that they would all meet him at once had kept her up most of the night, but by the time she and Ian set out, she had mostly convinced herself it was for the best. If he and her family were not compatible, it was best to discover it now rather than later.

A few blocks into their walk, Ian pulled a small flask out of his pocket and sipped from it. Martha frowned but said nothing. Ian's manner was cheery and loose but not sloppy, so it didn't seem worth a lecture. However, after the flask had made a few more surreptitious appearances, he couldn't help but catch her meaningful looks at the small container.

He looked down at her. "You don't approve, I take it?"

"Not really, no. Especially today of all days."

"That's exactly why I had to do it. Otherwise, I'd be a nervous wreck. I needed something to calm me down. Besides, I assure you I am not drunk, only a bit tipsy, perhaps." To punctuate this statement, he gave a tug of his lapels that was meant to look decisive but only made it appear as if he had to hold himself up.

Martha laughed but smothered it quickly. She looked at Ian out of the corner of her eye. He didn't seem to mind being the butt of her private joke.

"I'm glad to see I can bring a smile to your face, even if it is at my own expense," he said. He took another sip from the flask, then twisted on the cap and returned it to his jacket pocket.

They walked in companionable silence for a bit. They had just reached the fringes of Bloomsbury when Ian reached into his pocket and absentmindedly pulled out the flask.

Before he raised it to his lips, he caught Martha's look and hurriedly put it back in his pocket with an apologetic smile.

"Miss Cratchit," a voice called. Steven Heron stepped up to Martha's elbow and tipped his hat. His pointed glance at Ian's jacket pocket showed he had caught what had just transpired.

Martha introduced the two, referring to them only as her "friend" and her "neighbor." A current of tension ran between the two men. "Mr. Thatcher was just accompanying me home," she said, half turning to indicate they would continue on their way.

Steven planted himself in front of her. "He needn't put himself out any longer. We're very close, and I'm happy to accompany you from here."

"I hardly need an escort every step of the way."

"Be that as it may, we're headed to the same place, so I'm happy to do so."

"He's been invited to dinner, actually." She had hoped to avoid saying so but found there was no way around it. She glanced between them, trying to gauge their reactions. Ian appeared on edge, and Steven's puffed-out chest indicated he felt affronted that this man had been invited to dinner before he had.

"Invited to dinner? Why, you can smell the whiskey on him!" he declared.

Ian's jaw and fists clenched at the same time. It seemed prudent to extricate him from the situation before he erupted. Martha tugged on his elbow. "Let's go."

But Ian refused to move. "And who the hell are you?" he bellowed at Steven.

Martha cringed. People turned in the street to look at them. She tugged at his elbow again, but he shook her off.

"No! Who the hell are you, sir, to cast judgment on me?"

"I was merely stating a fact."

"Steven," she pleaded, trying a different tactic.

Steven at least glanced at her, and this seemed to mollify him. "You are proving my point, Mr. Thatcher. I think it would be best if you left and I escorted Miss Cratchit home."

In the next instant, Ian's fist came flying wide out to his side, knocking into Martha before connecting with Steven's jaw, sending both falling to the ground at Ian's feet.

"Oh my God, Martha," Ian said, leaning down to help her up.

It was Martha's turn to shake him off. She stood by her own power and brushed herself off. "I think it would be best if you went home, Ian."

Ian stared at her for a few seconds, then glanced at Steven, who by now had stood and was looking fierce. The blow, weakened by drink and its prior contact with Martha, had not left a mark—physically, at least. Ian's shoulders slumped. "I'm sorry, Martha. And Mr. . . . " he trailed off, having already forgotten Mr. Heron's name.

Rather than supplying it, Steven simply said, "I think you had best comply with the lady's request."

Ian looked between them again, then sadly turned and walked back the way they had come. He kicked the dirt while he walked, as if he were a child pouting after a lost sporting game.

Once he was sufficiently far away, Martha said, "I'm so sorry. He's never been like that before."

"It wasn't your fault by any means." Steven held out his arm for Martha to take. "I hope you understand that it was probably for the best to see him like that now rather than later."

Martha didn't respond. She had no idea what to think of the situation. It had happened so fast. Her hands shook slightly from the adrenaline.

Rather than pushing her any further, Steven asked, "By the way, how are things with the search for Mr. Scrooge?"

Martha, jolted out of her own thoughts, threw him a puzzled look.

"You haven't heard? He's missing, from what I understand. Your father has been out at all hours looking for him. My mother was over there yesterday to help yours with the children since he's been gone so much."

"I hadn't heard."

"Sorry to be the one to tell you. I assumed you knew."

They reached their houses. After all that had happened, Martha felt it was only right to invite Steven in. They would have Mr. Heron to dinner instead of Mr. Thatcher.

"Ian was unable to come," was all Martha said to the anticipated questions when she entered with Steven instead. Surprised but eager to appear polite, the Cratchits welcomed Steven and ushered him to his seat at the dinner table with as much gusto as if they had expected him all along. To avoid any more inquiries, once they sat down, Martha asked about the situation with Scrooge. Her father launched into an explanation clearly designed to assure everyone that he had everything under control, but once he finished and the conversation had moved on (aided by Mrs. Cratchit, who seemed loathe to discuss Mr. Scrooge even in this), Martha saw that Bob's thoughts had not moved on. He stayed quiet, his eyes seeming to look inward rather than out, his brow furrowed. It was the same look he always had when mulling over an intractable problem. It was a posture he had taken many times at the dinner table when Martha was young, trying to work out how to meet some unexpected small expense, what scraps they could get rid of, or who could do without. And somehow, he always figured it out. If he were devoting his faculties to solving this problem of Scrooge, then Martha was sure that Scrooge would be found. She sighed quietly. She doubted Mr. Scrooge had adequate appreciation for her father's dedication to him.

This last thought threw her into a fit of pique, and she determined to dislodge her father's train of thought. "How was your business visit with Mr. Werther yesterday?" she asked.

Bob looked startled, and it took him a second to come back to himself. "Fine, fine," he said. "All well."

Martha didn't respond immediately. She was still formulating her next question: Why hadn't she known? What had the two men discussed?

Before she could ask, Bob said, "It may be good for you. If this warehouse project goes well."

Martha frowned. She at least knew what it was all about now—she had heard nothing about a warehouse, but then again, she had no reason to hold any interest in her employer's business as long as it continued to pay her salary. But there was an unacknowledged reverse to Bob's statement: If it did not go well, then it might affect her badly.

She hated, *hated* Mr. Scrooge.

After dinner, Martha helped with the washing up, then joined her parents and Steven chatting over coffee—a new extravagance in the Cratchit household, one she was pleased to be considered adult enough to join. Once their cups were empty, Martha and Mrs. Cratchit put the children to bed. With all that had happened that day, Martha was exhausted. She couldn't face the thought of the walk home, so she determined to stay the night. She said goodbye to Steven, then crawled into bed beside her sister Belinda. The younger girl stirred but didn't wake. Martha's mind attempted to parse through the day's events, but her body overrode it, and she was snoring within five minutes.

Martha was up before dawn to return to work, but even so, her mother hurried down, still in her nightdress. "Did you see your father leave?" she asked.

"No," Martha replied. "Why, is something wrong?"

"He's gone off so early this morning."

"You know about the whole business with Scrooge—"

"Yes, but why is he spending so much time worrying about this man who never once worried about him? Something else must be going on."

Martha frowned, unconvinced. "Like what?"

"I don't know. A woman, maybe."

Martha laughed. The younger children began to stir upstairs, and she lowered her voice. "Don't be ridiculous. You know Father would never do that. He's just doing what he feels is his duty. Once he's done everything he can, maybe he'll accept that Scrooge is out of the picture. Then the business will be his, and all our problems will be solved." She kissed her mother's forehead. "You're the one who's worrying too much."

Martha walked out the door with a smile on her face, but it quickly fell away. On the street in front of her house stood Steven Heron.

"What are you doing here?" She hurried down the front steps and past him. He started walking with her.

"I have to catch the train again. I figured you would be leaving early. I thought I'd walk with you the first bit of the way."

"I really am quite capable of taking care of myself."

"Yes, but that doesn't mean you have to take care of yourself—all by yourself," he stumbled. "You can let others help, I mean."

Martha sighed. "And you are the person to do it, I suppose?" In the dim predawn light, Steven's face appeared covered in a dark veil. Even so, Martha could see the hurt her words had caused. "I didn't mean to be rude," she said quickly.

"I'm not sure what you have against me. I've never done anything but be nice to you, I think. And I took a punch for you yesterday."

"I think we took equal amounts of the punch, to be fair."

Steven laughed. "You're right about that."

"I'm sorry," she said, "You've been very kind. But you have to understand that for a woman in my position, most men are not kind without wanting something in return."

The silence was thoughtful for a moment.

"I admit," Steven said, "I do have an ulterior motive. I admire you greatly, and I'd like to call on you officially, if that would be all right. That way, we will all know where we stand, and I won't be relegated to trying to meet you on the street as much as possible."

She let out a brief laugh. "I knew these meetings were hardly happenstance... But I'm not available to be called on by anyone. I have a position—"

"I know. Can I come by there sometime? Just let me know when and I'll come. I promise you, I'm not like my mother."

"I know you aren't. But I don't think it's a good idea. Ian is there sometimes."

Steven raised one eyebrow. "Still?"

"He makes deliveries to the house."

"Right. I suppose I will have to be content with next Sunday, then. I'll let you continue on your way." He tipped his hat and headed back the way they had come, not toward the train station at all. Martha laughed to herself at the false pretense he had forgotten to keep up.

She was happy to have the rest of the walk to herself. The morning was warm, and the few people she passed seemed to also be put in a good mood by the quiet morning, greeting her cheerily as they walked by. She tried her best to put the uncheery things out of her mind—Ian, Mr. Scrooge, what on earth to do about the ever-eager Steven Heron. But at the Werthers' corner, those thoughts came screeching back. She paused and listened to two familiar voices drifting over the wall: Kitty's high-pitched giggle and Ian's deep tones. Martha steeled herself and walked into the courtyard.

Both Kitty and Ian stopped talking the instant she appeared. Kitty's gaze was haughty; clearly, Ian had told her some version of yesterday's story that was not very flattering to Martha.

Martha said, "Good morning," but continued on her way.

Ian's heavy footsteps followed her. He darted around her, blocking the back door so that she couldn't go in. "I came to see you," he said. "I wanted to talk about yesterday."

Kitty came up beside Martha and gave Ian a meaningful look. He stepped aside and let her in. "Just give us a moment," he said to her as she passed. She smiled too big in response, so the expression rang false.

"What's there to talk about?" Martha asked once Kitty had left.

"I want to apologize. I would never hit a woman. That was an accident, I swear."

"But you aren't sorry for hitting Mr. Heron?"

"I didn't even know who he was. He just came up and started being rude to me."

"I introduced you!"

"Well, he seemed awfully protective of you."

"Clearly, I can't control what the men around me do," she said dryly. "And you can't really blame him, can you? All he saw was a man drinking from a flask on a Sunday afternoon."

"What's the harm in that? I wasn't causing any trouble. And you know what he really saw was someone too low class for his fancy neighborhood."

Martha rubbed her forehead. She had not been prepared for this onslaught. She had thought his speech would involve a lot more begging for her forgiveness.

"Have you been seeing him, too?"

"No. I barely know him. Besides, how would I be seeing him when I'm here all the time?"

"You go home every Sunday. Is that why?"

She shot him an exasperated look. "I've been going home every Sunday afternoon since I got this position at fourteen. And I don't appreciate this interrogation."

He ran his hand through his hair several times before he spoke again. "I guess that's it, then."

"What do you mean?"

He stood straighter. "I'm taking Kitty out this Sunday."

The declaration surprised her even more than the onslaught had. But she thought of Miss Spencer and her independence and the advice she had given Martha. There were other things a woman could devote herself to. Perhaps this was for the best. "Well, I hope it works out for you two."

Ian stared at her for a long moment as if waiting for her to change her mind, then spun around with a flourish of his arms and stomped off the property. Martha went inside and started her work without giving him another thought.

That evening after the workday was done, Martha asked the housekeeper, Mrs. Kellan, for pen, ink, and paper. Once in possession of these items, she retreated to the small basement room she shared with Kitty. She changed and got into her narrow bed, propping the sheet of paper up on her knees. Martha was not in the habit of writing letters, so despite the coldness that had lingered between them all day, Kitty couldn't contain her curiosity. Martha wouldn't say whom she was writing to, so Kitty speculated out loud.

"You do have another man, don't you? A wealthy one?" It was information she must have gotten from Ian, but she said it the same friendly, conspiratorial tone she used when passing on any other gossip she had heard.

Martha relaxed. Their friendship wasn't over, then. She struggled to keep the corners of her mouth from curling into a smile. It was much more fun to keep her face serious and let her friend speculate as Martha considered each sentence.

"Gosh, is he married?" Kitty asked. "Is that what all the drama is about? I wish I was pretty and blonde like you and had multiple beaus. It must be wonderful." Kitty played with a lock of her hair. It was a dull, mousy brown, ringing a face that was continually flushed red no matter what she was doing. But she had a fine nose and brilliant green eyes, so she wasn't quite the ogre she often made herself out to be.

Ian must not have told Kitty the whole story if she didn't know what the "drama" was about, Martha mused. Of course, he would want to come off well in his tale. But Martha wasn't going to ruin her friend's new relationship by filling in the holes in Ian's story. Kitty, unlike Martha, wanted a beau more than anything, and Martha knew Kitty would never forgive her if she was the one who took it away.

"It's not a beau," Martha finally said.

Kitty frowned. "Who, then? Oh, you're not applying for another place, are you?"

"No, of course not!"

"I'm out of guesses, then." There was silence for several minutes as Martha's pen scratched across the page. "You really aren't going to tell me."

"It's not that exciting, I promise." She folded up the page and addressed it. She would put it out for tomorrow's post.

Kitty snatched the letter from her hand. "Who is Miss Alice Spencer?" Her mouth fell as she read the name until she had acquired quite a pout.

"I told you it's not exciting," Martha said, taking the letter back from her and receiving no protest.

A knock came at their door, and Mrs. Kellan opened it and leaned her head in. "Martha," she said, "Mr. Werther wants to see you in his office."

Both girls froze, mouths agape. After a few seconds, Martha looked down at her nightgown. "Get dressed and go up quickly," Mrs. Kellan said and left, closing the door behind her.

The tiny room became a flurry of activity as Martha rushed to make herself presentable with the occasional assistance of Kitty, whose intervention was of questionable helpfulness. But eventually, Martha was ready, and she hurried upstairs to Mr. Werther's office. The door was closed. She knocked and was told to enter. She had never been in the room when Mr. Werther was there. The room felt different, as if his presence behind the desk on one side of the room had thrown everything a bit off-balance.

"Draw the door closed behind you," he said.

Martha hesitated. That was, perhaps, not appropriate.

"Don't worry. This is a business matter, that's all. Don't want any prying ears around here."

She smiled nervously and shut the door. He waved her to the seat in front of the desk.

"I assume you know that I have engaged the firm Scrooge and Cratchit in some business."

"Yes, I saw my father when he came by on Saturday."

Mr. Werther nodded. He took a moment to light a cigar and take his first puff. "Your father has been very helpful to me in getting the deal to move forward. Much more so than that Mr. Scrooge. An eccentric at best, a criminal at worst, that one is. Anyway, I'm glad to say we broke ground on the new warehouse this morning."

"That's wonderful." Martha had no idea whether it was wonderful or not, but she felt she should say something.

"It is wonderful. For you, too, my dear." He leaned forward and pointed the end of his cigar at her. "I owe your father a favor now, you see. And I'm a man of my word." He leaned back in his chair. "I shall make you head maid, overseeing that mousy one and that god-awful Irish one. Comes with an extra five shillings a month."

Martha leaped a few inches above her chair but quickly sat again and clasped her hands together to hold herself in place. "Thank you so much, sir. I won't let you down."

Mr. Werther only shrugged and puffed on his cigar.

His nonchalance irritated her. "By the way, their names are Kitty and Margaret."

"What?"

"The maids." Receiving no response, she simply stood, curtsied, and started to leave the room.

"Wait," he called after her.

She turned.

"In the future, always negotiate," he said. "I would have given you ten."

She smiled. "Thanks for the advice."

He winked at her. She rushed downstairs to tell Kitty the news but was stopped by Mrs. Kellan, who waited in the basement hall.

One she had explained the conversation to Mrs. Kellan's satisfaction—which involved about three retellings—Mrs. Kellan said, "I shall have to move people around."

"What do you mean?"

"Kitty and Margaret will have to room together now. I'll have to find someplace else for you." More quietly, she said, "God, I wish he would tell me these things first." She gathered herself and nodded to Martha. "Good night."

Martha's heart had sunk at the news of her impending move. She walked much more slowly to her room. Just as she thought she had salvaged her friendship with Kitty, she learned that it would never be the same again.

Though much had changed for Martha, for others affected by Scrooge's disappearance, life was starting to return to normal. Bob conducted his regular business. Fred returned to his place of employment, dining at home with his wife as usual; both were starting to worry that they would never find answers but were buoyed by the promises made during Miss Spencer's visit. Michaels and Crane unloaded a new shipment of goods at the docks. Mrs. Minston stopped by Scrooge's house to dust and throw out old food, as it hadn't been touched in days, but found there wasn't much else to do and left by midmorning.

While all these lives trundled along in the capital, in a forgotten quadrant of a northern city, in a hulk of a building surrounding a dark, forgotten courtyard, in an upstairs room, Ebenezer Scrooge waited for the doctor to arrive.

An orderly had cleaned Scrooge up after serving him supper and informing him that the doctor would arrive soon. Soon, of course, was a relative term in this place. Even after only a few days, Scrooge's sense of time had gotten slippery, with his pocket watch confiscated and not even the sound of church bells ringing the hour penetrating the walls. There was one small window, high up in the room, that only allowed in the little light that penetrated the courtyard.

Down the hall, someone shouted, with two or three more voices quickly joining in. The constant noise of his fellow inmates was the most disconcerting thing about the place. Though he didn't enjoy the freezing cold baths, either—he was afraid he might be catching a chill. But he had his own private room, which was a blessing even though it was cramped and dim and the bucket in the corner was not emptied as often as it should be. This was what he had been hoarding his money for all his life, he told himself—to maintain some standard of decency during his imprisonment. That pocket watch had been worth a pretty penny by itself. He wasn't sure if the thought was comforting or incredibly depressing.

Boots scraped in the hall. Then keys turned and the door opened. A man entered—not Dr. Burnhope as he had expected. Scrooge had not seen that gentleman since Scrooge had arrived. The orderly closed the door behind the man, leaving Scrooge alone with him.

The visitor set a black case on the floor beside his feet. "I'm Dr. Harris."

Scrooge rose from his seat on the cot to greet him. Scrooge extended his hand, and for an instant, he feared the doctor wasn't going to take it. But after that moment's hesitation, Dr. Harris accepted a firm handshake.

The doctor looked around and dragged a short wooden stool out of the corner by the bucket.

"I wouldn't sit on that if I were you."

"Why not?"

"I just wouldn't."

The doctor looked at the hand that had touched the stool, as if he were afraid it would burst into flame. Then he returned his focus to Scrooge with a forced smile. "Well, let's just stand, shall we?"

Scrooge folded his hands neatly in front of him.

Dr. Harris pulled a folder out of his case. "Mr. Scrooge, is it?"

"Yes."

"I'm told you've been very docile while you've been here."

"Would you rather I wasn't?"

"No, but most men in your position don't take their enforced residence here quite so well." He looked up expectantly from his folder, but Scrooge offered no response. "You believe you were visited by ghosts, is that right?"

"Spirits, really, but yes."

"Ah. Can you explain the difference to me?"

"I've thought about that quite a bit. The spirits I met with were not the souls of specific people who have died, which I think the word 'ghost' implies. They are spiritual entities but were never human."

"I see. And was this a frightening experience?"

"At first, yes, but then I realized they were trying to help me."

"Did they help you?"

"Oh, yes. Immensely."

"And yet you're here."

"I suppose I could hardly expect there to be no punishment for all the ills I've wrought in the world. I'm happy to have my penance be temporary here on earth rather than eternal on the other side."

"You're quite the philosopher."

"When will I be able to see my family? Or send them a letter?"

"We discourage contact with the outside world. It can upset the treatment process."

"At least send a note to Bob to let him know I'm well, and he can spread the news to everyone else."

"Who is Bob?"

"My business partner."

Dr. Harris flipped to a different page in the folder. "Is that Mr. Cratchit? He knows perfectly well that you're here. According to this, he was the one who arranged with Dr. Burnhope to have you collected."

"Bob . . . what?" Scrooge blinked furiously, trying to make sense of this new information.

"I'm sure he only had your best interests in mind. If you adhere to your treatment, I think you're a very good candidate to be released once we've cleared you of this mania."

"I do not have a mania."

"I'll try to come see you this time next week." He picked up his case and knocked on the door. It swung mysteriously open with no orderly appearing.

When the doctor left, Scrooge thought his cell seemed even darker than it had before that awful meeting.

Chapter 22

While Bob had dedicated himself to the tedious everyday affairs of the business on Monday, he had all the while been turning over in his mind the problem with Archie, whom Scrooge had trusted and taken under his wing, and the others determined to damage the business beyond repair. Over the course of the day, Bob's plan coalesced, with only a few notes sent and one slightly nefarious meeting required to set it in motion.

On Tuesday morning, the dominos began to fall. While Bob waited for the plan to unfold, he spent more time imagining the chaos ensuing at Mr. Parker's place of business than he did focusing on the papers in front of him. His feelings about these imaginings alternated between a knot in his stomach and a smile on his face. He could only hope that he had done the right thing.

Eventually, he heard a scuffle at the front door. He stayed at his desk in the Tank. "In here, gentlemen," he called.

Two men, dressed in passable imitations of constable uniforms, wrestled a man into the chair across from Bob. One lifted a burlap sack off the man's head to reveal Mr. Parker.

Archie looked crazily around the room. "This isn't debtors' prison."

Bob had to stop himself from grinning at the success of his own ruse. "No, it's not, because I'm much kinder than I could have been. In fact, I've brought you here to make a deal."

Archie scowled. "And what, pray tell, is that?"

"I've found out all about your little plot with your friend Michaels and that awful Crane. Honestly, I'm surprised you would let yourself get pulled into such a thing. I've talked to all your minions, so they won't be part of it anymore. Now I just need you out of the way, too."

"Out of the way?" Archie jumped out of his chair, and the two goons wrestled him back down.

"Not like that, you fool. In case you haven't noticed, this place has been quite kind to everyone you've brought us, especially yourself. You can admit that, at least?"

"Yes, but it remains to be seen if that can make up for all the bad this hellhole has done."

"You must let us see. Why stop the good work when it has barely begun?"

Archie regarded him for a moment. "What do you want me to do?"

"Talk to Michaels and Crane. Tell them you won't participate any longer. And do what you need to call them off the scent." Archie hesitated, so Bob continued. "I have more than enough reason to sign an order for you to be put in debtors' prison in actuality. And I won't hesitate to exercise that power if I'm given a reason to. A lawyer might even tell me to take action regarding the forgery of those contracts you gave Mr. Lauriston."

Archie stood, much more calmly this time. His two handlers approached, but Bob waved them away.

"I'll do as you ask," Archie said. "But I can't speak for the other two men."

"I'm sure you'll find a way to convince them. A man always does when his livelihood is at stake."

"Where is the old bastard, anyway?" Archie twisted to peek across the hall at Scrooge's office.

Bob flicked a finger in the direction of the door and the two men escorted Archie out, only slightly less roughly than they had dragged him in. When they had left, Bob dropped his head into shaking hands. He couldn't believe he had done that. But it proved what he told Mr. Parker. A man will always find a way when his life—or livelihood—is at stake.

Archie hated being this close to the docks. The smell lingered on your clothes long after you had left. He feared it could be catching—the poverty, that is, or the lure of criminality.

He didn't know exactly where to find Michaels, but he imagined his old friend would find him. Sure enough, after one or two passes along the waterfront, Crane appeared on a street corner, looking for all the world as if he were just out enjoying the day. Well, enjoying might be too strong of a word, as Crane's face seemed a stranger to a smile. Archie approached him. "I need to talk to you," he said.

Crane led him away from the water. They turned into a narrow street and entered an equally narrow three-story building. On the top floor, Crane escorted him into a small kitchen where Michaels sat smoking a cigarette. He motioned to the chair across from him. Archie sat.

"I hear you've been doing a good job," Michaels said. "Really getting under that bastard's skin."

Archie jerked forward in his seat. "You have to stop this vendetta."

"Why on earth would I do that?"

"He knows I'm involved, and he's threatened to bring me down with you."

"And how did he convey this information to you, seeing as he's securely locked up somewhere?"

Archie looked back and forth between the other two men. "What?" When no explanation was forthcoming, he continued. "His business partner told me. He's been to see all my employees who owe the firm money. Somebody grassed."

"Guess that Cratchit fellow wasn't smart enough to take our offer," Crane said.

Archie whipped his head around to look at Crane, startled by the sound of his voice. Crane showed no inclination to add further words.

Michaels took a final drag of his cigarette, then snuffed it out on the tabletop, which was already covered in scratches and burn marks. "What is it with people falling under the spell of that awful man? My sister was here yesterday saying the same thing. 'Oh, he's actually so nice, and he's trying really hard.'" Michaels scoffed. "You all are fucking idiots."

"As your oldest friend, I am asking you to please let this go." Archie paused for emphasis. "And if you insist on pursuing this folly, I'll make sure you go down with me. I know a lot about what you're trading in. And I won't be afraid to share it with the right people. I, for one, still have connections in reputable places."

Michaels and Crane exchanged a glance. Michaels shrugged. "I don't know why you think anyone is going down except that miserable old Scrooge. But fine, I release you from your promise. We'll figure something else out."

Archie started to protest the last statement, but Michaels began inspecting his fingernails, refusing to meet Archie's gaze. Seeing there was no point in forcing the conversation to continue, Archie gave up and left. He had to stop himself from running once his feet hit the street. He couldn't get away from the docks and those two men fast enough. He resolved to never get sucked in by them again. Any favors he owed his old friend had surely been repaid.

The rapid footsteps through the front door of the office and across the foyer could only signal the arrival of Fred. Bob looked up calmly as Scrooge's nephew entered, not surprised to see Fred in the grip of another restless mania, desperate to do something. Bob was grateful for the distraction to take his mind off that morning's events.

"Any news?" Bob asked.

Fred held up a forefinger. "Miss Spencer and I have come up with a plan," he announced. "Well, Clara, too," he added. "More Clara than me, actually, if I'm honest." He paused and grinned at Bob.

Bob clapped his hands once in appreciation of this news. "What's the plan?"

"We're going to raise a petition and publish it in the paper. Use the public in our favor, just like Dr. Burnhope did."

"A petition by whom?"

"All the people my uncle has helped this year. They can certify that he is perfectly sane and that it's in their best interest that he continues to do business in the city." Fred looked around the Tank. "I'll need your books."

Bob rubbed his hands together, his palms sweaty, his whole body tense. He sensed this complicated his plan immensely.

When Bob didn't respond, Fred added helpfully, "Miss Spencer said there were a lot of small loan holders we could ask. And a lawyer who's been helping out, and that chap Martha works for. What's his name?"

"I don't think any of that is a good idea."

Fred looked as if Bob had thrown a bucket of cold water over him. For once, he held still for more than three seconds. "Whyever not?" he asked.

"Things with the business are more complicated than that. The agreement with the lawyer didn't turn out so well, as I think Miss Spencer is aware, and I would prefer that Mr. Werther didn't get dragged into this again now that I've mollified him."

"Mollified... what are you talking about, Bob?"

Bob sighed and gave a brief outline of what had occurred with the lawyer and the small loan holders, omitting his confrontation with Archie that morning.

Fred's frown deepened as the story unfurled. By the end, he was standing as straight as possible, his fists clenched at his sides. "This is all recorded and accounted for, I assume?"

"Y-yes, of course."

"Show me."

Fred had never once expressed interest in his uncle's business, but Bob saw there was no way around it now. He took the account book he had brought with him on his rounds to the loan holders down from a shelf and opened it across his desk. He ran his finger down the column of entries.

Fred leaned over Bob's shoulder to view the numbers the older man indicated. "What do these marks mean?" He indicated a few entries where Bob had crossed out future amounts due.

"To get the payments and information from these men, I had to promise to forgive their future installments."

"Would my uncle approve of that?"

"He is not here. I had to take action."

Fred frowned but continued looking down the column of numbers. When he had reached the end, he asked, "Where is all this money, then?"

"I had to give it to Mr. Werther for his line of credit."

"All of it?"

"Yes. It was for a line of credit that your uncle approved without informing me, mind you, and then refused to pay. And keep in mind that this is my daughter's employer he was playing these games with."

Fred ran his fingers back and forth through his hair quickly. The corners of his eyes were red and moist. After a few minutes, he said, "I don't know what to think. It seems he is lost. Everyone is against him."

"No, I don't think that. Let's still try your idea about the letter to the editor." Desperate to redeem himself in Fred's eyes, he said, "Come back tomorrow. I'll bring Peter. He worked at a newspaper before he came here, so he can probably help us get the letter in the paper as soon as possible."

"He's just a boy."

"Yes, but he makes himself useful. And everyone likes him."

Fred dropped his hands to his sides. "All right. It's worth a try." He cast a withering glance at Bob. "I'm still not sure of you, Bob, but yes, let's regroup here in the morning and see what we can do."

Bob bowed his head. Saying more now wouldn't help anything. With Fred gone, he collapsed at his desk once again. His heart beat an unsteady rhythm in his chest. He took deep, slow breaths for a few minutes until his heart calmed. It made no sense that he was making himself so unwell over problems that were not of his own doing, especially when no one appreciated his efforts. Once he cleaned up this mess, perhaps it would be better if Scrooge never reappeared. He felt immensely guilty the instant he thought it. No one deserved what Scrooge was probably experiencing at that moment.

He couldn't sit there any longer without going insane himself. When he had sufficiently recovered, he locked up and went home early. The walk cleared his head, so when he arrived home to a surprised but pleased Mrs. Cratchit, he gave the impression that nothing much was amiss and that Scrooge wasn't the only thing consuming his thoughts.

Chapter 23

As promised, the next day, Peter accompanied Bob to work. The boy had been chomping at the bit to return, hating being stuck at home with the children when he was so sure he was now a man himself. Bob was both relieved and worried when they turned the corner and saw that Fred was not waiting for them.

In spite of everything, Bob knew that the regular business of the company couldn't be delayed forever. They would have to return to some semblance of normalcy. Perhaps this was that chance. Father and son spent the morning silently copying letters, a dull, repetitive task that helped them pretend it was a day like any other.

That illusion didn't last long, however. Fred showed up before lunch. His greeting to the two Cratchits was colder than usual. He approached Bob's desk slowly, as if Bob were a potentially aggressive animal. He held out a sheet of paper and laid it on Bob's desk. "I went by Miss Spencer's this morning. Here is the letter she wrote for the paper." As Bob read the letter, Fred continued, "Listen, Bob, I want to apologize for yesterday. I know you've been helping my uncle in any way you can, when, really, who could blame you if you resented him . . ."

Bob waved away the comment, though the clenching in his chest released in gratitude. "This situation has put all of us on edge." He finished reading the letter and laid it down. "It's good."

Fred nodded. "I think so, too. The awful thing, the thing we need to combat, is that Dr. Burnhope is very respected in his field. Even though the papers have reported on this travesty, no one is willing to do anything. If Dr. Burnhope thinks this man needs to be committed, they say it must be true."

"Still no help from Dr. Burnhope's office?"

"No. I went there this morning after I visited Miss Spencer. I thought if I stayed long enough, I would have to see him, but his staff always say he's either occupied or away, or the place is locked up completely. I think he's hiding from us, hoping we'll give up."

"Dr. Burnhope, you say?" Peter asked from his desk in the corner.

"Yes," Fred said, turning to look at the boy. "Why?"

"I remember that name."

"Yes, it's the same man we've been talking about for days," Bob said.

"No, I don't think I've heard you say his name before. If I had, I would have said I remember it. Because I do. From the newspaper."

He now had both men's full attention.

"When I worked at the paper, I would do deliveries and sometimes errands within the office. When I had a chance, I would read some of the articles to practice my letters. Mostly they were very dull, but the ones about Dr. Burnhope were cracking. Almost like an adventure story."

Fred looked newly energized. He bounced on the balls of his feet. "Do you think the newspaper has an archive?" Without waiting for an answer, he said, "Take us there." He dashed toward the door, then dashed back to rescue Miss Spencer's letter from Bob's desk, before following the Cratchits out.

The front desk clerk at the newspaper office met Fred's explanation with skepticism. After additional pleading from Peter, the clerk led them to a back room filled with filing cabinets and six-foot stacks of newspaper. "Feel free to look around," he said with a look that showed he thought they were wasting their time.

"Is Mr. Harper here?" Peter asked.

"Yes."

Peter darted toward the door.

"But don't you go bothering him!"

Peter was already past the clerk, who watched after Peter for a few seconds, then shook his head and headed back to his desk.

A few minutes later, Peter returned, leading a pale, balding man by the hand. "This is Mr. Harper," he announced. "The one who wrote those articles about Dr. Burnhope. This is Mr., uh, Fred, and my father."

The three men shook hands while Bob apologized for the boldness of his son's behavior, which the newspaperman brushed off.

"Can you help us find the archived copies in this mess?" Fred asked.

"I think trying to find anything in here is a waste of time. But I can tell you what was in the articles."

Everyone followed Mr. Harper to his desk. After a few minutes of scrounging up extra chairs, they sat in a tight half circle in the small space in front of the desk.

"Dr. Burnhope is a complicated figure," Mr. Harper began. "While his methods are sometimes questionable, he's done a lot of well-respected work in reforming asylums and improving conditions for residents. That makes it difficult to accuse him of much of anything that sticks. And his dedication to this cause and his questionable methods stem from his childhood experiences. His mother was committed to an asylum involuntarily by his father, and it was many years into his adulthood before he found out where she was held. By that time, as I understand, any faculties she may have still had when she entered the institution were long gone from the inhumane treatment she received."

Bob and Fred exchanged worried looks. The journalist held up a hand.

"I'm not saying this to scare you. The person you're looking for has only been missing for what, a week?" The others nodded. "And like I say, Dr. Burnhope is not quite the evil genius you probably think he is."

"Do you know where he might take someone?" Fred asked.

Mr. Harper pulled a sheet of paper out of a drawer and began writing. "At least at the time I wrote the articles, he was a visiting physician at these three institutions. I would start there."

He slid the paper across the desk. Fred took it and stood.

"These types of places don't typically allow visitors," Mr. Harper added. "You'll need someone with power to get you in. A peer, a member of government, that sort of thing."

After profuse thanks, Fred broached the next subject. "We would like to publish our own rebuttal. Since Dr. Burnhope fired the first volley in the papers, we need to fire back the same way." He pulled the letter out of his jacket pocket and handed it over. "Could you help us, by any chance?"

Mr. Harper glanced over the page. "It's well written." He smiled at Fred. "I'll bring it to my editor and see what we can do."

Fred, Bob, and Peter returned to the street outside the newspaper office, buoyed and bonded by their success.

"We need to pay a visit to Miss Spencer next," Bob said, and the little group headed in that direction. "She'll know who to call on to get us in these places."

In the parlor of Miss Spencer's boarding house, the story came out jumbled, with the three talking over each other at various points. Peter, in particular, was eager to share the part he had played in their discovery. Eventually, they made it through their tale, and Miss Spencer sat with the list from Mr. Harper in her hand while the others finally paused long enough for her to speak.

"I see why it's been so hard to find him," she said. "None of these are even in London."

"Not in London! What a trick!" the others exclaimed.

Miss Spencer tapped a finger next to one of the names. "I know Mr. Perim, the MP for this area, and I think he might be willing to help us. Let me grab my reticule and we'll go."

Tired of running around the city, the little group splurged on a carriage to take them to Westminster. With their newly hopeful outlook, the air inside the vehicle felt fresh and light.

"Peter," Fred said jovially, "when you're old enough, I owe you a drink."

Peter just grinned. Bob, not being a man who frequented the pub himself, frowned but made no comment.

The carriage dropped them off in the square in front of the House of Parliament. The noise was deafening. The whole area was a construction site, with materiel being maneuvered through the crowd and workers shouting from the scaffolding to their colleagues on the pavement below, all with a regular background of hammering and another shrill noise the group couldn't quite place.

"It's been ten years since the fire," Bob shouted more than said. "Do you think they'll ever actually finish this?"

"Not in our lifetime, I think," Fred replied with a friendly pat on the shoulder. "Onward!" he shouted.

Inside, the noise was not much reduced. Everything had the feeling of the temporary and make-do. Furniture filled spaces much too small for it. Stacks of boxes and crates were shoved into every corner. Along one wall teetered several towers of chairs that threatened to topple the next time somebody walked too close—which was likely to happen soon, as there was hardly space to move. In one stretch of the lobby, the group had to wait for a man to walk through a narrow passage between two desks before they could pass through.

Miss Spencer explained their mission to a clerk they found in the lobby. The others followed like ducklings, taking in their surroundings in awe. Bob stepped on Fred's heels several times as they walked, and Peter nearly got lost three times, as it was very difficult to keep him from heading toward the next interesting thing he saw.

There was some confusion over where Mr. Perim's office was located. When Miss Spencer had visited that particular MP a few months before, he had been lodged in an east wing that they were now told had been taken over by some committee or another. After stretches of waiting in a series of lobbies and offices, they were eventually brought to a tiny office crammed with papers, where Miss Spencer introduced them to Mr. Perim, MP. He was a short, pudgy man with an overabundance of thick gray hair.

"I have heard something about this case," he said once Miss Spencer had oriented him to their cause. "I read about a businessman who had developed an admirable duty to the poor. But from what I understand, there was some damning evidence given against him that led to his certification."

"Where did you read that?" Fred asked. His voice came across with too hard of an edge, so he followed it with a gentle smile and waited expectantly for Mr. Perim's response.

"I don't know. Papers somewhere." He absentmindedly rifled through a few of the paper stacks on his desk, then gave up on finding anything.

Bob leaned forward in his seat. "It was probably me. I set up the meeting between him and the doctor."

"No, not you. Woman, I think. His housekeeper, perhaps?"

"Damn," Fred said. "None of us have even talked to her, have we?"

Everyone shook their heads.

"And we know about the Morodys," Bob added.

"I can at least find out for you which of these institutions he is placed at." The MP managed to locate a few scraps of paper and began scribbling on them. "And if you can convince me he is worth saving, perhaps I can do more."

Fred and Bob exchanged nervous glances at this requirement. Miss Spencer looked unperturbed, her gaze steady and calm.

Mr. Perim rang a little bell teetering on one of the stacks of papers. His secretary came in, a notepad at the ready. Mr. Perim handed him the scraps of paper with instructions to send them as telegrams ASAP. "Call us a cab, too," he instructed.

Once the secretary had left, Mr. Perim addressed the group. "Where shall we go first?"

They knocked several times before a quivering Mrs. Minston came to the door.

Mr. Perim tipped his hat to her and introduced himself. Upon hearing a member of Parliament was on her front step, she looked stricken.

"We need to talk to you," Mr. Perim said. "You're not in trouble."

"Like hell she isn't," Fred said, coming forward from behind the others. Miss Spencer whacked him on the shoulder in reprimand.

"Oh!" Mrs. Minston said, suddenly coming back to herself. "Mr. Williamson, thank goodness you're here. Have you gone by the house?"

"What house? What are you talking about?"

"Why, Mr. Scrooge's house. You didn't get my messages? I've been to your house and your office and Mr. Scrooge's office."

The pair stared at each other for a moment. Mr. Perim finally broke the confused silence. "May we come in and get all this sorted?"

Mrs. Minston fixed them with a steely gaze Peter would later say made him sure she was a witch silently cursing them. Eventually, she stepped back and opened the door the rest of the way.

"I think I better ask the questions," Mr. Perim said once they were inside, "to prevent feeling from getting too much into it."

Fred frowned but nodded.

"My business first. I read you said some damning things against your employer."

"Yes... but I didn't mean them. He was awkward and condescending sometimes, but he did try to help me and my family. He was a good employer."

"Then why on earth did you say it?"

She chewed her lower lip before answering. "I didn't know he would be taken away. I thought it was just about money." She tilted her head so that she could look around Mr. Perim and lock her gaze on Bob.

Mr. Perim turned and followed her line of sight. "Do you know what the devil she's talking about?" he asked Bob.

"No."

Mrs. Minston crossed her arms and looked down. "My brother told me what you said to Mr. Parker and the others. That you found them out, so they called it off."

Bob stepped forward with enough determination that Mrs. Minston flinched. "Don't tell me you're related to one of those—" He glanced at the two women and thought better of the word he had been about to use.

"Mr. Michaels is my brother."

Bob rubbed his forehead. It was good to hear that Archie had succeeded in getting Michaels and Crane to call off their revenge, but somehow, that news didn't make him feel much better. He launched into an explanation of all that had happened with the business and the vendetta against Scrooge. Fred chewed a nail as he listened to this story a second time.

"My God," Mr. Perim said when Bob had finished. "Your Mr. Scrooge really built himself quite a cadre of enemies."

"But he has worked so hard to make up for it," Miss Spencer said. "Won't you help us?"

Mr. Perim nodded. "Yes. We all deserve the chance to make amends, or else we'd have given up hope, I imagine. Now," he said to Mrs. Minston, "what is all this about the house?"

"Well, you see, I went by the house this morning to check on it, and . . ."

"Out with it, please," Mr. Perim said.

"It's destroyed." When no one responded to this vague description, she added, "Burned to a crisp." Once everyone had finished exclaiming over this revelation, she ventured, "I think, you see, that maybe my brother called off one plan only to implement another. It would be very hard for him to let go of his revenge against Mr. Scrooge."

"You're accusing this Mr. Michaels of arson?" Mr. Perim sighed and pointed at the door. "Let's deal with one thing at a time. Mr. Scrooge's personal safety is of higher importance than his dwelling. Let's head back to my office to see if any of my telegrams have been answered."

The others mutely followed him—but not before Fred shot Mrs. Minston a look of ire and Bob lingered one of anguish on her countenance.

There were no telegrams when they returned to the tiny office. The group consumed many pots of tea while they waited for answers. Mr. Perim and his secretary stepped around the others as they went about their usual business. In the cramped space, Fred couldn't pace, so he alternated between jittering his legs up and down, resting his elbows on his knees, and letting his face sag into his hands.

The first telegrammed response was definitively negative. The second was equivocal ("Don't think he's a patient here") but still offered no hope. An hour after the second arrived, the entire group watched intensely as the secretary handed a third slip of paper to Perim.

Mr. Perim read it with no change of expression, then slowly set it on the nearest stack of papers. "Looks like we're taking the train north in the morning." He broke into a grin.

Fred leaped out of his chair and whooped. Peter copied him, relishing being allowed to shout indoors. Miss Spencer sank back in her chair. Bob dropped his head in his hands and sobbed in relief, but in the circumstances, no one chastised him for such an unmanly display.

When the room had settled down, they began making plans. It soon became clear to Peter that the thing little boys dread most was occurring: he was being left out. "Come on, Father. You have to let me come. You wouldn't know where Mr. Scrooge was if it weren't for me!"

Bob's eyes were still moist and red-rimmed, but there was no mistaking the love and pride in them as he looked down at his son. "All right. I suppose it's only fair. But you must do as we say."

"Oh, boy!" In his joy at joining the adventure, he hugged everyone in the room and was on the verge of running into the hall to continue before Bob restrained him.

"Until the morning," Mr. Perim said, shaking each hand in turn, taking the longest time with Peter, who beamed under such preeminent attention.

The four left Mr. Perim to his own business. The sun was setting once they made it outside, but they resolved to go view Scrooge's house to assess the damage.

They walked quietly, each absorbed in their own worries and their own happy thoughts of the next day's rescue. When they reached the awkward courtyard in front of Scrooge's building, they all inadvertently paused before entering.

Across the courtyard, the house loomed a gray shell of its former self. It still stood, but the front door hung awkwardly on its hinges, allowing a glimpse of the charred interior. It was lucky that the house was off on its own because it had kept the fire from spreading to other buildings.

"It's in remarkably good shape, considering," Miss Spencer said, trying to sound cheerful as they neared.

"Someone didn't want it to get out of hand," Fred said. "This is a message more than anything else. Mrs. Minston was probably right about her brother being behind this."

Bob stepped into the doorway. "It's not livable either way," he said.

Miss Spencer looked over his shoulder. "I wouldn't go any farther inside. It's probably not safe."

The four stood at the entranceway for several minutes, peering into the darkness as if searching for some clue that would help make sense of it all. Eventually, Bob looked behind them, back out to the courtyard. The sky had darkened.

"Well," Bob said. "Well."

"We had better all be getting home," Miss Spencer said. But it took another moment before anyone made a motion to move.

"I'll see you all on the train in the morning," Fred said. He sounded close to tears.

Bob rubbed Fred's shoulder. "It's all right. We'll have him tomorrow."

Fred just nodded and stomped off into the night. The others slowly followed, then went their separate ways.

Alone in his cell, the object of all these people's attention had had another night and day to reflect on things big and small: his last conversation with Mr. Harris, every conversation he had ever had with Bob. What he would have for supper if he were ever released, the future position he would take in the swirl of humanity.

In a brief fit of sleep, he dreamed a scene similar to the one he had conjured at the seaside about Belle. Except this time, it was his asylum room filling with smoke, and it was the Ghost of Christmas Past that appeared. Scrooge sat up in bed to get a better look at this specter. Even through the gray clouds of smoke, the spirit glowed blindingly bright. Scrooge's tongue stuck to the roof of his mouth, too dry to form any words.

"You still haven't seen," the specter said in its high, faint voice. "You have to release the past to change the future."

In the next instant, Scrooge awoke in bed, though he would have sworn he had been awake a second before. He had the same sensation he had when he woke up on Christmas morning: he didn't know what day it was or how much time had passed. This time, there was no boy for him to shout to through the window.

A swift movement caught his eye, and he turned to see it. A light blinked like a glowworm, then disappeared.

He sat on the cot until his breakfast arrived, contemplating what the spirit had said. It had to be an important message for the spirit to return, so he tried his best to puzzle it out. As the door to his cell scraped open, he resolved that when he was released—which he felt sure would happen—he would change his life completely. Let go of his fears, his old grudges, his shame at his past. He would forge a new identity, as a person rather than simply a businessman.

Chapter 24

Everyone arrived at the train station with plenty of time to spare, as they were all anxious to begin the journey. Mrs. Cratchit had wrapped some warm buns in cloth, which Bob handed out to everyone as they waited. Clara came with Fred, which caused a little surprise since she had largely absented herself during the proceedings. She was more subdued than usual and a little pale. "I wouldn't have missed this trip for the world," she declared to the group with a forced smile.

Fred fretted around her constantly, making sure she was all right, until Mr. Perim whispered in his ear, "I believe many thousands of ladies have taken trains or made even more difficult journeys while in her condition and survived." He finished with a wink. Fred looked sheepish and wandered over to Peter, trying to occupy himself by answering the boy's multitude of questions about every conceivable part of the train and the station. When Fred didn't know the answer, he made it up, at one point telling the boy the train could navigate on its own with the driver only there for backup, and Peter didn't seem any less satisfied by it.

Mr. Perim disappeared for a few minutes and returned carrying a newspaper. "It seems you all have moved your case into the public eye."

Fred halted in his conversation with Peter. "Did they publish it?" he asked, hurrying over to Mr. Perim, with Miss Spencer close behind him.

Mr. Perim held the paper open for the others to view.

"I told you Mr. Harper was the man to ask," Peter said.

Fred placed a companionable hand on Peter's back. "You did a good job, Mr. Cratchit."

Peter giggled at being referred to so formally.

The train whistle blew, and Mr. Perim folded the paper. Once the group boarded, the heavy reality of their situation fell over them again. The train ride was spent mostly in tense but expectant silence. Even Peter, after a few ill-received exclamations of interesting things passing by in the countryside, settled into quietness.

A constable met them at the train station and loaded them into a carriage to convey them to the asylum. The vehicle was cramped, with Peter unhappily required to take his seat in his father's lap.

"You were right, sir," the constable said to Mr. Perim as they rode along. "Word of your interest has got out. Dr. Burnhope arrived this morning."

"And he hasn't left with anyone?"

"No, sir. We've had eyes on the building all morning."

The courtyard they arrived at was so dark inside its confines, it felt like early evening instead of midday. Mr. Perim marched at the head of the group, exuding authority. He rang the doorbell with purpose. With their attention fixed on the door, they jumped when a second policeman appeared from the shadows behind them and began to speak.

"No movement," he reported to his colleague as he stationed himself at the rear of the group.

Mr. Perim rang the bell again. Eventually, footsteps shuffled on the other side of the door. A series of locks clicked before the door swung open to reveal an elderly man with long gray hair dressed in a tidy if old-fashioned suit. Behind him, the lobby was eerily silent, though hints of bumps and voices drifted from the upper floors.

"I am Mr. Perim, MP. I am here to see the manager of this establishment. And if Dr. Burnhope is here, too, all the better."

The old man swung his eyes along the group gathered behind Mr. Perim, then back at him, in a wordless question.

"These people are the interested parties in the case. The constables are here to ensure our complaints are addressed properly."

With no change in expression, the man stepped aside and allowed them to enter. Once they were inside, the man slowly went about the business of relatching all the locks down the length of the door. The man dropped the ring of keys into his pocket. Bob and Fred glanced nervously at each other as they realized they were now shut in.

The man led them down a series of long corridors until they reached a row of offices along the back of the building. Here, far from the courtyard, light managed to penetrate the windows. He directed them to a large corner office. Inside, a man sat in the crook of an L-shaped mahogany desk. Beside him stood Dr. Burnhope and another man.

"Good," Mr. Perim said. "It looks like we've been expected." He introduced himself to the three men, who reciprocated by stating they were Mr. Grant, the superintendent, Dr. Burnhope, and Dr. Harris, both consulting physicians. Mr. Perim made no attempt to introduce his own little group. The others hung back, letting Mr. Perim lead the proceedings. Bob glowered at Dr. Burnhope but wisely said nothing. If Dr. Burnhope remembered him, his face gave no flicker of recognition.

"I believe you have in your care, against his and his family's will, Mr. Ebenezer Scrooge."

"I wouldn't be so sure about him being here against his will," Dr. Harris said. "I've spoken with him several times, and he's quite philosophical about why he's here."

"Snatching a man from his place of business hardly counts as consent, I think."

"This man knew when I would be arriving." Dr. Burnhope pointed at Bob.

Without looking behind him, Mr. Perim responded, "Yes, but he didn't know what you intended once you arrived."

"This place is meant to care for the insane who are not fit to be in society," Mr. Grant said. "I put it to you, would a sane man think he deserved to be here?"

Mr. Perim straightened, as if wishing for extra height. "I did not come here to debate these points. I demand to see Mr. Scrooge immediately. And you shall answer for your conduct toward him."

Mr. Grant nodded, and Dr. Harris squeezed past the group and out the door. Those remaining in the office stood in awkward silence until he returned several minutes later. Behind him came Scrooge in a simple linen shirt and black, ill-fitting trousers. He looked freshly washed, but his face was gaunt and hollow. He had lost weight during his short time there. He grinned as he recognized his visitors.

Fred pushed through the group and embraced him. "Thank God we found you! Are you all right?" Clara followed close behind and hugged Scrooge as well.

Scrooge nodded. He looked around those gathered in the room, and his smile faded when he saw the two men stationed behind the desk. Fred stepped back, sensing there was probably more these men had to answer for than Fred would have liked.

Mr. Perim stepped forward and introduced himself, shaking Scrooge's hand firmly. "I'm sure you'll be happy to go home?"

"Why wouldn't I be? Bah!"

"I see." Mr. Perim looked pointedly at Dr. Harris, now standing behind the patient. He turned back to Dr. Burnhope and Mr. Grant. "I trust there will be no argument against us taking this man home?"

Dr. Burnhope set his chin in a way that indicated he was indeed preparing his argument, but Mr. Grant stepped forward. "We don't want any trouble, gentlemen. This is a reputable institution, and we would like to keep it that way."

"Good. I'm glad we understand one another," Mr. Perim said.

"Perhaps," Dr. Harris broke in, glancing at Mr. Grant quickly, "you would consent to letting one of our London colleagues check in on Mr. Scrooge occasionally."

Mr. Perim glanced at Fred, who scowled. "I will leave that up to the family to see if there is a neutral third party who could conduct such work." He reached into his pocket and pulled out his card. "Come by my office next week," he said, handing the card to Dr. Burnhope. "We can talk about your ideas on asylum reform for the next legislative session."

Dr. Burnhope frowned but accepted the card and slid it into his breast pocket.

"In the meantime, I trust nothing like this will happen again." Still getting no response, Mr. Perim added, "I'm sure our constable friends here will keep a close eye on you. In fact, I may send a delegation up to tour the facility. If they like what they see, they may be able to do good things for you." He turned back to Scrooge. "Did you have any belongings on you when you arrived?"

"Yes. My clothes, my watch, and my wallet, with exactly nine pounds, eight shillings, and four pence in it."

For an instant, Mr. Perim looked taken aback by the preciseness of the response, but he quickly wiped the surprise from his face.

Without being prompted, Mr. Grant sighed and stood. "I'll go see what I can find."

While they waited, the others came up to greet Scrooge, offering quiet words and tentative pats on the back. Peter barged through and wrapped his arms tightly around Scrooge's waist. Startled, Scrooge set a hand on Peter's head, but he found nothing to say.

As Bob stepped forward, Scrooge gave him a curt nod. "We need to talk later, Bob."

"Sir, I promise—"

"Later." He looked away.

Mr. Grant returned. "The clothes have been burned as is standard protocol, but here are the watch and the wallet. All accounted for." He forced a smile briefly, then turned a sour look in Dr. Burnhope's direction.

"Thank you, gentlemen," Mr. Perim said. "I hope I shall never have reason to make such a visit again."

The group shuffled out the office door, where they again picked up their elderly escort. The little group, with Scrooge protected at its center, gave a collective sigh of relief as the locks on the front door opened easily. Even the sight of the bleak courtyard brought voiceless praises to their hearts.

The first hour of the train trip back to London was spent with everyone excitedly telling Scrooge what had happened since they had last seen him, and vice versa. The others told Scrooge of their oft-thwarted efforts to find him. Bob remained rather quiet, not eager to share what had been going on with the business in case it should make Scrooge even more upset with him than he likely already was. Upon prodding from Fred, Bob gave some of the basics of the situation. Fortunately, Scrooge didn't seem eager to discuss business matters and asked no follow-up questions. Scrooge told them a little about his journey and the accommodations at the asylum but was hazy on the details for the sake of his loved ones' peace of mind. Once this flow of information was mostly exhausted, Scrooge suggested an idea to Mr. Perim.

"I couldn't help but notice there was no real punishment for Dr. Burnhope's behavior," Scrooge began.

Mr. Perim shifted in his seat. "Sometimes it's better in these situations to work with the person rather than against him."

"Exactly what I was thinking! Perhaps when you discuss reform ideas with him, you can also—suggest, shall we say?—that he provide some free services to those of the lower classes, the underresourced institutions."

Mr. Perim looked surprised at the enthusiastic proposal. "I can certainly convey that such work would be in his best interest."

"And Dr. Harris isn't such a bad fellow. He may want to help as well. Miss Spencer has plenty of connections to places in need."

Mr. Perim smiled at the mentioned lady. "Oh, yes, I'm aware of all of Miss Spencer's good works."

Scrooge settled back in his seat and complained of being tired. His companions let him snooze undisturbed for the next three-quarters of an hour. Even his snores were comforting to those watching over him.

He awoke at one of Peter's exclamations at some interesting scene passing by the window before Bob had a chance to shush him.

"It's all right," Scrooge said. He regarded Bob carefully for a moment before sitting forward and stretching. "Actually, Bob, why don't we talk down here?" he asked, motioning to the far end of the carriage, which was unoccupied.

Clara stopped Scrooge with a light touch on his arm. "Since we are nearing London, there's something else we need to tell you first."

"The surprises never end, it seems," Scrooge said with a grin, but the corners of it wavered as he registered Fred and Clara's serious expressions.

"There has been a fire at your house," Clara said simply. "It is no longer habitable."

"But you are welcome to stay with Clara and me for as long as you like," Fred added.

Scrooge thought about this for a moment before nodding. "It is for the best," he said.

Mr. Perim raised an eyebrow at Miss Spencer. He clearly was beginning to see that the man they had rescued was indeed an odd duck.

"Yes," Scrooge continued. "It's better for me to start over completely, away from the influence of Jacob Marley." He paused. After a moment, his eyes lit up, and he turned toward Fred and Clara. "And I'll be there to help with the baby! Won't that be wonderful!" He settled back into his seat, a contented smile on his face.

"It seems convincing him to stay with us won't be an issue," Clara teased her husband.

"Now, back to our purpose, Bob," Scrooge said abruptly. As he stepped between the others' legs, he smiled softly down at them. "Business, you know." But the others could sense tension creeping beneath his throwaway words.

Bob and Scrooge sat across from each other at the back of the car. The end of the carriage they had just come from was suddenly quiet as the others strained to hear what was said.

Scrooge kept his voice low. "It seems there are men all around who would see me undone. It might not be quite as easy as I hoped for a man to change his life."

"Given time, sir..."

Scrooge fixed a fierce gaze on Bob. "Are you one of those men who would see me undone?"

"No, sir, never!" The words carried, and tittering came from the front of the carriage as the others whispered about what they had heard.

Ignoring them, Scrooge relaxed slightly, relieved at Bob's answer. "I wouldn't blame you if you were. I was cruel to your family for many years."

"Never, sir. I hope you know I'm not the type of man to hold a grudge. I was simply naive about Dr. Burnhope, is all—"

Scrooge patted Bob's knee. "You have explained yourself on that point enough. I've been too trusting, too, I think. No, not with you. With these doctors. Fred hasn't said anything, but I'm sure he's bursting with 'I told you so.' He told me to stop telling everyone about my encounter with the spirits."

"I'm sure he's just happy you're safe." Bob hesitated, unsure whether it was a good time to bring up the other business matters that had consumed him since Scrooge's forced departure.

"Yes, yes. Fred is better than all of us put together. I shall just have to let my actions speak for themselves in the future and not be so concerned with providing an explanation." The train slowed. Scrooge looked out the window. "Ah! London at last!" He clapped his hands on his thighs, stood, and made his way up the aisle to the others, leaving Bob alone with the words he hadn't yet said.

On the London train platform, everyone gathered around Scrooge as they prepared to separate for the night. When it was time for Bob to say his goodbye, he gripped Scrooge's hand. "Listen, there are business matters we must discuss," he said.

"That can wait. I'm sure you've done a fine job while I was away."

Fred stepped forward and wrapped his hand around his uncle's elbow. "Yes, let's not make him worry about work just yet." He shot Bob a meaningful look, then tugged gently on Scrooge's elbow to lead him away.

"Thank you, everyone," Scrooge called behind him. He waved as he walked away.

Bob sighed and rubbed his forehead.

"It'll be all right, Bob," Miss Spencer said. "Maybe he doesn't need to know how many people were working against him."

"He'll find out once he returns to work."

"I suspect that may not happen."

"What?" Bob stared at her, dumbfounded. The idea of Scrooge without his business was absurd.

Miss Spencer nodded in the direction of Peter, who was in the middle of a huge yawn. "It's been a long day," she said.

"Right. Thank you again." Bob put a hand on Peter's shoulder and led the sleepy boy home through the streets of London. He rolled Miss Spencer's suspicion over in his mind but could make no sense of it.

The following morning, after she had been at work for a couple of hours already but the family had only just risen, Martha was once again called to Mr. Werther's office. He brandished a letter at her in a way she couldn't place as either threatening or excitable.

"You'll be glad to know I've had a letter from your father this morning, and they've found Mr. Scrooge." He set the letter down. "Though, at least in business terms, I'm not sure how pleased I am."

"Me either, to be honest, sir."

He stared at her for a moment, then guffawed. "I knew I liked you," he said. "Keep at it and you'll be housekeeper in no time." He pulled another letter off his desk, this one still sealed. "This arrived for you this morning as well. I had the butler give it to me since I was going to call you in anyway."

Martha accepted the letter—a treat she rarely received. She smothered her excitement at the thought of what it could be. The response from Miss Spencer, most likely. Back in the hallway, she quickly tucked it into her bodice. There was work to do and no time to dawdle over silly bits of news or her own personal drama.

That evening, Martha returned to her basement room. The room was quiet in a way it had never been before. Kitty had moved into Margaret's room the day before, leaving Martha all to herself. Solitude wasn't something she had experienced much of in her life, and she wasn't sure she liked it. She lit the room's one candle, an extravagance she rarely allowed herself. At least she had Miss Spencer's reply to occupy her. She pulled the letter out of her bodice and sat on the bed to read it.

The first part of the letter described their successful rescue of Mr. Scrooge. While it would be a thrilling story to read in the paper about a stranger, having her own opinion of the rescued, Martha couldn't bring herself to care. She scanned the page to find the point where the subject changed to her own concerns.

How nice that you would like to get more involved in charity work. I am happy to introduce you to any institutions that could use your assistance. Even having a little time to commit to a cause is worthwhile. Where does your interest lie—the poor? Orphans? The insane? Fallen women? Let me know and I will find you an appropriate placement.

Now, on to what I believe was the real reason for your letter. I hope you realize how odd it is to ask an old maid for advice on courting. Prudence would suggest you should also ask a long-married woman and compare our answers. I am sorry to hear it didn't work out with your Mr. Thatcher, but it is much better to find out a man has a penchant for drink prior to entering into an engagement. For my part, I would caution you not to discount the value of a life of comfort and companionship. While these may seem like mercenary concerns, they have been the basis of many a happy marriage—or so I have been led to believe. Mr. Heron seems like he would fit this profile quite nicely. However, the fact that you need to ask me for advice indicates that you are not certain about him. I would hesitate to spend my life with anyone who thought I needed to change—to be more one way or the other—as I am quite set in my ways. It may be worth waiting for the person who thinks you just right, like the Goldilocks story.

As for myself, I have in mind a specific change in my condition that, if offered, I would accept. We must each make our decisions for ourselves.

Miss Spencer was right in her assessment. Martha knew in that instant that she had no desire to marry Steven Heron, and therefore there was no reason to allow their courtship to continue—or to begin, really, as she had never given him permission to call on her officially as he had hoped to do. But Martha puzzled over Miss Spencer's last statement. Was Miss Spencer hinting that she would marry? Then her mind hit on a memory—a remark her father had made teasing Scrooge about Miss Spencer. Surely, a woman like that wouldn't seriously consider—

Martha folded up the letter and blew out the candle in her rush to get into bed and away from such strange thoughts.

Chapter 25

Scrooge stayed quietly in his new bedroom at Fred and Clara's for the next few days, declining to go out. He claimed he only needed to rest, but he often seemed thoughtful and a bit distant, as if his mind were working on solving a particularly troubling mathematics problem in the background of all he did. He made no mention of his own home except to inquire whether the insurance had been dealt with, which Fred promised to tackle. Fred and Clara thought it best not to discuss anything that had happened unless he brought it up, which he seemed increasingly unlikely to do as each day passed.

However, on the morning of the third day, he appeared in Fred and Clara's bedroom doorway as they were readying themselves to go to church. He cleared his throat. "Now, what about Mrs. Minston," he began, asking about her station, as she no longer had a house to keep for him. His niece and nephew halted their toilette to answer his inquiry.

"You don't need to worry about her," Clara said.

The brusqueness of her response told Scrooge there was more beneath the remark than a simple desire that he not worry himself. Fred stepped in and explained what they had learned about Mrs. Minston's intentions.

Scrooge tapped his index finger against his chin as he digested this information. "No, I think she should return," he said eventually. "She can be your housekeeper. You'll need a bigger house with me here and the baby coming. I can help you pay for it. We shall simply combine households."

"But Uncle, she tried to get you committed!" Fred exclaimed. He threw his wife an exasperated look.

"If a covetous old sinner like me can be given a second chance, then certainly she deserves one since she felt remorse so much sooner than I."

Clara shrugged and looked at her husband. "I suppose she'll be on her best behavior from now on."

"Next you'll tell me you want to forgive the Morodys, too," Fred said.

Scrooge laughed. "I am not quite so sympathetic there. But I would advocate for them being given the opportunity to explain themselves."

"We'll invite them to supper," Fred declared to his wife, his characteristic good humor restored at the prospect of this social visit.

Scrooge flinched. "I don't think they want to see me."

"Simple," Fred said. "We won't tell them you're here."

The trio laughed at the little joke they were going to play.

"I'll just be happy not to have to be the host," Scrooge said. "I will leave that up to you, my dears. You are much better at it than I."

Fred and Clara embraced him, but for once, the tenderness brought a smile unclouded by tears to Scrooge's face. Somehow, he finally felt like he deserved their affection. And he would continue to make sure he deserved it for the remainder of his life, however long that was to be.

"Now," Clara said. "Will you accompany us to church?"

"You know, I think I will." Always dressed in the same basic wardrobe that would do equally well for the office or church, he felt no need to change and went to his room to pull on his coat. When he returned to the hallway, Fred was there, holding a simple green cravat. Fred didn't need to say anything. Scrooge took it and put it on using the hall mirror. It was the first article of color he had ever worn, and it looked nice on him.

The church was much less crowded on this unimportant Sunday than it had been three months before when they visited on Easter. The three found seats quickly and were in no danger of sitting on anyone's lap. The same service proceeded, reassuring in its repetition. Scrooge did not listen closely to the words of the sermon but took in the beauty of the small church and its sole pair of stained-glass windows. Feeling the serenity of the space and the ritual, for the first time, he understood how something could be sacred.

When Communion came, he accepted the wafer and the small sip of wine. He noticed Fred and Clara, kneeling beside him, exchange glances at this difference. Clara tried to hide her smile but was not very successful at it.

The day was bright and warm when they returned to the street, mirroring how Scrooge felt inside. He was ready, he thought, to begin to move on.

Back at Fred and Clara's that afternoon and feeling invigorated from his renewal at the church, Scrooge crossed the street and knocked on the Cratchits' front door. Mrs. Cratchit answered. She did not look happy to see him, but she asked him to come in all the same.

"Not necessary," Scrooge said. "If you'll just send Bob out for a moment, that's all I need."

Shortly, Bob replaced his wife in the doorway. "All well, sir?" he asked.

"Yes, yes. I was hoping we could take some time to talk. Shall we meet at the pub down the street?"

Bob glanced into his living room. "All right. Give me half an hour or so." As he closed the door, his face looked gloomy, as if he had just made an appointment with the Grim Reaper.

Unconcerned about having to wait, Scrooge walked directly to the pub and nursed a cup of tea while he read the paper. When Bob arrived, closer to an hour later, Scrooge switched to a pint of ale, which his partner joined him in.

After a few minutes' pleasantries, Scrooge broached the subject he had intended to talk about. "From the bits and pieces I have gathered so far, it seems a great deal has gone on with the business while I was away—and to be fair, before that, while I was not paying close enough attention—that we need to discuss."

Bob nodded solemnly. He launched into the entire story of what he had discovered and how he had leveraged Archie to call off the assault of Michaels and Crane. He recited this tale with no stumbles, unlike his previous partial retellings, and Scrooge got the distinct impression Bob had practiced. Bob then summarized how Mr. Werther had threatened to end their business relationship and Bob had mollified him—though Bob omitted how he found the money to do so. He guessed Fred had not told Scrooge anything, probably so as not to worry him, and indeed, Scrooge made no reference to that incident.

When Bob had finished, Scrooge said, "It seems you have saved the business, Bob."

Bob let out a sigh of relief. "I have tried my best, sir."

"And I'm very sorry Martha got mixed up in it. I promised you that wouldn't happen."

"It turned out all right for her in the end, sir."

"Good. You have saved the business," he repeated. "Now we must decide what to do about it." Scrooge took a gulp of his ale and gazed off into the corner of the room for a moment. When he turned his gaze back to Bob, his jaw was set in determination. "We must figure out a way to keep them from doing any such thing again. Not debtors' prison. Something else." He tapped his index finger against his lower lip. "How did you say Michaels and Crane acquired all this money they used against us?"

"I'm not sure exactly. Some sort of import business down by the docks. Probably not importing anything legal."

"Right." He leaped out of his seat. "Let's go back to my room. We shall write a letter to Archie." Bob, a little bewildered, followed dutifully behind him, though he looked back a little sadly at his half-finished pint.

The next day, Scrooge waited on a corner by the docks, not far from the customs house. Archie Parker had given him the information he needed, and Scrooge had arranged a meeting with the cargo inspector. Part of him felt his task here was petty, but he pushed those thoughts away and reassured himself that he was doing this for the greater good. To take down a couple of smugglers, even temporarily, was certainly a good thing.

Scrooge saw the end of a cigar flash through the fog before he saw the man smoking it. The man was dressed in a linen shirt and vest, with a clean necktie contrasted with a rather ratty cap. Scrooge held out his hand, but the man didn't shake it, so Scrooge was forced to return it to his pocket.

"You in shipping?" the man asked.

"Not myself, no. But I wish to have a certain level of . . . influence on what comes in and out here. I hear you are the man to make that happen."

The inspector sucked on his cigar. His expression remained impassive.

"There's a pair of business owners I believe you are acquainted with, Mr. Michaels and Mr. Crane?"

"Could be."

Scrooge pursed his lips. He was not sure how to proceed with this subterfuge. He had always been a man to tell exactly what he thought, blast what other people might think. "I will just come out with my request, then. I don't want their cargo let through anymore."

"Why would I do that?"

"I assume you make money off such shipments. I simply want to know how much it would cost to undo your agreement with them."

The man considered Scrooge carefully, taking in his fine clothes and the gold watch chain hanging across his waistcoat. "You got that kind of money?"

"I assure you I do. How much?"

The man named an amount. Scrooge reached into the interior pocket of his jacket and pulled out his wallet. He hadn't been sure how much the man would say, so he had withdrawn as much money at one of his banks—he had accounts at institutions all over the city, just in case one should go bust—yesterday as he could. He flipped open his wallet, careful not to let the inspector see its contents, and began counting out twenty-pound notes. He kept his eyes trained on the man as he did so.

The man looked nervous. He had probably guessed that he could have asked for more. But the amount Scrooge was counting out would set him up for at least a year. "I want that pocket watch," the man said, trying to recoup some of his negotiating power. "And that nice top hat you're wearing, too."

Scrooge nodded. He calmly folded the notes and handed them to the inspector, then tucked his wallet back into his pocket. He took the top hat off his head, unhooked his pocket watch, and dropped it into the hat before handing it over. Once the inspector took it, Scrooge said, "Do you know when their next shipment is coming in? I should like to read the shipping news in the paper, see how it transpires."

"Should be three days from now. These things aren't always exact, though. The sea has its own schedule."

"Quite right. Well, I shall keep an eye out." He reached up to tip his hat to him, then realized there was no longer anything to tip.

"How about them gloves, too?"

They were a fine pair, of smoke-gray silk. Scrooge hesitated, then pulled them off quickly and handed them over.

"Pleasure doing business with you," the inspector said.

Scrooge watched him disappear back into the fog. What a stupid use of a fortune, he thought. But it was a small price to pay for a little healthy revenge, wasn't it?

As he walked home, guilt snuck into his thoughts. Despite everything they had done, he would hate to prove Michaels and Crane right by ruining their lives once again. The remaining bills in his wallet began to feel as if they would burn through his clothes. Maybe money could solve some things, after all.

He made his way back to the bank and brought out the pound notes he had not been forced to give to the cargo inspector. He explained his purpose to the clerk, who brought Scrooge round to meet with a banker at a desk in a back room. Within an hour, the documents were drawn up and the funds deposited. Scrooge scribbled off a short note, signing it only "A friend," though he was sure the two men would know from where the beneficence came. Whether they accepted it was up to them. He only hoped they were not so stubborn as to refuse it. Their illegitimate business might be going away, but this trust would help set Michaels and Crane up with a proper business venture, plus a little something left over for themselves—for a quiet house in the country or a ship of their own if they decided to stay in the world of maritime trade. They would see, finally, that Scrooge was no longer the ogre they had made him out to be.

That same night, Mrs. and Miss Morody attended Fred and Clara's dinner while Scrooge remained tucked safely away upstairs. The old Scrooge and Marley sign Fred had salvaged from Scrooge's office was propped up on the sideboard, taking pride of place in its symbolism but also occupying space that rightly should have been filled with the platters that instead lay across the table. The row of dishes created a sort of embankment between the two warring factions: Williamson and Morody.

After tense pleasantries over the soup, Fred dove into the uncomfortable subject he had been waiting to discuss. "I assume you've heard that my uncle is returned to us?"

"Yes," Mrs. Morody said, leaning so far forward her lace collar nearly dipped into her soup. "Praise God he has been rescued." At the last instant, she realized her precarious situation. She sat bolt upright and checked her lace for spots of broth. Once satisfied of its cleanliness, she said to her daughter, "You could go pay him a visit. I'm sure he would appreciate that."

"I'm sure he wouldn't," Fred broke in.

"I know they haven't had the most intimate relationship thus far, but—"

"Mrs. Morody, I do not like that you have made me into a vindictive man. But I will not stand for all these lies!"

Miss Morody dropped her head and made a good show of weeping into her palms. "I'm ashamed to have taken part in this, but it was all because of my mother's influence." When she looked up from this pretty little speech, her eyes were wide and innocent but surprisingly dry.

"How dare you!" her mother hissed.

Clara stood, directing everyone's attention to herself. "Mrs. Morody, what my husband is trying to say is that we are aware of all your little deceits. We know of the untrue report you made to the police against our uncle, and the fact that you come here in a show of pity for him is, quite frankly, disgraceful. You may be part of my sister's family, but I am glad you're not part of mine. I must ask you to please leave and never darken our door again." She stepped out from in front of her chair to indicate to the Morodys that movement on their part should indeed occur.

Both ladies so chastened stood and made their way slowly to the door. Mrs. Morody was pale as cream as she collected her wrap from the coat rack. Once she had it on, she said, "We can go to the police and recant, can't we, Lucretia?"

"I hope you will," Fred said, swinging open the door. "But that will not change our position."

Mrs. Morody's glance darted from Fred's face to Clara's and back again. Seeing no hope in either, she pushed through the door and down the stairs in a huff, dragging her daughter along.

Fred shut the door behind them with a satisfying click and an almost too-gleeful grin. Once they were gone, he called, "Did you hear that?"

"Oh, yes," Scrooge responded, coming down the stairs. "You were quite firm with them. That's good."

"You don't think they're deserving of a second chance, do you?" Fred asked warily.

"Of course not. I never liked them to begin with. They have never been sincere in anything they've done. Whether a person is right or wrong, if they are sincere in their convictions, I can at least respect that."

"Right." Fred laughed, thinking about the "sincere convictions" his uncle had held for so many years. "We are done with them then, I think."

"Thank God," Clara said. The two men laughed and agreed.

"Aren't you going to the office?" Mrs. Cratchit asked her husband as she cleared the breakfast table the next day.

"I'll go in later," Bob said, opening the newspaper and settling back in his chair. "I think I deserve a break after the chaos of the last few weeks, don't you?"

"Yes. Honestly, I was starting to think . . ."

The newspaper came down immediately. "Think what?"

"I don't know. That you didn't want to be here. That you were picking business over your family. Or even worse, that there was someone else."

Bob stood and wrapped his arms around her waist from behind as she half-heartedly scrubbed the dishes in a bucket of hot water. "How could you think that? You and the children are the center of my world. It's just been so mad lately."

"I know all that's been going on. It's just been a bit lonely here, not knowing anyone, and the neighbors I do know look down on us so . . . Anyway, it's easy to start thinking all sorts of things."

He turned her gently round and kissed her. "I promise to never give you any cause for those kinds of thoughts again. Once Scrooge decides on his future—"

"Let's not talk of him."

"Right." He paused. "I'd like to see the children off to school for once."

"Well, hurry up. They'll be running out of here any moment."

Bob accompanied the children down the road to the day school. He offered to take Tiny Tim up on his shoulders, but Tim declined and ran after his brother and sister instead. The scene brought happy tears to Bob's eyes. His children, all healthy and happy and getting an education. He could never ask for anything better.

He walked leisurely back home after he had dropped them off. Near the house, he ran into Steven Heron.

"Mr. Cratchit." Steven tipped his hat at the older man but hesitated before he spoke again. "I was wondering if I could talk to you about a somewhat delicate matter."

Bob frowned. He did not want to get dragged into any more "delicate matters."

Steven cleared his throat. "It's about Martha—Miss Cratchit, I mean."

"I know who you mean." Bob smiled, and Steven relaxed.

"She's a lovely young woman, and I had asked permission to court her—I don't know if she told you . . . Anyway, I've had a letter from her this morning, and she's declined my advances."

"I'm sorry to hear that."

Steven's eyes brightened, making him look like an eager puppy. "Are you? I'm so glad to hear it. Could you talk to her, perhaps, see if she can be persuaded—"

"Martha knows her own mind. I wouldn't presume to interfere. She would resent me for it."

Steven's shoulders slumped. "Right, well, thanks anyway." He started to walk away.

"There will be someone else," Bob called after him.

Steven didn't respond, just waved and continued on his way to wherever he was going.

During his days at Fred and Clara's, Scrooge had spent hours musing over his situation. He had mostly made up his mind on what his future should hold while he had been alone for so long at the asylum, but it still took him several days before he worked up the courage to put his final decisions into action. A week after his return, he left the house early and walked across the city to call on Miss Spencer at home, hoping to catch her before she went out for the day. He succeeded, and she came downstairs to meet him with what he dared hope was an eager manner.

The day was pleasantly warm, so they went for a leisurely walk, tending in the direction of the nearest park, but Scrooge reckoned he would have his answer before they made it there.

"Miss Spencer," he began.

"Please, after all that has happened in the short time we have known each other, I hope you can call me Alice."

He smiled. This was an encouraging sign. "I would say you can call me Ebenezer, but as it is quite a mouthful, Scrooge will do equally as well."

"Yes, your parents made a bold choice."

His laugh was so jovial the couple walking nearest them turned to look, with the man tipping his hat to them. "I suppose they did," Scrooge said as the couple passed on. "As I'm sure you recall, I nearly asked you this question once before." He watched her face closely, but it remained impassive. "I never pursued it because I realized my motives at that time were not entirely pure. Now that so much has befallen me and I have had so much time left to my own thoughts, I can now say I know exactly what I want."

They stepped separately around two men who had stopped to talk on the sidewalk, then returned to each other's sides.

"Your total commitment to the betterment of society is inspiring to me. It is also what I want to dedicate my life to, and while I am much too old to think of children, I think that as partners in life, we could do wondrous things together." He saw a smile tugging at the corners of her mouth. His heart sang. There was hope after all! "What I am, probably rather foolishly, asking is, will you marry me?"

He walked two steps farther on before realizing she had stopped. He halted and turned to face her.

She was grinning. "You know I will be a tough taskmaster."

"I don't doubt it."

"You old fool, I'm saying yes."

For a second, he felt so lightheaded he thought he might faint. He didn't know what to do.

"You may kiss me now," she said.

He did.

---

hey hurried to Fred and Clara's to share the good news. The younger couple alternated between congratulating and teasing them. They opened a bottle of wine even though it was before 10:00 a.m. After they had consumed its contents, Scrooge said, "I have a proposal to make to Bob as well. Let's go surprise him together."

The merry group made their way across the street. Fortunately, Bob had not yet left for the office, as he was enjoying his new routine of accompanying the children to school. Scrooge had not gone in at all since his return, so Bob felt no compunction to rush each morning. He was, effectively, his own boss for the time being.

Everyone squeezed into the little parlor along with the younger children scattered across the floor, their books and slates set among them, providing plenty of opportunities for the others to trip. Ignoring these hazards, Mrs. Cratchit watched Scrooge disapprovingly from the kitchen door.

"Bob," Scrooge began. "I have come to a decision. It was business that so destroyed my character, and if I want to achieve the tasks set before me, it is business I must give up. It is too great a temptation for me. Therefore, I will retire and let you purchase my half of the business. We can do it over time, in a plan that works for you. I am in no hurry. Except in the determination that it should be yours."

Bob stood open-mouthed for a moment. "I don't know what to say."

"It doesn't feel too burdensome, I hope? I promise we will work out a plan in writing tomorrow. Which I will not hold you to, of course, should circumstances change."

"No, it's certainly not burdensome. It's too good for me." Behind him, his wife looked rather pleased with herself, thinking she had predicted exactly this as the best possible future for her husband.

"Bah, humbug. You singlehandedly saved the business from every attempt to destroy it. You are the best of us here. The ladies, perhaps, excepted." He inclined his head to Mrs. Cratchit, who offered a tentative smile.

"What a glorious future we have ahead of us," Fred declared, resting his hand on his wife's rounded belly.

Amid the shouts of agreement and "hear, hear," from a stool next to the unlit fireplace, Tiny Tim said, "God bless us, everyone."

"Oh, my dear child," Scrooge said. "He already has."

www.ingramcontent.com/pod-product-compliance
Ingram Content Group UK Ltd.
Pitfield, Milton Keynes, MK11 3LW, UK
UKHW031258060225
4478UKWH00030B/398